EFFI BRIEST

Theodor Fontane

CHAPTER I

In front of the old manor house occupied by the von Briest family since the days of Elector George William, the bright sunshine was pouring down upon the village road, at the quiet hour of noon. The wing of the mansion looking toward the garden and park cast its broad shadow over a white and green checkered tile walk and extended out over a large round bed, with a sundial in its centre and a border of Indian shot and rhubarb. Some twenty paces further, and parallel to the wing of the house, there ran a churchyard wall, entirely covered with a small-leaved ivy, except at the place where an opening had been made for a little white iron gate. Behind this arose the shingled tower of Hohen-Cremmen, whose weather vane glistened in the sunshine, having only recently been regilded. The front of the house, the wing, and the churchyard wall formed, so to speak, a horseshoe, inclosing a small ornamental garden, at the open side of which was seen a pond, with a small footbridge and a tied-up boat. Close by was a swing, with its crossboard hanging from two ropes at either end, and its frame posts beginning to lean to one side. Between the pond and the circular bed stood a clump of giant plane trees, half hiding the swing.

The terrace in front of the manor house, with its tubbed aloe plants and a few garden chairs, was an agreeable place to sit on cloudy days, besides affording a variety of things to attract the attention. But, on days when the hot sun beat down there, the side of the house toward the garden was given a decided preference, especially by the mother and the daughter of the house. On this account they were today sitting on the tile walk in the shade, with their backs to the open windows, which were all overgrown with wild grape-vines, and by the side of a little projecting stairway, whose four stone steps led from the garden to the ground floor of the wing of the mansion. Both mother and daughter were busy at work, making an altar cloth out of separate squares, which they were piecing together. Skeins of woolen yarn of various colors, and an equal variety of silk thread lay in confusion upon a large round table, upon which were still standing the luncheon dessert plates and a majolica dish filled with fine large gooseberries.

Swiftly and deftly the wool-threaded needles were drawn back and forth, and the mother seemed never to let her eyes wander from the work. But the daughter, who bore the Christian name of Effi, laid aside her needle from time to time and arose from her seat to practice a course of healthy home gymnastics, with every variety of bending and stretching. It was apparent that she took particular delight in these exercises, to which she gave a somewhat comical turn, and whenever she stood there thus engaged, slowly raising her arms and bringing the palms of her hands together high above her head, her mother would occasionally glance up from her needlework, though always but for a moment and that, too, furtively, because she did not wish to show how fascinating she considered her own child, although in this feeling of motherly pride she was fully justified. Effi wore a bl and white striped linen dress, a sort of smock-frock, which would have shown no waist line at all but for the bronze-colored leather belt which she drew up tight. Her neck was bare and a broad sailor collar fell over her shoulders and back. In everything she did there was a union of haughtiness and gracefulness, and her laughing brown eyes betrayed great natural cleverness and abundant enjoyment of life and goodness of heart. She was called the "little girl," which she had to suffer only because her beautiful slender mother was a full hand's breadth taller than she.

Effi had just stood up again to perform her calisthenic exercises when her mother, who at the moment chanced to be looking up from her embroidery, called to her: "Effi, you really ought to have been an eqstrienne, I'm thinking. Always on the trapeze, always a daughter of the air. I almost believe you would like something of the sort."

"Perhaps, mama. But if it were so, whose fault would it be? From whom do I get it? Why, from no one but you. Or do you think, from papa? There, it makes you laugh yourself. And then, why do you always dress me in this rig, this boy's smock? Sometimes I fancy I shall be put back in short clothes yet. Once I have them on again I shall courtesy like a girl in her early teens, and when our friends in Rathenow come over I shall sit in Colonel Goetze's lap and ride a trot horse. Why not? He is three-fourths an uncle and only one-fourth a suitor. You are to blame. Why don't I have any party clothes? Why don't you make a lady of me?"

"Should you like me to?"

"No." With that she ran to her mother, embraced her effusively and kissed her.

"Not so savagely, Effi, not so passionately. I am always disturbed when I see you thus."

At this point three young girls stepped into the garden through the little iron gate in the churchyard wall and started along the gravel walk toward the round bed and the sundial. They all waved their umbrellas at Effi and then ran up to Mrs. von Briest and kissed her hand. She hurriedly asked a few qstions and then invited the girls to stay and visit with them, or at least with Effi, for half an hour. "Besides, I have something else that I must do and young folks like best to be left to themselves. Fare ye well." With these words she went up the stone steps into the house.

Two of the young girls, plump little creatures, whose freckles and good nature well matched their curly red hair, were daughters of Precentor Jahnke, who swore by the Hanseatic Leag, Scandinavia, and Fritz Reuter, and following the example of his favorite writer and fellow countryman, had named his twin daughters Bertha and

4

Hertha, in imitation of Mining and Lining. The third young lady was Hulda Niemeyer, Pastor Niemeyer's only child. She was more ladylike than the other two, but, on the other hand, tedious and conceited, a lymphatic blonde, with slightly protruding dim eyes, which, nevertheless, seemed always to be seeking something, for which reason the Hussar Klitzing once said: "Doesn't she look as though she were every moment expecting the angel Gabriel?" Effi felt that the rather captious Klitzing was only too right in his criticism, yet she avoided making any distinction between the three girl friends. Nothing could have been farther from her mind at this moment. Resting her arms on the table, she exclaimed: "Oh, this tedious embroidery! Thank heaven, you are here."

"But we have driven your mama away," said Hulda.

"Oh no. She would have gone anyhow. She is expecting a visitor, an old friend of her girlhood days. I must tell you a story about him later, a love story with a real hero and a real heroine, and ending with resignation. It will make you open your eyes wide with amazement. Moreover, I saw mama's old friend over in Schwantikow. He is a district councillor, a fine figure, and very manly."

"Manly? That's a most important consideration," said Hertha.

"Certainly, it's the chief consideration. 'Women womanly, men manly,' is, you know, one of papa's favorite maxims. And now help me put the table in order, or there will be another scolding."

It took but a moment to put the things in the basket and, when the girls sat down again, Hulda said: "Now, Effi, now we are ready, now for the love story with resignation. Or isn't it so bad?"

"A story with resignation is never bad. But I can't begin till Hertha has taken some gooseberries; she keeps her eyes gld on them. Please take as many as you like, we can pick some more afterward. But be sure to throw the hulls far enough away, or, better still, lay them here on this newspaper supplement, then we can wrap them up in a bundle and dispose of everything at once. Mama can't bear to see hulls lying about everywhere. She always says that some one might slip on them and break a leg."

"I don't believe it," said Hertha, applying herself closely to the berries.

"Nor I either," replied Effi, confirming the opinion. "Just think of it, I fall at least two or three times every day and have never broken any bones yet. The right kind of leg doesn't break so easily; certainly mine doesn't, neither does yours, Hertha. What do you think, Hulda?"

"One ought not to tempt fate. Pride will have a fall."

5

"Always the governess. You are just a born old maid."

"And yet I still have hopes of finding a husband, perhaps even before you do."

"For aught I care. Do you think I shall wait for that? The idea! Furthermore one has already been picked out for me and perhaps I shall soon have him. Oh, I am not worrying about that. Not long ago little Ventivegni from over the way said to me: 'Miss Effi, what will you bet we shall not have a charivari and a wedding here this year yet?'"

"And what did you say to that?"

"Quite possible, I said, quite possible; Hulda is the oldest; she may be married any day. But he refused to listen to that and said: 'No, I mean at the home of another young lady who is just as decided a brunette as Miss Hulda is a blonde.' As he said this he looked at me quite seriously--But I am wandering and am forgetting the story."

"Yes, you keep dropping it all the while; may be you don't want to tell it, after all?"

"Oh, I want to, but I have interrupted the story a good many times, chiefly because it is a little bit strange, indeed, almost romantic."

"Why, you said he was a district councillor."

"Certainly, a district councillor, and his name is Geert von Innstetten, Baron von Innstetten."

All three laughed.

"Why do you laugh?" said Effi, nettled. "What does this mean?"

"Ah, Effi, we don't mean to offend you, nor the Baron either. Innstetten did you say? And Geert? Why, there is nobody by that name about here. And then you know the names of noblemen are often a bit comical."

"Yes, my dear, they are. But people do not belong to the nobility for nothing. They can endure such things, and the farther back their nobility goes, I mean in point of time, the better they are able to endure them. But you don't know anything about this and you must not take offense at me for saying so. We shall contin to be good friends just the same. So it is Geert von Innstetten and he is a Baron. He is just as old as mama, to the day."

"And how old, pray, is your mama?"

"Thirty-eight."

"A fine age."

"Indeed it is, especially when one still looks as well as mama. I consider her truly a beautiful woman, don't you, too? And how accomplished she is in everything, always so sure and at the same time so ladylike, and never unconventional, like papa. If I were a young lieutenant I should fall in love with mama."

"Oh, Effi, how can you ever say such a thing?" said Hulda. "Why, that is contrary to the fourth commandment."

"Nonsense. How can it be? I think it would please mama if she knew I said such a thing."

"That may be," interrupted Hertha. "But are you ever going to tell the story?"

"Yes, compose yourself and I'll begin. We were speaking of Baron von Innstetten. Before he had reached the age of twenty he was living over in Rathenow, but spent much of his time on the seignioral estates of this region, and liked best of all to visit in Schwantikow, at my grandfather Belling's. Of course, it was not on account of my grandfather that he was so often there, and when mama tells about it one can easily see on whose account it really was. I think it was mutual, too."

"And what came of it?"

"The thing that was bound to come and always does come. He was still much too young and when my papa appeared on the scene, who had already attained the title of baronial councillor and the proprietorship of Hohen-Cremmen, there was no need of further time for consideration. She accepted him and became Mrs. von Briest."

"What did Innstetten do?" said Bertha, "what became of him? He didn't commit suicide, otherwise you could not be expecting him today."

"No, he didn't commit suicide, but it was something of that nature."

"Did he make an unsuccessful attempt?"

"No, not that. But he didn't care to remain here in the neighborhood any longer, and he must have lost all taste for the soldier's career, generally speaking. Besides, it was an era of peace, you know. In short, he asked for his discharge and took up the study of the law, as papa would say, with a 'true beer zeal.' But when the war of seventy broke out he

7

returned to the army, with the Perleberg troops, instead of his old regiment, and he now wears the cross. Naturally, for he is a smart fellow. Right after the war he returned to his documents, and it is said that Bismarck thinks very highly of him, and so does the Emperor. Thus it came about that he was made district councillor in the district of Kessin."

"What is Kessin? I don't know of any Kessin here."

"No, it is not situated here in our region; it is a long distance away from here, in Pomerania, in Farther Pomerania, in fact, which signifies nothing, however, for it is a watering place (every place about there is a summer resort), and the vacation journey that Baron Innstetten is now enjoying is in reality a tour of his cousins, or something of the sort. He wishes to visit his old friends and relatives here."

"Has he relatives here?"

"Yes and no, depending on how you look at it. There are no Innstettens here, there are none anywhere any more, I believe. But he has here distant cousins on his mother's side, and he doubtless wished above all to see Schwantikow once more and the Belling house, to which he was attached by so many memories. So he was over there the day before yesterday and today he plans to be here in Hohen-Cremmen."

"And what does your father say about it?"

"Nothing at all. It is not his way. Besides, he knows mama, you see. He only teases her."

At this moment the clock struck twelve and before it had ceased striking, Wilke, the old factotum of the Briest family, came on the scene to give a message to Miss Effi: "Your Ladyship's mother sends the reqst that your Ladyship make her toilet in good season; the Baron will presumably drive up immediately after one o'clock." While Wilke was still delivering this message he began to put the ladies' work-table in order and reached first for the sheet of newspaper, on which the gooseberry hulls lay.

"No, Wilke, don't bother with that. It is our affair to dispose of the hulls--Hertha, you must now wrap up the bundle and put a stone in it, so that it will sink better. Then we will march out in a long funeral procession and bury the bundle at sea."

Wilke smiled with satisfaction. "Oh, Miss Effi, she's a trump," was about what he was thinking. But Effi laid the paper bundle in the centre of the quickly gathered up tablecloth and said: "Now let all four of us take hold, each by a corner, and sing something sorrowful."

"Yes, Effi, that is easy enough to say, but what, pray, shall we sing?"

8

"Just anything. It is quite immaterial, only it must have a rime in 'oo;' 'oo' is always a sad vowel. Let us sing, say:

'Flood, flood,

Make it all good.'"

While Effi was solemnly intoning this litany, all four marched out upon the landing pier, stepped into the boat tied there, and from the further end of it slowly lowered into the pond the pebble-weighted paper bundle.

"Hertha, now your guilt is sunk out of sight," said Effi, "in which connection it occurs to me, by the way, that in former times poor unfortunate women are said to have been thrown overboard thus from a boat, of course for unfaithfulness."

"But not here, certainly."

"No, not here," laughed Effi, "such things do not take place here. But they do in Constantinople and it just occurs to me that you must know about it, for you were present in the geography class when the teacher told about it."

"Yes," said Hulda, "he was always telling us about such things. But one naturally forgets them in the course of time."

"Not I, I remember things like that."

CHAPTER II

The conversation ran on thus for some time, the girls recalling with mingled disgust and delight the school lessons they had had in common, and a great many of the teacher's uncalled-for remarks. Suddenly Hulda said: "But you must make haste, Effi; why, you look--why, what shall I say--why, you look as though you had just come from a cherry picking, all rumpled and crumpled. Linen always gets so badly creased, and that large white turned down collar--oh, yes, I have it now; you look like a cabin boy."

"Midshipman, if you please. I must derive some advantage from my nobility. But midshipman or cabin boy, only recently papa again promised me a mast, here close by the swing, with yards and a rope ladder. Most assuredly I should like one and I should

9

not allow anybody to interfere with my fastening the pennant at the top. And you, Hulda, would climb up then on the other side and high in the air we would shout: 'Hurrah!' and give each other a kiss. By Jingo, that would be a sweet one."

"'By Jingo.' Now just listen to that. You really talk like a midshipman. However, I shall take care not to climb up after you, I am not such a dare-devil. Jahnke is quite right when he says, as he always does, that you have too much Billing in you, from your mother. I am only a preacher's daughter."

"Ah, go along. Still waters run deep--But come, let us swing, two on a side; I don't believe it will break. Or if you don't care to, for you are drawing long faces again, then we will play hide-and-seek. I still have a quarter of an hour. I don't want to go in, yet, and anyhow it is merely to say: 'How do you do?' to a district councillor, and a district councillor from Further Pomerania to boot. He is elderly, too. Why he might almost be my father; and if he actually lives in a seaport, for, you know, that is what Kessin is said to be, I really ought to make the best impression upon him in this sailor costume, and he ought almost to consider it a delicate attention. When princes receive anybody, I know from what papa has told me, they always put on the uniform of the country of their gst. So don't worry--Quick, quick, I am going to hide and here by the bench is the base."

Hulda was about to fix a few boundaries, but Effi had already run up the first gravel walk, turning to the left, then to the right, and suddenly vanishing from sight. "Effi, that does not count; where are you? We are not playing run away; we are playing hide-and-seek." With these and similar reproaches the girls ran to search for her, far beyond the circular bed and the two plane trees standing by the side of the path. She first let them get much farther than she was from the base and then, rushing suddenly from her hiding place, reached the bench, without any special exertion, before there was time to say: "one, two, three."

"Where were you?"

"Behind the rhubarb plants; they have such large leaves, larger even than a fig leaf."

"Shame on you."

"No, shame on you, because you didn't catch me. Hulda, with her big eyes, again failed to see anything. She is always slow." Hereupon Effi again flew away across the circle toward the pond, probably because she planned to hide at first behind a dense-growing hazelnut hedge over there, and then from that point to take a long roundabout way past the churchyard and the front house and thence back to the wing and the base. Everything was well calculated, but before she was half way round the pond she heard some one at the house calling her name and, as she turned around, saw her mother waving a handkerchief from the stone steps. In a moment Effi was standing by her.

"Now you see that I knew what I was talking about. You still have that smock-frock on and the caller has arrived. You are never on time."

"I shall be on time, easily, but the caller has not kept his appointment. It is not yet one o'clock, not by a good deal," she said, and turning to the twins, who had been lagging behind, called to them: "Just go on playing; I shall be back right away."

The next moment Effi and her mama entered the spacious drawing-room, which occupied almost the whole ground floor of the side wing.

"Mama, you daren't scold me. It is really only half past. Why does he come so early? Cavaliers never arrive too late, much less too early."

Mrs. von Briest was evidently embarrassed. But Effi cuddled up to her fondly and said: "Forgive me, I will hurry now. You know I can be quick, too, and in five minutes Cinderella will be transformed into a princess. Meanwhile he can wait or chat with papa."

Bowing to her mother, she was about to trip lightly up the little iron stairway leading from the drawing-room to the story above. But Mrs. von Briest, who could be unconventional on occasion, if she took a notion to, suddenly held Effi back, cast a glance at the charming young creature, still all in a heat from the excitement of the game, a perfect picture of youthful freshness, and said in an almost confidential tone: "After all, the best thing for you to do is to remain as you are. Yes, don't change. You look very well indeed. And even if you didn't, you look so unprepared, you show absolutely no signs of being dressed for the occasion, and that is the most important consideration at this moment. For I must tell you, my sweet Effi--" and she clasped her daughter's hands--"for I must tell you--"

"Why, mama, what in the world is the matter with you? You frighten me terribly."

"I must tell you, Effi, that Baron Innstetten has just asked me for your hand."

"Asked for my hand? In earnest?"

"That is not a matter to make a jest of. You saw him the day before yesterday and I think you liked him. To be sure, he is older than you, which, all things considered, is a fortunate circumstance. Besides, he is a man of character, position, and good breeding, and if you do not say 'no,' which I could hardly expect of my shrewd Effi, you will be standing at the age of twenty where others stand at forty. You will surpass your mama by far."

11

Effi remained silent, seeking a suitable answer. Before she could find one she heard her father's voice in the adjoining room. The next moment Councillor von Briest, a well preserved man in the fifties, and of pronounced *bonhomie*, entered the drawing-room, and with him Baron Innstetten, a man of slender figure, dark complexion, and military bearing.

When Effi caught sight of him she fell into a nervous tremble, but only for an instant, as almost at the very moment when he was approaching her with a friendly bow there appeared at one of the wide open vine-covered windows the sandy heads of the Jahnke twins, and Hertha, the more hoidenish, called into the room: "Come, Effi." Then she ducked from sight and the two sprang from the back of the bench, upon which they had been standing, down into the garden and nothing more was heard from them except their giggling and laughing.

CHAPTER III

Later in the day Baron Innstetten was betrothed to Effi von Briest. At the dinner which followed, her jovial father found it no easy matter to adjust himself to the solemn rÃ´le that had fallen to him. He proposed a toast to the health of the young couple, which was not without its touching effect upon Mrs. von Briest, for she obviously recalled the experiences of scarcely eighteen years ago. However, the feeling did not last long. What it had been impossible for her to be, her daughter now was, in her stead. All things considered, it was just as well, perhaps even better. For one could live with von Briest, in spite of the fact that he was a bit prosaic and now and then showed a slight streak of frivolity. Toward the end of the meal--the ice was being served--the elderly baronial councillor once more arose to his feet to propose in a second speech that from now on they should all address each other by the familiar pronoun "Du." Thereupon he embraced Innstetten and gave him a kiss on the left cheek. But this was not the end of the matter for him. On the contrary, he went on to recommend, in addition to the "Du," a set of more intimate names and titles for use in the home, seeking to establish a sort of basis for hearty intercourse, at the same time preserving certain well-earned, and hence justified, distinctions. For his wife he suggested, as the best solution of the problem, the continuation of "Mama," for there are young mamas, as well as old; whereas for himself, he was willing to forego the honorable title of "Papa," and could not help feeling a decided preference for the simple name of Briest, if for no other reason, because it was so beautifully short. "And then as for the children," he said--at which word he had to give himself a jerk as he exchanged gazes with Innstetten, who was only about a dozen years his junior--"well, let Effi just remain Effi, and Geert, Geert. Geert, if I am not mistaken, signifies a tall and slender trunk, and so Effi may be the ivy destined to twine about it." At these words the betrothed couple looked at each other somewhat embarrassed, Effi's face showing at the same time an expression of childlike mirth, but Mrs. von Briest said: "Say what you like, Briest, and formulate your toasts to suit your own taste, but if you will allow me one reqst, avoid poetic imagery; it is beyond your sphere." These silencing words were received by von Briest with more assent than dissent. "It is possible that you are right, Luise."

Immediately after rising from the table, Effi took leave to pay a visit over at the pastor's. On the way she said to herself: "I think Hulda will be vexed. I have got ahead of her after all. She always was too vain and conceited."

But Effi was not quite right in all that she expected. Hulda behaved very well, preserving her composure absolutely and leaving the indication of anger and vexation to her mother, the pastor's wife, who, indeed, made some very strange remarks. "Yes, yes, that's the way it goes. Of course. Since it couldn't be the mother, it has to be the daughter. That's nothing new. Old families always hold together, and where there is a beginning there will be an increase." The elder Niemeyer, painfully embarrassed by these and similar pointed remarks, which showed a lack of culture and refinement, lamented once more the fact that he had married a mere housekeeper.

After visiting the pastor's family Effi naturally went next to the home of the precentor Jahnke. The twins had been watching for her and received her in the front yard.

"Well, Effi," said Hertha, as all three walked up and down between the two rows of amaranths, "well, Effi, how do you really feel?"

"How do I feel? O, quite well. We already say 'Du' to each other and call each other by our first names. His name is Geert, but it just occurs to me that I have already told you that."

"Yes, you have. But in spite of myself I feel so uneasy about it. Is he really the right man?"

"Certainly he is the right man. You don't know anything about such matters, Hertha. Any man is the right one. Of course he must be a nobleman, have a position, and be handsome."

"Goodness, Effi, how you do talk! You used to talk quite differently."

"Yes, I used to."

"And are you quite happy already?"

"When one has been two hours betrothed, one is always quite happy. At least, that is my idea about it."

13

"And don't you feel at all--oh, what shall I say?--a bit awkward?"

"Yes, I do feel a bit awkward, but not very. And I fancy I shall get over it."

After these visits at the parsonage and the home of the precentor, which together had not consumed half an hour, Effi returned to the garden veranda, where coffee was about to be served. Father-in-law and son-in-law were walking up and down along the gravel path by the plane trees. Von Briest was talking about the difficulties of a district councillor's position, saying that he had been offered one at various times, but had always declined. "The ability to have my own way in all matters has always been the thing that was most to my liking, at least more--I beg your pardon, Innstetten--than always having to look up to some one else. For in the latter case one is always obliged to bear in mind and pay heed to exalted and most exalted superiors. That is no life for me. Here I live along in such liberty and rejoice at every green leaf and the wild grape-vine that grows over those windows yonder."

He spoke further in this vein, indulging in all sorts of anti-bureaucratic remarks, and excusing himself from time to time with a blunt "I beg your pardon, Innstetten," which he interjected in a variety of ways. The Baron mechanically nodded assent, but in reality paid little attention to what was said. He turned his gaze again and again, as though spellbound, to the wild grape-vine twining about the window, of which Briest had just spoken, and as his thoughts were thus engaged, it seemed to him as though he saw again the girls' sandy heads among the vines and heard the saucy call, "Come, Effi."

He did not believe in omens and the like; on the contrary, he was far from entertaining superstitious ideas. Nevertheless he could not rid his mind of the two words, and while Briest's peroration rambled on and on he had the constant feeling that the little incident was something more than mere chance.

Innstetten, who had taken only a short vacation, departed the following morning, after promising to write every day. "Yes, you must do that," Effi had said, and these words came from her heart. She had for years known nothing more delightful than, for example, to receive a large number of birthday letters. Everybody had to write her a letter for that day. Such expressions as "Gertrude and Clara join me in sending you heartiest congratulations," were tabooed. Gertrude and Clara, if they wished to be considered friends, had to see to it that they sent individual letters with separate postage stamps, and, if possible, foreign ones, from Switzerland or Carlsbad, for her birthday came in the traveling season.

Innstetten actually wrote every day, as he had promised. The thing that made the receipt of his letters particularly pleasurable was the circumstance that he expected in return only one very short letter every week. This he received regularly and it was always full of charming trifles, which never failed to delight him. Mrs. von Briest undertook to carry on the correspondence with her future son-in-law whenever there was any serious matter to be discussed, as, for example, the settling of the details of the wedding, and

14

qstions of the dowry and the furnishing of the new home. Innstetten was now nearly three years in office, and his house in Kessin, while not splendidly furnished, was nevertheless very well suited to his station, and it seemed advisable to gain from correspondence with him some idea of what he already had, in order not to buy anything superfluous. When Mrs. von Briest was finally well enough informed concerning all these details it was decided that the mother and daughter should go to Berlin, in order, as Briest expressed himself, to buy up the trousseau for Princess Effi.

Effi looked forward to the sojourn in Berlin with great pleasure, the more so because her father had consented that they should take lodgings in the Hotel du Nord. "Whatever it costs can be deducted from the dowry, you know, for Innstetten already has everything." Mrs. von Briest forbade such "mesquineries" in the future, once for all, but Effi, on the other hand, joyously assented to her father's plan, without so much as stopping to think whether he had meant it as a jest or in earnest, for her thoughts were occupied far, far more with the impression she and her mother should make by their appearance at the table d'hÃ´te, than with Spinn and Mencke, Goschenhofer, and other such firms, whose names had been provisionally entered in her memorandum book. And her demeanor was entirely in keeping with these frivolous fancies, when the great Berlin week had actually come.

Cousin von Briest of the Alexander regiment, an uncommonly jolly young lieutenant, who took the *Fliegende Blatter* and kept a record of the best jokes, placed himself at the disposal of the ladies for every hour he should be off duty, and so they would sit with him at the corner window of Kranzler's, or perhaps in the CafÃ© Bar, when permissible, or would drive out in the afternoon to the Zoological Garden, to see the giraffes, of which Cousin von Briest, whose name, by the way, was Dagobert, was fond of saying: "They look like old maids of noble birth." Every day passed according to program, and on the third or fourth day they went, as directed, to the National Gallery, because Dagobert wished to show his cousin the "Isle of the Blessed." "To be sure, Cousin Effi is on the point of marrying, and yet it may perhaps be well to have made the acquaintance of the 'Isle of the Blessed' beforehand." His aunt gave him a slap with her fan, but accompanied the blow with such a gracious look that he saw no occasion to change the tone.

These were heavenly days for all three, no less for Cousin Dagobert than for the ladies, for he was a past master in the art of escorting and always knew how quickly to compromise little differences. Of the differences of opinion to be expected between mother and daughter there was never any lack during the whole time, but fortunately they never came out in connection with the purchases to be made. Whether they bought a half dozen or three dozen of a particular thing, Effi was uniformly satisfied, and when they talked, on the way home, about the prices of the articles bought, she regularly confounded the figures. Mrs. von Briest, ordinarily so critical, even toward her own beloved child, not only took this apparent lack of interest lightly, she even recognized in it an advantage. "All these things," said she to herself, "do not mean much to Effi. Effi is unpretentious; she lives in her own ideas and dreams, and when one of the

Hohenzollern princesses drives by and bows a friendly greeting from her carriage that means more to Effi than a whole chest full of linen."

That was all correct enough, and yet only half the truth. Effi cared but little for the possession of more or less commonplace things, but when she walked up and down Unter den Linden with her mother, and, after inspecting the most beautiful show-windows, went into Demuth's to buy a number of things for the honeymoon tour of Italy, her tr, character showed itself. Only the most elegant articles found favor in her sight, and, if she could not have the best, she forewent the second-best, because this second meant nothing to her. Beyond qstion, she was able to forego,--in that her mother was right,--and in this ability to forego there was a certain amount of unpretentiousness. But when, by way of exception, it became a qstion of really possessing a thing, it always had to be something out of the ordinary. In this regard she was pretentious.

CHAPTER IV

Cousin Dagobert was at the station when the ladies took the train for Hohen-Cremmen. The Berlin sojourn had been a succession of happy days, chiefly because there had been no suffering from disagreeable and, one might almost say, inferior relatives. Immediately after their arrival Effi had said: "This time we must remain incognito, so far as Aunt Therese is concerned. It will not do for her to come to see us here in the hotel. Either Hotel du Nord or Aunt Therese; the two would not go together at all." The mother had finally agreed to this, had, in fact, sealed the agreement with a kiss on her daughter's forehead.

With Cousin Dagobert, of course, it was an entirely different matter. Not only did he have the social grace of the Guards, but also, what is more, the peculiarly good humor now almost a tradition with the officers of the Alexander regiment, and this enabled him from the outset to draw out both the mother and the daughter and keep them in good spirits to the end of their stay. "Dagobert," said Effi at the moment of parting, "remember that you are to come to my nuptial-eve celebration; that you are to bring a cortÃ¨ge goes without saying. But don't you bring any porter or mousetrap seller. For after the theatrical performances there will be a ball, and you must take into consideration that my first grand ball will probably be also my last. Fewer than six companions--superb dancers, that goes without saying--will not be approved. And you can return by the early morning train." Her cousin promised everything she asked and so they bade each other farewell.

Toward noon the two women arrived at their Havelland station in the middle of the marsh and after a drive of half an hour were at Hohen-Cremmen. Von Briest was very happy to have his wife and daughter at home again, and asked qstions upon qstions, but in most cases did not wait for the answers. Instead of that he launched out into a long account of what he had experienced in the meantime. "A while ago you were telling me about the National Gallery and the 'Isle of the Blessed.' Well, while you were away, there was something going on here, too. It was our overseer Pink and the gardener's wife. Of course, I had to dismiss Pink, but it went against the grain to do it. It is very unfortunate that such affairs almost always occur in the harvest season. And Pink was otherwise an uncommonly efficient man, though here, I regret to say, in the wrong place. But enough of that; Wilke is showing signs of restlessness too."

At dinner von Briest listened better. The friendly intercourse with Cousin Dagobert, of whom he heard a good deal, met with his approval, less so the conduct toward Aunt Therese. But one could see plainly that, at the same time that he was declaring his disapproval, he was rejoicing; for a little mischievous trick just suited his taste, and Aunt Therese was unqstionably a ridiculous figure. He raised his glass and invited his wife and daughter to join him in a toast. After dinner, when some of the handsomest purchases were unpacked and laid before him for his judgment, he betrayed a great deal of interest, which still remained alive, or, at least did not die out entirely, even after he had glanced over the bills. "A little bit dear, or let us say, rather, very dear; however, it makes no difference. Everything has so much style about it, I might almost say, so much inspiration, that I feel in my bones, if you give me a trunk like that and a traveling rug like this for Christmas, I shall be ready to take our wedding journey after a delay of eighteen years, and we, too, shall be in Rome for Easter. What do you think, Luise? Shall we make up what we are behind? Better late than never."

Mrs. von Briest made a motion with her hand, as if to say: "Incorrigible," and then left him to his own humiliation, which, however, was not very deep.

* * * * *

The end of August had come, the wedding day (October the 3d) was drawing nearer, and in the manor house, as well as at the parsonage and the schoolhouse, all hands were incessantly occupied with the preparations for the pre-nuptial eve. Jahnke, faithful to his passion for Fritz Reuter, had fancied it would be particularly "ingenious" to have Bertha and Hertha appear as Lining and Mining, speaking Low German, of course, whereas Hulda was to present the elder-tree scene of *Kä¤thchen von Heilbronn*, with Lieutenant Engelbrecht of the Hussars as Wetter vom Strahl. Niemeyer, who by rights was the father of the idea, had felt no hesitation to compose additional lines containing a modest application to Innstetten and Effi. He himself was satisfied with his effort and at the end of the first rehearsal heard only very favorable criticisms of it, with one exception, to be sure, viz., that of his patron lord, and old friend, Briest, who, when he had heard the admixture of Kleist and Niemeyer, protested vigorously, though not on literary grounds. "High Lord, and over and over, High Lord--what does that mean? That is misleading and it distorts the whole situation. Innstetten is unqstionably a fine specimen of the race, a man of character and energy, but, when it comes to that, the Briests are not of base parentage either. We are indisputably a historic family--let me add: 'Thank God'--and

17

the Innstettens are not. The Innstettens are merely old, belong to the oldest nobility, if you like; but what does oldest nobility mean? I will not permit that a von Briest, or even a figure in the wedding-eve performance, whom everybody must recognize as the counterpart of our Effi--I will not permit, I say, that a Briest either in person or through a representative speak incessantly of 'High Lord.' Certainly not, unless Innstetten were at least a disguised Hohenzollern; there are some, you know. But he is not one and hence I can only repeat that it distorts the whole situation."

For a long time von Briest really held fast to this view with remarkable tenacity. But after the second rehearsal, at which KÃ¤thchen was half in costume, wearing a tight-fitting velvet bodice, he was so carried away as to remark: "KÃ¤thchen lies there beautifully," which turn was pretty much the equivalent of a surrender, or at least prepared the way for one. That all these things were kept secret from Effi goes without saying. With more curiosity on her part, however, it would have been wholly impossible. But she had so little desire to find out about the preparations made and the surprises planned that she declared to her mother with all emphasis: "I can wait and see," and, when Mrs. von Briest still doubted her, Effi closed the conversation with repeated assurances that it was really tr and her mother might just as well believe it. And why not? It was all just a theatrical performance, and prettier and more poetical than *Cinderella*, which she had seen on the last evening in Berlin--no, on second thought, it couldn't be prettier and more poetical. In this play she herself would have been glad to take a part, even if only for the purpose of making a chalk mark on the back of the ridiculous boarding-school teacher. "And how charming in the last act is 'Cinderella's awakening as a princess,' or at least as a countess! Really, it was just like a fairy tale." She often spoke in this way, was for the most part more exuberant than before, and was vexed only at the constant whisperings and mysterious conduct of her girl friends. "I wish they felt less important and paid more attention to me. When the time comes they will only forget their lines and I shall have to be in suspense on their account and be ashamed that they are my friends."

Thus ran Effi's scoffing remarks and there was no mistaking the fact that she was not troubling herself any too much about the pre-nuptial exercises and the wedding day. Mrs. von Briest had her own ideas on the subject, but did not permit herself to worry about it, as Effi's mind was, to a considerable extent, occupied with the future, which after all was a good sign. Furthermore Effi, by virt of her wealth of imagination, often launched out into descriptions of her future life in Kessin for a quarter of an hour at a time,--descriptions which, incidentally, and much to the amusement of her mother, revealed a remarkable conception of Further Pomerania, or, perhaps it would be more correct to say, they embodied this conception, with clever calculation and definite purpose. For Effi delighted to think of Kessin as a half-Siberian locality, where the ice and snow never fully melted.

"Today Goschenhofer has sent the last thing," said Mrs. von Briest, sitting, as was her custom, out in front of the wing of the mansion with Effi at the work-table, upon which the supplies of linen and underclothing kept increasing, whereas the newspapers, which merely took up space, were constantly decreasing. "I hope you have everything now,

Effi. But if you still cherish little wishes you must speak them out, if possible, this very hour. Papa has sold the rape crop at a good price and is in an unusually good humor."

"Unusually? He is always in a good humor."

"In an unusually good humor," repeated the mother. "And it must be taken advantage of. So speak. Several times during our stay in Berlin I had the feeling that you had a very special desire for something or other more."

"Well, dear mama, what can I say? As a matter of fact I have everything that one needs, I mean that one needs *here*. But as it is once for all decided that I am to go so far north-- let me say in passing that I have no objections; on the contrary I look forward with pleasure to it, to the northern lights and the brighter splendor of the stars--as this has been definitely decided, I should like to have a set of furs."

"Why, Effi, child, that is empty folly. You are not going to St. Petersburg or Archangel."

"No, but I am a part of the way."

"Certainly, child, you are a part of the way; but what does that mean? If you go from here to Nan you are, by the same train of reasoning, a part of the way to Russia. However, if you want some furs you shall have them. But let me tell you beforehand, I advise you not to buy them. Furs are proper for elderly people; even your old mother is still too young for them, and if you, in your seventeenth year, come out in mink or marten the people of Kessin will consider it a masqrade."

It was on the second of September that these words were spoken, and the conversation would doubtless have been contind, if it had not happened to be the anniversary of the battle of Sedan. But because of the day they were interrupted by the sound of drum and fife, and Effi, who had heard before of the proposed parade, but had meanwhile forgotten about it, rushed suddenly away from the work-table, past the circular plot and the pond, in the direction of a balcony built on the churchyard wall, to which one could climb by six steps not much broader than the rungs of a ladder. In an instant she was at the top and, surely enough, there came all the school children marching along, Jahnke strutting majestically beside the right flank, while a little drum major marched at the head of the procession, several paces in advance, with an expression on his countenance as though it were incumbent upon him to fight the battle of Sedan all over again. Effi waved her handkerchief and he promptly returned the greeting by a salute with his shining baton.

A week later mother and daughter were again sitting in the same place, busy, as before, with their work. It was an exceptionally beautiful day; the heliotrope growing in a neat bed around the sundial was still in bloom, and the soft breeze that was stirring bore its fragrance over to them.

"Oh, how well I feel," said Effi, "so well and so happy! I can't think of heaven as more beautiful. And, after all, who knows whether they have such wonderful heliotrope in heaven?"

"Why, Effi, you must not talk like that. You get that from your father, to whom nothing is sacred. Not long ago he even said: 'Niemeyer looks like Lot.' Unheard of. And what in the world can he mean by it? In the first place he doesn't know how Lot looked, and secondly it shows an absolute lack of consideration for Hulda. Luckily, Niemeyer has only the one daughter, and for this reason the comparison really falls to the ground. In one regard, to be sure, he was only too right, viz., in each and every thing that he said about 'Lot's wife,' our good pastor's better half, who again this year, as was to be expected, simply ruined our Sedan celebration by her folly and presumption. By the by it just occurs to me that we were interrupted in our conversation when Jahnke came by with the school. At least I cannot imagine that the furs, of which you were speaking at that time, should have been your only wish. So let me know, darling, what further things you have set your heart upon."

"None, mama."

"Truly, none?"

"No, none, truly; perfectly in earnest. But, on second thought, if there were anything--"

"Well?"

"It would be a Japanese bed screen, black, with gold birds on it, all with long crane bills. And then perhaps, besides, a hanging lamp for our bedroom, with a red shade."

Mrs. von Briest remained silent.

"Now you see, mama, you are silent and look as though I had said something especially improper."

"No, Effi, nothing improper. Certainly not in the presence of your mother, for I know you so well. You are a fantastic little person, you like nothing better than to paint fanciful pictures of the future, and the richer their coloring the more beautiful and desirable they appear to you. I saw that when we were buying the traveling articles. And now you fancy it would be altogether adorable to have a bed screen with a variety of fabulous beasts on it, all in the dim light of a red hanging lamp. It appeals to you as a fairy tale and you would like to be a princess."

Effi took her mother's hand and kissed it. "Yes, mama, that is my nature."

"Yes, that is your nature. I know it only too well. But, my dear Effi, we must be circumspect in life, and we women especially. Now when you go to Kessin, a small place, where hardly a streetlamp is lit at night, the people will laugh at such things. And if they would only stop with laughing! Those who are ill-disposed toward you--and there are always some--will speak of your bad bringing-up, and many will doubtless say even worse things."

"Nothing Japanese, then, and no hanging lamp either. But I confess I had thought it would be so beautiful and poetical to see everything in a dim red light."

Mrs. von Briest was moved. She got up and kissed Effi. "You are a child. Beautiful and poetical. Nothing but fancies. The reality is different, and often it is well that there should be dark instead of light and shimmer."

Effi seemed on the point of answering, but at this moment Wilke came and brought some letters. One was from Kessin, from Innstetten. "Ah, from Geert," said Effi, and putting the letter in her pocket, she contind in a calm tone: "But you surely will allow me to set the grand piano across one corner of the room. I care more for that than for the open fireplace that Geert has promised me. And then I am going to put your portrait on an easel. I can't be entirely without you. Oh, how I shall be homesick to see you, perhaps even on the wedding tour, and most certainly in Kessin. Why, they say the place has no garrison, not even a staff surgeon, and how fortunate it is that it is at least a watering place. Cousin von Briest, upon whom I shall rely as my chief support, always goes with his mother and sister to Warnemunde. Now I really do not see why he should not, for a change, some day direct our dear relatives toward Kessin. Besides, 'direct' seems to suggest a position on the staff, to which, I believe, he aspires. And then, of course, he will come along and live at our house. Moreover Kessin, as somebody just recently told me, has a rather large steamer, which runs over to Sweden twice a week. And on the ship there is dancing (of course they have a band on board), and he dances very well."

"Who?"

"Why, Dagobert."

"I thought you meant Innstetten. In any case the time has now come to know what he writes. You still have the letter in your pocket, you know."

"That's right. I had almost forgotten it." She opened the letter and glanced over it.

"Well, Effi, not a word? You are not beaming and not even smiling. And yet he always writes such bright and entertaining letters, and not a word of fatherly wisdom in them."

"That I should not allow. He has his age and I have my youth. I should shake my finger at him and say: 'Geert, consider which is better.'"

"And then he would answer: 'You have what is better.' For he is not only a man of most refined manners, he is at the same time just and sensible and knows very well what youth means. He is always reminding himself of that and adapting himself to youthful ways, and if he remains the same after marriage you will lead a model married life."

"Yes, I think so, too, mama. But just imagine--and I am almost ashamed to say it--I am not so very much in favor of what is called a model married life."

"That is just like you. And now tell me, pray, what are you really in favor of?"

"I am--well, I am in favor of like and like and naturally also of tenderness and love. And if tenderness and love are out of the qstion, because, as papa says, love is after all only fiddle-faddle, which I, however, do not believe, well, then I am in favor of wealth and an aristocratic house, a really aristocratic one, to which Prince Frederick Charles will come for an elk or grouse hunt, or where the old Emperor will call and have a gracious word for every lady, even for the younger ones. And then when we are in Berlin I am for court balls and gala performances at the Opera, with seats always close by the grand central box."

"Do you say that out of pure sauciness and caprice?"

"No, mama, I am fully in earnest. Love comes first, but right after love come splendor and honor, and then comes amusement--yes, amusement, always something new, always something to make me laugh or weep. The thing I cannot endure is *ennui*."

"If that is the case, how in the world have you managed to get along with us?"

"Why, mama, I am amazed to hear you say such a thing. To be sure, in the winter time, when our dear relatives come driving up to see us and stay for six hours, or perhaps even longer, and Aunt Gundel and Aunt Olga eye me from head to foot and find me impertinent--and Aunt Gundel once told me that I was--well, then occasionally it is not very pleasant, that I must admit. But otherwise I have always been happy here, so happy--"

As she said the last words she fell, sobbing convulsively, at her mother's feet and kissed her hands.

"Get up, Effi. Such emotions as these overcome one, when one is as young as you and facing her wedding and the uncertain future. But now read me the letter, unless it contains something very special, or perhaps secrets."

"Secrets," laughed Effi and sprang to her feet in a suddenly changed mood. "Secrets! Yes, yes, he is always coming to the point of telling me some, but the most of what he writes might with perfect propriety be posted on the bulletin board at the mayor's office, where the ordinances of the district council are posted. But then, you know, Geert is one of the councillors."

"Read, read."

"Dear Effi: The nearer we come to our wedding day, the more scanty your letters grow. When the mail arrives I always look first of all for your handwriting, but, as you know, all in vain, as a rule, and yet I did not ask to have it otherwise. The workmen are now in the house who are to prepare the rooms, few in number, to be sure, for your coming. The best part of the work will doubtless not be done till we are on our journey. Paper-hanger Madelung, who is to furnish everything, is an odd original. I shall tell you about him the next time. Now I must tell you first of all how happy I am over you, over my sweet little Effi. The very ground beneath my feet here is on fire, and yet our good city is growing more and more quiet and lonesome. The last summer gst left yesterday. Toward the end he went swimming at nine degrees above zero (Centigrade), and the attendants were always rejoiced when he came out alive. For they feared a stroke of apoplexy, which would give the baths a bad reputation, as though the water were worse here than elsewhere. I rejoice when I think that in four weeks I shall row with you from the Piazzetta out to the Lido or to Murano, where they make glass beads and beautiful jewelry. And the most beautiful shall be yours. Many greetings to your parents and the tenderest kiss for yourself from your Geert."

Effi folded the letter and put it back into the envelope.

"That is a very pretty letter," said Mrs. von Briest, "and that it observes d moderation throughout is a further merit."

"Yes, d moderation it surely does observe."

"My dear Effi, let me ask a qstion. Do you wish that the letter did not observe d moderation? Do you wish that it were more affectionate, perhaps gushingly affectionate?"

"No, no, mama. Honestly and truly no, I do not wish that. So it is better as it is."

"So it is better as it is. There you go again. You are so qer. And by the by, a moment ago you were weeping. Is something troubling you? It is not yet too late. Don't you love Geert?"

"Why shouldn't I love him? I love Hulda, and I love Bertha, and I love Hertha. And I love old Mr. Niemeyer, too. And that I love you and papa I don't even need to mention. I love all who mean well by me and are kind to me and humor me. No doubt Geert will humor me, too. To be sure, in his own way. You see he is already thinking of giving me jewelry in Venice. He hasn't the faintest suspicion that I care nothing for jewelry. I care more for climbing and swinging and am always happiest when I expect every moment that something will give way or break and cause me to tumble. It will not cost me my head the first time, you know."

"And perhaps you also love your Cousin von Briest?"

"Yes, very much. He always cheers me."

"And would you have liked to marry Cousin von Briest?"

"Marry? For heaven's sake no. Why, he is still half a boy. Geert is a man, a handsome man, a man with whom I can shine and he will make something of himself in the world. What are you thinking of, mama?"

"Well, that is all right, Effi, I am glad to hear it. But there is something else troubling you."

"Perhaps."

"Well, speak."

"You see, mama, the fact that he is older than I does no harm. Perhaps that is a very good thing. After all he is not old and is well and strong and is so soldierly and so keen. And I might almost say I am altogether in favor of him, if he only--oh, if he were only a little bit different."

"How, pray, Effi."

"Yes, how? Well, you must not laugh at me. It is something that I only very recently overheard, over at the parsonage. We were talking about Innstetten and all of a sudden old Mr. Niemeyer wrinkled his forehead, in wrinkles of respect and admiration, of course, and said: 'Oh yes, the Baron. He is a man of character, a man of principles."

"And that he is, Effi."

"Certainly. And later, I believe, Niemeyer said he is even a man of convictions. Now that, it seems to me, is something more. Alas, and I--I have none. You see, mama, there is something about this that worries me and makes me uneasy. He is so dear and good to me and so considerate, but I am afraid of him."

CHAPTER V

The days of festivity at Hohen-Cremmen were past; all the gsts had departed, likewise the newly married couple, who left the evening of the wedding day.

The nuptial-eve performance had pleased everybody, especially the players, and Hulda had been the delight of all the young officers, not only the Rathenow Hussars, but also their more critically inclined comrades of the Alexander regiment. Indeed everything had gone well and smoothly, almost better than expected. The only thing to be regretted was that Bertha and Hertha had sobbed so violently that Jahnke's Low German verses had been virtually lost. But even that had made but little difference. A few fine connoisseurs had even expressed the opinion that, "to tell the truth, forgetting what to say, sobbing, and unintelligibility, together form the standard under which the most decided victories are won, particularly in the case of pretty, curly red heads." Cousin von Briest had won a signal triumph in his self-composed rÃ´le. He had appeared as one of Demuth's clerks, who had found out that the young bride was planning to go to Italy immediately after the wedding, for which reason he wished to deliver to her a traveling trunk. This trunk proved, of course, to be a giant box of bonbons from HÃ¶vel's. The dancing had contind till three o'clock, with the effect that Briest, who had been gradually talking himself into the highest pitch of champagne excitement, had made various remarks about the torch dance, still in vog at many courts, and the remarkable custom of the garter dance. Since these remarks showed no signs of coming to an end, and kept getting worse and worse, they finally reached the point where they simply had to be choked off. "Pull yourself together, Briest," his wife had whispered to him in a rather earnest tone; "you are not here for the purpose of making indecent remarks, but of doing the honors of the house. We are having at present a wedding and not a hunting party." Whereupon von Briest answered: "I see no difference between the two; besides, I am happy."

The wedding itself had also gone well, Niemeyer had conducted the service in an exquisite fashion, and on the way home from the church one of the old men from Berlin, who half-way belonged to the court circle, made a remark to the effect that it was truly wonderful how thickly talents are distributed in a state like ours. "I see therein a triumph of our schools, and perhaps even more of our philosophy. When I consider how this Niemeyer, an old village preacher, who at first looked like a hospitaler--why, friend, what do you say? Didn't he speak like a court preacher? Such tact, and such skill in antithesis, quite the equal of KÃ¶gel, and in feeling even better. KÃ¶gel is too cold. To be sure, a man in his position has to be cold. Generally speaking, what is it that makes wrecks of the lives of men? Always warmth, and nothing else." It goes without saying that these remarks were assented to by the dignitary to whom they were addressed, a gentleman as yet unmarried, who doubtless for this very reason was, at the time being, involved in his fourth "relation." "Only too tr, dear friend," said he. "Too much warmth--most excellent--Besides, I must tell you a story, later."

The day after the wedding was a clear October day. The morning sun shone bright, yet there was a feeling of autumn chilliness in the air, and von Briest, who had just taken breakfast in company with his wife, arose from his seat and stood, with his hands behind his back, before the slowly dying open fire. Mrs. von Briest, with her fancy work in her hands, moved likewise closer to the fireplace and said to Wilke, who entered just at this point to clear away the breakfast table: "And now, Wilke, when you have everything in order in the dining hall--but that comes first--then see to it that the cakes are taken over to the neighbors, the nutcake to the pastor's and the dish of small cakes to the Jahnkes'. And be careful with the goblets. I mean the thin cut glasses."

Briest had already lighted his third cigarette, and, looking in the best of health, declared that "nothing agrees with one so well as a wedding, excepting one's own, of course."

"I don't know why you should make that remark, Briest. It is absolutely news to me that you suffered at your wedding. I can't imagine why you should have, either."

"Luise, you are a wet blanket, so to speak. But I take nothing amiss, not even a thing like that. Moreover, why should we be talking about ourselves, we who have never even taken a wedding tour? Your father was opposed to it. But Effi is taking a wedding tour now. To be envied. Started on the ten o'clock train. By this time they must be near Ratisbon, and I presume he is enumerating to her the chief art treasures of the Walhalla, without getting off the train--that goes without saying. Innstetten is a splendid fellow, but he is pretty much of an art crank, and Effi, heaven knows, our poor Effi is a child of nature. I am afraid he will annoy her somewhat with his enthusiasm for art."

"Every man annoys his wife, and enthusiasm for art is not the worst thing by a good deal."

"No, certainly not. At all events we will not quarrel about that; it is a wide field. Then, too, people are so different. Now you, you know, would have been the right person for that. Generally speaking, you would have been better suited to Innstetten than Effi. What a pity! But it is too late now."

"Extremely gallant remark, except for the fact that it is not apropos. However, in any case, what has been has been. Now he is my son-in-law, and it can accomplish nothing to be referring back all the while to the affairs of youth."

"I wished merely to rouse you to an animated humor."

"Very kind of you, but it was not necessary. I am in an animated humor."

"Likewise a good one?"

"I might almost say so. But you must not spoil it.--Well, what else is troubling you? I see there is something on your mind."

"Were you pleased with Effi? Were you satisfied with the whole affair? She was so peculiar, half naÃ¯ve, and then again very self-conscious and by no means as demure as she ought to be toward such a husband. That surely must be d solely to the fact that she does not yet fully know what she has in him. Or is it simply that she does not love him very much? That would be bad. For with all his virts he is not the man to win her love with an easy grace."

Mrs. von Briest kept silent and counted the stitches of her fancy work. Finally she said: "What you just said, Briest, is the most sensible thing I have heard from you for the last three days, including your speech at dinner. I, too, have had my misgivings. But I believe we have reason to feel satisfied."

"Has she poured out her heart to you?"

"I should hardly call it that. Tr, she cannot help talking, but she is not disposed to tell everything she has in her heart, and she settles a good many things for herself. She is at once communicative and reticent, almost secretive; in general, a very peculiar mixture."

"I am entirely of your opinion. But how do you know about this if she didn't tell you?"

"I only said she did not pour out her heart to me. Such a general confession, such a complete unburdening of the soul, it is not in her to make. It all came out of her by sudden jerks, so to speak, and then it was all over. But just because it came from her soul so unintentionally and accidentally, as it were, it seemed to me for that very reason so significant."

"When was this, pray, and what was the occasion?"

"Unless I am mistaken, it was just three weeks ago, and we were sitting in the garden, busied with all sorts of things belonging to her trousseau, when Wilke brought a letter from Innstetten. She put it in her pocket and a quarter of an hour later had wholly forgotten about it, till I reminded her that she had a letter. Then she read it, but the expression of her face hardly changed. I confess to you that an anxious feeling came over me, so intense that I felt a strong desire to have all the light on the matter that it is possible to have under the circumstances."

"Very tr, very tr."

27

"What do you mean by that?"

"Well, I mean only--But that is wholly immaterial. Go on with your story; I am all ears."

"So I asked her straight out how matters stood, and as I wished to avoid anything bordering on solemnity, in view of her peculiar character, and sought to take the whole matter as lightly as possible, almost as a joke, in fact, I threw out the qstion, whether she would perhaps prefer to marry Cousin von Briest, who had showered his attentions upon her in Berlin."

"And?"

"You ought to have seen her then. Her first answer was a saucy laugh. Why, she said, her cousin was really only a big cadet in lieutenant's uniform. And she could not even love a cadet, to saying nothing of marrying one. Then she spoke of Innstetten, who suddenly became for her a paragon of manly virts."

"How do you explain that?"

"It's quite simple. Lively, emotional, I might almost say, passionate as she is, or perhaps just because she is so constituted, she is not one of those who are so particularly dependent upon love, at least not upon what truly deserves the name. To be sure, she speaks of love, even with emphasis and a certain tone of conviction, but only because she has somewhere read that love is indisputably the most exalted, most beautiful, most glorious thing in the world. And it may be, perhaps, that she has merely heard it from that sentimental person, Hulda, and repeats it after her. But she does not feel it very deeply. It is barely possible that it will come later. God forbid. But it is not yet at hand."

"Then what is at hand? What ails her?"

"In my judgment, and according to her own testimony, she has two things: mania for amusement and ambition."

"Well, those things can pass away. They do not disturb me."

"They do me. Innstetten is the kind of a man who makes his own career. I will not call him pushing, for he is not, he has too much of the real gentleman in him for that. Let us say, then, he is a man who will make his own career. That will satisfy Effi's ambition."

"Very well. I call that good."

"Yes, it is good. But that is only the half. Her ambition will be satisfied, but how about her inclination for amusement and adventure? I have my doubts. For the little entertainment and awakening of interest, demanded every hour, for the thousand things that overcome ennui, the mortal enemy of a spiritual little person, for these Innstetten will make poor provision. He will not leave her in the midst of an intellectual desert; he is too wise and has had too much experience in the world for that, but he will not specially amuse her either. And, most of all, he will not even bother to ask himself seriously how to go about it. Things can go on thus for a while without doing much harm, but she will finally become aware of the situation and be offended. And then I don't know what will happen. For gentle and yielding as she is, she has, along with these qualities, a certain inclination to fly into a fury, and at such times she hazards everything."

At this point Wilke came in from the dining hall and reported that he had counted everything and found everything there, except that one of the fine wine glasses was broken, but that had occurred yesterday when the toast was drunk. Miss Hulda had clinked her glass too hard against Lieutenant Nienkerk's.

"Of course, half asleep and always has been, and lying under the elder tree has obviously not improved matters. A silly person, and I don't understand Nienkerk."

"I understand him perfectly."

"But he can't marry her."

"No."

"His purpose, then?"

"A wide field, Luise."

This was the day after the wedding. Three days later came a scribbled little card from Munich, with all the names on it indicated by two letters only. "Dear mama: This morning we visited the Pinakothek. Geert wanted to go over to the other museum, too, the name of which I will not mention here, because I am in doubt about the right way to spell it, and I dislike to ask him. I must say, he is angelic to me and explains everything. Generally speaking, everything is very beautiful, but it's a strain. In Italy it will probably slacken somewhat and get better. We are lodging at the 'Four Seasons,' which fact gave Geert occasion to remark to me, that 'outside it was autumn, but in me he was having spring.' I consider that a very graceful compliment. He is really very attentive. To be sure, I have to be attentive, too, especially when he says something or is giving me an explanation. Besides, he knows everything so well that he doesn't even need to consult a guide book. He delights to talk of you two, especially mama. He considers

Hulda somewhat affected, but old Mr. Niemeyer has completely captivated him. A thousand greetings from your thoroughly entranced, but somewhat weary Effi."

Similar cards now arrived daily, from Innsbruck, from Vicenza, from Padua. Every one began: "We visited the famous gallery here this morning," or, if it was not the gallery, it was an arena or some church of "St. Mary" with a surname. From Padua came, along with the card, a real letter. "Yesterday we were in Vicenza. One must see Vicenza on account of Palladio. Geert told me that everything modern had its roots in him. Of course, with reference only to architecture. Here in Padua, where we arrived this morning, he said to himself several times in the hotel omnibus, 'He lies in Padua interred,' and was surprised when he discovered that I had never heard these words. But finally he said it was really very well and in my favor that I knew nothing about them. He is very just, I must say. And above all he is angelic to me and not a bit overbearing and not at all old, either. I still have pains in my feet, and the consulting of guide books and standing so long before pictures wears me out. But it can't be helped, you know. I am looking forward to Venice with much pleasure. We shall stay there five days, perhaps even a whole week. Geert has already begun to rave about the pigeons in St. Mark's Square, and the fact that one can buy there little bags of peas and feed them to the pretty birds. There are said to be paintings representing this scene, with beautiful blonde maidens, 'a type like Hulda,' as he said. And that reminds me of the Jahnke girls. I would give a good deal if I could be sitting with them on a wagon tong in our yard and feeding *our* pigeons. Now, you must not kill the fan tail pigeon with the big breast; I want to see it again. Oh, it is so beautiful here. This is even said to be the most beautiful of all. Your happy, but somewhat weary Effi."

When Mrs. von Briest had finished reading the letter she said: "The poor child. She is homesick."

"Yes," said von Briest, "she is homesick. This accursed traveling--"

"Why do you say that now! You might have hindered it, you know. But it is just your way to play the wise man after a thing is all over. After a child has fallen into the well the aldermen cover up the well."

"Ah, Luise, don't bother me with that kind of stuff. Effi is our child, but since the 3d of October she has been the Baroness of Innstetten. And if her husband, our son-in-law, desires to take a wedding tour and use it as an occasion for making a new catalog of every gallery, I can't keep him from doing it. That is what it means to get married."

"So now you admit it. In talking with me you have always denied, yes, always denied that the wife is in a condition of restraint."

"Yes, Luise, I have. But what is the use of discussing that now? It is really too wide a field."

CHAPTER VI

Innstetten's leave of absence was to expire the 15th of November, and so when they had reached Capri and Sorrento he felt morally bound to follow his usual habit of returning to his duties on the day and at the hour designated. So on the morning of the 14th they arrived by the fast express in Berlin, where Cousin von Briest met them and proposed that they should make use of the two hours before the departure of the Stettin train to pay a visit to the Panorama and then have a little luncheon together. Both proposals were accepted with thanks. At noon they returned to the station, shook hands heartily and said good-by, after both Effi and her husband had extended the customary invitation, "Do come to see us some day," which fortunately is never taken seriously. As the train started Effi waved a last farewell from her compartment. Then she leaned back and made herself comfortable, but from time to time sat up and held out her hand to Innstetten.

It was a pleasant journey, and the train arrived on time at the Klein-Tantow station, from which a turnpike led to Kessin, ten miles away. In the summer time, especially during the tourist season, travelers were accustomed to avoid the turnpike and take the water route, going by an old sidewheel steamer down the Kessine, the river from which Kessin derived its name. But the "Phoenix"--about which the wish had long been vainly cherished, that, at some time when there were no passengers on board, it might justify its name and burn to ashes--regularly stopped running on the 1st of October. For this reason Innstetten had telegraphed from Stettin to his coachman Kruse: "Five o'clock, Klein-Tantow station. Open carriage, if good weather."

It certainly was good weather, and there sat Kruse in the open carriage at the station. He greeted the newly arrived couple with all the prescribed dignity of a first-class coachman.

"Well, Kruse, everything in order?"

"At your service, Sir Councillor."

"Then, Effi, please get in." As Effi was doing as bid, and one of the station porters was finding a place for a small satchel by the coachman, in front, Innstetten left orders to send the rest of the luggage by the omnibus. Then he, too, took his seat and after condescendingly asking one of the bystanders for a light called to Kruse: "Drive on, Kruse." The carriage rolled quickly over the rails of the many tracks at the crossing, then slantingly down the slope of the embankment, and on the turnpike past an inn called "The Prince Bismarck." At this point the road forked, one branch leading to the right to Kessin, the other to the left to Varzin. In front of the inn stood a moderately tall, broad-shouldered man in a fur coat and a fur cap. The cap he took off with great deference as the District Councillor drove by. "Pray, who was that?" said Effi, who was extremely interested in all she saw and conseqntly in the best of humor. "He looked like a starost, though I am forced to confess I never saw a starost before."

"Which is no loss, Effi. You gssed very well just the same. He does really look like a starost and is something of the sort, too. I mean by that, he is half Polish. His name is Golchowski, and whenever we have an election or a hunt here, he is at the top of the list. In reality he is a very unsafe fellow, whom I would not trust across the road, and he doubtless has a great deal on his conscience. But he assumes an air of loyalty, and when the quality of Varzin go by here he would like nothing better than to throw himself before their carriages. I know that at the same time he is hostile to the Prince. But what is the use? We must not have any misunderstandings with him, for we need him. He has this whole region in his pocket and understands electioneering better than any one else. Besides, he is considered well-to-do and lends out money at usury which is contrary to the ordinary practice of the Poles."

"But he was good-looking."

"Yes, good-looking he is. Most of the people here are good-looking. A handsome strain of human beings. But that is the best that can be said of them. Your Brandenburg people look more unostentatious and more ill-humored, and in their conduct they are less respectful, in fact, are not at all respectful, but their yes is yes and no is no, and one can depend upon them. Here everybody is uncertain."

"Why do you tell me that, since I am obliged to live here among them now?"

"Not you. You will not hear or see much of them. For city and country are here very different, and you will become acquainted with our city people only, our good people of Kessin."

"Our good people of Kessin. Is that sarcasm, or are they really so good?"

"That they are really good is not exactly what I mean to say, but they are different from the others; in fact, they have no similarity whatever to the country inhabitants here."

"How does that come?"

"Because they are entirely different human beings, by ancestry and association. The people you find in the country here are the so-called Cassubians, of whom you may have heard, a Slavic race, who have been living here for a thousand years and probably much longer. But all the inhabitants of our seaports, and the commercial cities near the coast, have moved here from a distance and trouble themselves very little about the

Cassubian backwoods, because they derive little profit from that source and are dependent upon entirely different sources. The sources upon which they are dependent are the regions with which they have commercial relations, and as their commerce brings them into touch with the whole world you will find among them people from every nook and corner of the earth, even here in our good Kessin, in spite of the fact that it is nothing but a miserable hole."

"Why, that is perfectly charming, Geert. You are always talking about the miserable hole, but I shall find here an entirely new world, if you have not exaggerated. All kinds of exotics. That is about what you meant, isn't it?"

He nodded his head.

"An entirely new world, I say, perhaps a negro, or a Turk, or perhaps even a Chinaman."

"Yes, a Chinaman, too. How well you can gss! It may be that we still have one. He is dead now and buried in a little fenced-in plot of ground close by the churchyard. If you are not easily frightened I will show you his grave some day. It is situated among the dunes, with nothing but lyme grass around it, and here and there a few immortelles, and one always hears the sea. It is very beautiful and very uncanny."

"Oh, uncanny? I should like to know more about it. But I would better not. Such stories make me have visions and dreams, and if, as I hope, I sleep well tonight, I should certainly not like to see a Chinaman come walking up to my bed the first thing."

"You will not, either."

"Not, either? Upon my word, that sounds strange, as though, after all, it were possible. You seek to make Kessin interesting to me, but you carry it a trifle too far. And have you many such foreigners in Kessin?"

"A great many. The whole population is made up of such foreigners, people whose parents and grandparents lived in an entirely different region."

"Most remarkable. Please tell me more about them. But no more creepy stories. I feel that there is always something creepy about a Chinaman."

"Yes, there is," laughed Geert, "but the rest, thank heaven, are of an entirely different sort, all mannerly people, perhaps a little bit too commercial, too thoughtful of their own advantage, and always on hand with bills of qstionable val. In fact, one must be cautious with them. But otherwise they are quite agreeable. And to let you see that I have not been deceiving you I will just give you a little sample, a sort of index or list of names."

33

"Please do, Geert."

"For example, we have, not fifty paces from our house, and our gardens are even adjoining, the master machinist and dredger Macpherson, a real Scotchman and a Highlander."

"And he still wears the native costume?"

"No, thank heaven, he doesn't, for he is a shriveled up little man, of whom neither his clan nor Walter Scott would be particularly proud. And then we have, further, in the same house where this Macpherson lives, an old surgeon by the name of Beza, in reality only a barber. He comes from Lisbon, the same place that the famous general De Meza comes from. Meza, Beza; you can hear the national relationship. And then we have, up the river by the quay, where the ships lie, a goldsmith by the name of Stedingk, who is descended from an old Swedish family; indeed, I believe there are counts of the empire by that name. Further, and with this man I will close for the present, we have good old Dr. Hannemann, who of course is a Dane, and was a long time in Iceland, has even written a book on the last eruption of Hekla, or Krabla."

"Why, that is magnificent, Geert. It is like having six novels that one can never finish reading. At first it sounds commonplace, but afterward seems quite out of the ordinary. And then you must also have people, simply because it is a seaport, who are not mere surgeons or barbers or anything of the sort. You must also have captains, some flying Dutchman or other, or--"

"You are quite right. We even have a captain who was once a pirate among the Black Flags."

"I don't know what you mean. What are Black Flags?"

"They are people away off in Tonquin and the South Sea--But since he has been back among men he has resumed the best kind of manners and is quite entertaining."

"I should be afraid of him nevertheless."

"You don't need to be, at any time, not even when I am out in the country or at the Prince's for tea, for along with everything else that we have, we have, thank heaven, also Rollo."

"Rollo?"

"Yes, Bollo. The name makes you think of the Norman Duke, provided you have ever heard Niemeyer or Jahnke speak of him. Our Rollo has somewhat the same character.

34

But he is only a Newfoundland dog, a most beautiful animal, that loves me and will love you, too. For Rollo is a connoisseur. So long as you have him about you, you are safe, and nothing can get at you, neither a live man nor a dead one. But just see the moon over yonder. Isn't it beautiful?"

Effi, who had been leaning back quietly absorbed, drinking in every word, half timorously, half eagerly, now sat erect and looked out to the right, where the moon had just risen behind a white mass of clouds, which quickly floated by. Copper-colored hung the great disk behind a clump of alders and shed its light upon the expanse of water into which the Kessine here widens out. Or perhaps it might be looked upon as one of the fresh-water lakes connected with the Baltic Sea.

Effi was stupefied. "Yes, you are right, Geert, how beautiful! But at the same time there is something uncanny about it. In Italy I never had such a sensation, not even when we were going over from Mestre to Venice. There, too, we had water and swamps and moonlight, and I thought the bridge would break. But it was not so spooky. What is the cause of it, I wonder? Can it be the northern latitude?"

Innstetten laughed. "We are here seventy-five miles further north than in Hohen-Cremmen, and you have still a while to wait before we come to the first polar bear. I think you are nervous from the long journey and the Panorama, not to speak of the story of the Chinaman."

"Why, you didn't tell me any story."

"No, I only mentioned him. But a Chinaman is in himself a story."

"Yes," she laughed.

"In any case you will soon recover. Do you see the little house yonder with the light? It is a blacksmith's shop. There the road bends. And when we have passed the bend you will be able to see the tower of Kessin, or to be more exact, the two."

"Has it two?"

"Yes, Kessin is picking up. It now has a Catholic church also."

A half hour later the carriage stopped at the district councillor's residence, which stood clear at the opposite end of the city. It was a simple, rather old-fashioned, frame-house with plaster between the timbers, and stood facing the main street, which led to the sea-baths, while its gable looked down upon a grove, between the city limits and the dunes, which was called the "Plantation." Furthermore this old-fashioned frame-house was only Innstetten's private residence, not the real district councillor's office. The latter stood diagonally across the street.

It was not necessary for Kruse to announce their arrival with three cracks of his whip. The servants had long been watching at the doors and windows for their master and mistress, and even before the carriage stopped all the inmates of the house were grouped upon the stone doorstep, which took up the whole width of the sidewalk. In front of them was Rollo, who, the moment the carriage stopped, began to circle around it. Innstetten first of all helped his young wife to alight. Then, offering her his arm, he walked with a friendly bow past the servants, who promptly turned and followed him into the entrance-hall, which was furnished with splendid old wardrobes and cases standing around the walls. The housemaid, a pretty girl, no longer very young, whose stately plumpness was almost as becoming to her as the neat little cap on her blonde head, helped her mistress take off her muff and cloak, and was just stooping down to take off her fur-lined rubber shoes. But before she had time to make a beginning, Innstetten said: "I suppose the best thing will be for me to introduce to you right here all the occupants of our house, with the exception of Mrs. Kruse, who does not like to be seen, and who, I presume, is holding her inevitable black chicken again." Everybody smiled. "But never mind Mrs. Kruse. Here is my old Frederick, who was with me when I was at the university. Good times then, weren't they, Frederick?--This is Johanna, a fellow countrywoman of yours, if you count those who come from the region of Pasewalk as full-fledged Brandenburgians; and this is Christel, to whom we trust our bodily welfare every noon and evening, and who knows how to cook, I can assure you.--And this is Rollo. Well, Rollo, how goes it?"

Rollo seemed only to have waited for this special greeting, for the moment he heard his name he gave a bark for joy, stood up on his hind legs and laid his forepaws on his master's shoulders.

"That will do, Rollo, that will do. But look here; this is my wife. I have told her about you and said that you were a beautiful animal and would protect her." Hereupon Rollo ceased fawning and sat down in front of Innstetten, looking up curiously at the young wife. And when she held out her hand to him he frisked around her.

During this introduction scene Effi had found time to look about. She was enchanted, so to speak, by everything she saw, and at the same time dazzled by the abundant light. In the forepart of the hall were burning four or five wall lights, the reflectors themselves very primitive, simply of tin-plate, which, however, only improved the light and heightened the splendor. Two astral lamps with red shades, a wedding present from Niemeyer, stood on a folding table between two oak cupboards. On the front of the table was the tea service, with the little lamp under the kettle already lighted. There were, beside these, many, many other things, some of them very qer. From one side of the hall to the other ran three beams, dividing the ceiling into sections. From the front one was suspended a ship under full sail, high quarter-deck, and cannon ports, while farther toward the front door a gigantic fish seemed to be swimming in the air. Effi took her umbrella, which she still held in her hand, and pushed gently against the monster, so that it set up a slow rocking motion.

"What is that, Geert?" she asked.

"That is a shark."

"And that thing, clear at the end of the hall, that looks like a huge cigar in front of a tobacco store?"

"That is a young crocodile. But you can look at all these things better and more in detail tomorrow. Come now and let us take a cup of tea. For in spite of shawls and rugs you must have been chilled. Toward the last it was bitter cold."

He offered Effi his arm and the two maids retired. Only Frederick and Rollo followed the master of the house as he took his wife into his sitting room and study. Effi was as much surprised here as she had been in the hall, but before she had time to say anything, Innstetten drew back a portiere, which disclosed a second, larger room looking out on the court and garden. "Now this, Effi, is your room. Frederick and Johanna have tried to arrange it the best they could in accordance with my orders. I find it quite tolerable and should be happy if you liked it, too."

She withdrew her arm from his and stood up on her tip-toes to give him a hearty kiss. "Poor little thing that I am, how you do spoil me! This grand piano! and this rug! Why, I believe it is Turkish. And the bowl with the little fishes, and the flower table besides! Luxuries, everywhere I look."

"Ah, my dear Effi, you will have to put up with that. It is to be expected when one is young and pretty and amiable. And I presume the inhabitants of Kessin have already found out about you, heaven knows from what source. For of the flower table, at least, I am innocent. Frederick, where did the flower table come from?"

"Apothecary Gieshübler. There is a card on it."

"Ah, Gieshübler, Alonzo Gieshübler," said Innstetten, laughingly and almost boisterously handing the card with the foreign-sounding first name to Effi. "Gieshübler. I forgot to tell you about him. Let me say in passing that he bears the doctor's title, but does not like to be addressed by it. He says it only vexes the real doctors, and I presume he is right about that. Well, I think you will become acquainted with him and that soon. He is our best number here, a bel-esprit and an original, but especially a man of soul, which is after all the chief thing. But enough of these things; let us sit down and drink our tea. Where shall it be? Here in your room or over there in mine! There is no other choice. Snug and tiny is my cabin."

Without hesitating she sat down on a little corner sofa. "Let us stay here today; you will be my gst today. Or let us say, rather: Tea regularly in my room, breakfast in yours. Then each will secure his rights, and I am curious to know where I shall like it best."

"That will be a morning and evening qstion."

"Certainly. But the way it is put, or better, our attitude toward it, is the important thing."

With that she laughed and cuddled up to him and was about to kiss his hand.

"No, Effi, for heaven's sake, don't do that. It is not my desire to be a person looked up to with awe and respect. I am, for the inhabitants of Kessin, but for you I am--"

"What, pray?"

"Ah, let that pass. Far be it from me to say what."

CHAPTER VII

The sun was shining brightly when Effi awoke the next morning. It was hard for her to get her bearings. Where was she? Correct, in Kessin, in the house of District Councillor von Innstetten, and she was his wife, Baroness Innstetten. Sitting up she looked around with curiosity. During the evening before she had been too tired to examine very carefully all the half-foreign, half-old-fashioned things that surrounded her. Two pillars supported the ceiling beam, and green curtains shut off from the rest of the room the alcove-like sleeping apartment in which the beds stood. But in the middle a curtain was either lacking or pulled back, and this afforded her a comfortable orientation from her bed. There between the two windows stood the narrow, but very high, pier-glass, while a little to the right, along the hall wall, towered the tile stove, the door of which, as she had discovered the evening before, opened into the hall in the old-fashioned way. She now felt its warmth radiating toward her. How fine it was to be in her own home! At no time during the whole tour had she enjoyed so much comfort, not even in Sorrento.

But where was Innstetten? All was still round about her, nobody was there. She heard only the tick-tock of a small clock and now and then a low sound in the stove, from which she inferred that a few new sticks of wood were being shoved in from the hall. Gradually she recalled that Geert had spoken the evening before of an electric bell, for which she did not have to search long. Close by her pillows was the little white ivory button, and she now pressed softly upon it.

Johanna appeared at once. "At your Ladyship's service."

"Oh, Johanna, I believe I have overslept myself. It must be late."

"Just nine."

"And my--" She couldn't make herself speak straightway of her "husband." "His Lordship, he must have kept very quiet. I didn't hear anything."

"I'm sure he did. And your Ladyship has slept soundly. After the long journey--"

"Yes, I have. And his Lordship, is he always up so early?"

"Always, your Ladyship. On that point he is strict; he cannot endure late sleeping, and when he enters his room across the hall the stove must be warm, and the coffee must not be late."

"So he has already had his breakfast?"

"Oh, no, your Ladyship--His Lordship--"

Effi felt that she ought not to have asked the qstion and would better have kept to herself the suspicion that Innstetten might not have waited for her. So she was very eager to correct her mistake the best she could, and when she had got up and taken a seat before the pier-glass she resumed the conversation, saying: "Moreover, his Lordship is quite right. Always to be up early was likewise the rule in my parents' home. When people sleep away the morning, everything is out of gear the rest of the day. But his Lordship will not be so strict with me. For a long time last night I couldn't sleep, and was even frightened a little bit."

"What must I hear, your Ladyship? What was it, pray?"

"There was a very strange noise overhead, not loud, but very penetrating. At first it sounded as though gowns with long trains were dragging over the floor, and in my excitement it seemed a few times as though I heard little white satin slippers. It seemed as though they were dancing overhead, but quite softly."

As the conversation ran on thus Johanna glanced over the shoulder of the young wife at the tall narrow mirror in order the better to observe Effi's facial expressions. In reply she said: "Oh, yes, that is up in the social room. We used to hear it in the kitchen, too. But now we don't hear it any more; we have become accustomed to it."

"Is there anything unusual about it?"

"God forbid, not in the least. For a while no one knew for sure what it came from, and even the preacher looked embarrassed, in spite of the fact that Dr. Gieshübler always simply laughed at it. But now we know that it comes from the curtains. The room is inclined to be musty and damp, and for that reason the windows are always left open, except when there is a storm. And so, as there is nearly always a strong draft upstairs, the wind sweeps the old white curtains, which I think are much too long, back and forth over the floor. That makes a sound like silk dresses, or even satin slippers, as your Ladyship just said."

"That is it, of course. But what I cannot understand is why the curtains are not taken down. Or they might be made shorter. It is such a qer noise that it gets on one's nerves. And now, Johanna, give me the little cape and put just a little dab of powder on my forehead. Or, better still, take the 'refresher' from my traveling bag--Ah, that is fine and refreshes me. Now I am ready to go over. He is still there, isn't he, or has he been out?"

"His Lordship went out earlier; I believe he was over at the office. But he has been back for a quarter of an hour. I will tell Frederick to bring the breakfast."

With that Johanna left the room. Effi took one more look into the mirror and then walked across the hall, which in the daylight lost much of its charm of the evening before, and stepped into Geert's room.

He was sitting at his secretary, a rather clumsy cylindrical desk, which, however, he did not care to part with, as it was an heirloom. Effi was standing behind him, and had embraced and kissed him before he could rise from his chair.

"So early?"

"So early, you say. Of course, to mock me."

Innstetten shook his head. "How can I?" Effi took pleasure in accusing herself, however, and refused to listen to the assurances of her husband that his "so early" had been meant in all seriousness. "You must know from our journey that I have never kept you waiting in the morning. In the course of the day--well, that is a different matter. It is tr, I am not very punctual, but I am not a late sleeper. In that respect my parents have given me good training, I think."

"In that respect? In everything, my sweet Effi."

"You say that just because we are still on our honeymoon,--why no, we are past that already. For heaven's sake, Geert, I hadn't given it a single thought, and--why, we have

40

been married for over six weeks, six weeks and a day. Yes, that alters the case. So I shall not take it as flattery, I shall take it as the truth."

At this moment Frederick came in and brought the coffee. The breakfast table stood across the corner of the sitting room in front of a sofa made just in the right shape and size to fill that corner. They both sat down upon the sofa.

"The coffee is simply delicious," said Effi, as she looked at the room and its furnishings. "This is as good as hotel coffee or that we had at Bottegone's--you remember, don't you, in Florence, with the view of the cathedral? I must write mama about it. We don't have such coffee in Hohen-Cremmen. On the whole, Geert, I am just beginning to realize what a distinguished husband I married. In our home everything was just barely passable."

"Nonsense, Effi. I never saw better house-keeping than in your home."

"And then how well your house is furnished. When papa had bought his new weapon cabinet and hung above his writing desk the head of a buffalo, and beneath that a picture of old general Wrangel, under whom he had once served as an adjutant, he was very proud of what he had done. But when I see these things here, all our Hohen-Cremmen elegance seems by the side of them merely commonplace and meagre. I don't know what to compare them with. Even last night, when I took but a cursory look at them, a world of ideas occurred to me."

"And what were they, if I may ask?"

"What they were? Certainly. But you must not laugh at them. I once had a picture book, in which a Persian or Indian prince (for he wore a turban) sat with his feet under him on a silk cushion, and at his back there was a great red silk bolster, which could be seen bulging out to the right and left of him, and the wall behind the Indian prince bristled with swords and daggers and panther skins and shields and long Turkish guns. And see, it looks just like that here in your house, and if you will cross your legs and sit down on them the similarity will be complete."

"Effi, you are a charming, dear creature. You don't know how deeply I feel that and how much I should like to show you every moment that I do feel it."

"Well, there will be plenty of time for that. I am only seventeen, you know, and have not yet made up my mind to die."

"At least not before I do. To be sure, if I should die first, I should like to take you with me. I do not want to leave you to any other man. What do you say to that?"

41

"Oh, I must have some time to think about it. Or, rather, let us not think about it at all. I don't like to talk about death; I am for life. And now tell me, how shall we live here? On our travels you told me all sorts of qer things about the city and the country, but not a word about how we shall live here. That here nothing is the same as in Hohen-Cremmen and Schwantikow, I see plainly, and yet we must be able to have something like intercourse and society in 'good Kessin,' as you are always calling it. Have you any people of family in the city?"

"No, my dear Effi. In this regard you are going to meet with great disappointments. We have in the neighborhood a few noble families with which you will become acquainted, but here in the city there is nobody at all."

"Nobody at all? That I can't believe. Why, you are upward of three thousand people, and among three thousand people there certainly must be, beside such inferior individuals as Barber Beza (I believe that was his name), a certain Ã©lite, officials and the like."

Innstetten laughed. "Yes, officials there are. But when you examine them narrowly it doesn't mean much. Of course, we have a preacher and a judge and a school principal and a commander of pilots, and of such people in official positions I presume there may be as many as a dozen altogether, but they are for the most part, as the proverb says, good men, but poor fiddlers. And all the others are nothing but consuls."

"Nothing but consuls! I beg you, Geert, how can you say 'nothing but consuls?' Why, they are very high and grand, and, I might almost say, awe-inspiring individuals. Consuls, I thought, were the men with the bundles of rods, out of which an ax blade projected."

"Not quite, Effi. Those men are called lictors."

"Right, they are called lictors. But consuls are also men of very high rank and authority. Brutus was a consul, was he not?"

"Yes, Brutus was a consul. But ours are not very much like him and are content to handle sugar and coffee, or open a case of oranges and sell them to you at ten pfennigs apiece."

"Not possible."

"Indeed it is certain. They are tricky little tradesmen, who are always at hand with their advice on any qstion of business, when foreign vessels put in here and are at a loss to know what to do. And when they have given advice and rendered service to some Dutch or Portugse vessel, they are likely in the end to become accredited representatives of such foreign states, and so we have just as many consuls in Kessin as we have ambassadors and envoys in Berlin. Then whenever there is a holiday, and we have many

42

holidays here, all the flags are hoisted, and, if we happen to have a bright sunny morning, on such days you can see all Europe flying flags from our roofs, and the star-spangled banner and the Chinese dragon besides."

"You are in a scoffing mood, Geert, and yet you may be right. But I for my part, insignificant though I be, must confess, that I consider all this charming and that our Havelland cities are nothing in comparison. When the Emperor's birthday is celebrated in our region the only flags hoisted are just the black and white, with perhaps a bit of red here and there, but that is not to be compared with the world of flags you speak of. Generally speaking, I find over and over again, as I have already said, that everything here has a certain foreign air about it, and I have not yet seen or heard a thing that has not more or less amazed me. Yesterday evening, for example, there was that remarkable ship out in the hall, and behind it the shark and the crocodile. And here your own room. Everything so oriental and, I cannot help repeating, everything as in the palace of an Indian prince."

"Well and good! I congratulate you, Princess."

"And then upstairs the social room with its long curtains, which sweep over the floor."

"Now what, pray, do you know about that room?"

"Nothing beyond what I just told you. For about an hour while I lay awake in the night it seemed to me as though I heard shoes gliding over the floor, and as though there were dancing, and something almost like music, too. But all very quiet. I told Johanna about it this morning, merely in order to excuse myself for sleeping so long afterwards. She told me that it came from the long curtains up in the social room. I think we shall put a stop to that by cutting off a piece of the curtains or at least closing the windows. The weather will soon turn stormy enough, anyhow. The middle of November is the time, you know."

Innstetten was a trifle embarrassed and sat with a puzzled look on his face, seemingly undecided whether or not he should attempt to allay all these fears. Finally he made up his mind to ignore them. "You are quite right, Effi, we can shorten the long curtains upstairs. But there is no hurry about it, especially as it is not certain whether it will do any good. It may be something else, in the chimney, or a worm in the wood, or a polecat. For we have polecats here. But, in any case, before we undertake any changes you must first examine our whole house, under my guidance; that goes without saying. We can do it in a quarter of an hour. Then you make your toilette, dress up just a little bit, for in reality you are most charming as you are now. You must get ready for our friend GieshÃ¼bler. It is now past ten, and I should be very much mistaken in him if he did not put in his appearance here at eleven, or at twelve at the very latest, in order most devotedly to lay his homage at your feet. This, by the way, is the kind of language he indulges in. Otherwise he is, as I have already said, a capital man, who will become your friend, if I know him and you aright."

43

CHAPTER VIII

It was long after eleven, but nothing had been seen of Gieshübler as yet. "I can't wait any longer," Geert had said, whose duties called him away. "If Gieshübler comes while I am gone, receive him as kindly as possible and the call will go especially well. He must not become embarrassed. When he is ill at ease he cannot find a word to say, or says the qerest kind of things. But if you can win his confidence and put him in a good humor he will talk like a book. Well, you will do that easily enough. Don't expect me before three; there is a great deal to do over across the way. And the matter of the room upstairs we will consider further. Doubtless, the best thing will be to leave it as it is."

With that Innstetten went away and left his young wife alone. She sat, leaning back, in a quiet, snug corner by the window, and, as she looked out, rested her left arm on a small side leaf drawn out of the cylindrical desk. The street was the chief thoroughfare leading to the beach, for which reason there was a great deal of traffic here in the summer time, but now, in the middle of November, it was all empty and quiet, and only a few poor children, whose parents lived in thatched cottages clear at the further edge of the "Plantation" came clattering by in their wooden shoes. But Effi felt none of this loneliness, for her fancy was still engaged with the strange things she had seen a short time before during her examination of the house.

This examination began with the kitchen, which had a range of modern make, while an electric wire ran along the ceiling and into the maids' room. These two improvements had only recently been made, and Effi was pleased when Innstetten told her about them. Next they went from the kitchen back into the hall and from there out into the court, the first half of which was little more than a narrow passage-way running along between the two side wings of the house. In these wings were to be found all the other rooms set apart for house-keeping purposes. In the right the maids' room, the manservant's room, and the mangling room; to the left the coachman's quarters, situated between the stable and the carriage shed and occupied by the Kruse family. Over this room was the chicken house, while a trap door in the roof of the stable furnished ingress and egress for the pigeons. Effi had inspected all these parts of the house with a great deal of interest, but this interest was exceeded by far when, upon returning from the court to the front of the house, she followed Innstetten's leading and climbed the stairway to the upper story. The stairs were askew, ramshackly, and dark; but the hall, to which they led, almost gave one a cheerful sensation, because it had a great deal of light and a good view of the surrounding landscape. In one direction it looked out over the roofs of the outskirts of the city and the "Plantation," toward a Dutch windmill standing high up on a dune; in the other it looked out upon the Kessine, which here, just above its mouth, was rather broad and stately. It was a striking view and Effi did not hesitate to give lively expression to her pleasure. "Yes, very beautiful, very picturesq," answered

Innstetten, without going more into detail, and then opened a double door to the right, with leaves hanging somewhat askew, which led into the so-called social room. This room ran clear across the whole story. Both front and back windows were open and the oft-mentioned curtains swung back and forth in the strong draft. From the middle of one side wall projected an open fireplace with a large stone mantlepiece, while on the opposite wall there hung a few tin candlesticks, each with two candle sockets, just like those downstairs in the hall, except that everything looked dingy and neglected. Effi was somewhat disappointed and frankly said so. Then she remarked that she would rather look at the rooms across the hall than at this miserable, deserted social room. "To tell the truth, there is absolutely nothing over there," answered Innstetten, but he opened the doors nevertheless. Here were four rooms with one window each, all tinted yellow, to match the social room, and all completely empty, except that in one there stood three rush-bottomed chairs, with seats broken through. On the back of one was pasted a little picture, only half a finger long, representing a Chinaman in bl coat and wide yellow trousers, with a low-crowned hat on his head. Effi saw it and said: "What is the Chinaman doing here?" Innstetten himself seemed surprised at the picture and assured her that he did not know. "Either Christel or Johanna has pasted it there. Child's play. You can see it is cut out of a primer." Effi agreed with that and was only surprised that Innstetten took everything so seriously, as though it meant something after all.

Then she cast another glance into the social room and said, in effect, that it was really a pity all that room should stand empty. "We have only three rooms downstairs and if anybody comes to visit us we shall not know whither to turn. Don't you think one could make two handsome gst rooms out of the social room? This would just suit mama. She could sleep in the back room and would have the view of the river and the two moles, and from the front room she could see the city and the Dutch windmill. In Hohen-Cremmen we have even to this day only a German windmill. Now say, what do you think of it? Next May mama will surely come."

Innstetten agreed to everything, only he said finally: "That is all very well. But after all it will be better if we give your mama rooms over in the district councillor's office building. The whole second story is vacant there, just as it is here, and she will have more privacy there."

That was the result, so to speak, which the first walk around through the house accomplished. Effi then made her toilette, but not so quickly as Innstetten had supposed, and now she was sitting in her husband's room, turning her thoughts first to the little Chinaman upstairs, then to Gieshübler, who still did not come. To be sure, a quarter of an hour before, a stoop-shouldered and almost deformed little gentleman in an elegant short fur coat and a very smooth-brushed silk hat, too tall for his proportions, had walked past on the other side of the street and had glanced over at her window. But that could hardly have been Gieshübler. No, this stoop-shouldered man, who had such a distinguished air about him, must have been the presiding judge, and she recalled then that she had once seen such a person at a reception given by Aunt Therese, but it suddenly occurred to her that Kessin had only a lower court judge.

While she was still following out this chain of thought the object of her reflections, who had apparently been taking a morning stroll, or perhaps a promenade around the "Plantation" to bolster up his courage, came in sight again, and a minute later Frederick entered to announce Apothecary GieshÃ¼bler.

"Ask him kindly to come in."

The poor young wife's heart fluttered, for it was the first time that she had to appear as a housewife, to say nothing of the first woman of the city.

Frederick helped GieshÃ¼bler take off his fur coat and then opened the door.

Effi extended her hand to the timidly entering caller, who kissed it with a certain amount of fervor. The young wife seemed to have made a great impression upon him immediately.

"My husband has already told me--But I am receiving you here in my husband's room,-- he is over at the office and may be back any moment. May I ask you to step into my room?"

GieshÃ¼bler followed Effi, who led the way into the adjoining room, where she pointed to one of the arm chairs, as she herself sat down on the sofa. "I wish I could tell you what a great pleasure it was yesterday to receive the beautiful flowers with your card. I straightway ceased to feel myself a stranger here and when I mentioned the fact to Innstetten he told me we should unqstionably be good friends."

"Did he say that? The good councillor. In the councillor and you, most gracious Lady,--I beg your permission to say it--two dear people have been united. For what kind of a man your husband is, I know, and what kind of a woman you are, most gracious Lady, I see."

"Provided only you do not look at me with too friendly eyes. I am so very young. And youth--"

"Ah, most gracious Lady, say nothing against youth. Youth, even with all its mistakes, is still beautiful and lovable, and age, even with its virts, is not good for much. Personally I have, it is tr, no right to say anything about this subject. About age I might have, perhaps, but not about youth, for, to be frank, I was never young. Persons with my misfortune are never young. That, it may as well be said, is the saddest feature of the case. One has no tr spirit, one has no self-confidence, one hardly ventures to ask a lady for the honor of a dance, because one does not desire to cause her an embarrassment, and thus the years go by and one grows old, and life has been poor and empty."

Effi gave him her hand. "Oh, you must not say such things. We women are by no means so bad."

"Oh, no, certainly not."

"And when I recall," contind Effi, "what all I have experienced--it is not much, for I have gone out but little, and have almost always lived in the country--but when I recall it, I find that, after all, we always love what is worthy of love. And then I see, too, at once that you are different from other men. We women have sharp eyes in such matters. Perhaps in your case the name has something to do with it. That was always a favorite assertion of our old pastor Niemeyer. The name, he loved to say, especially the forename, has a certain mysterious determining inflnce; and Alonzo GieshÃ¼bler, in my opinion, opens to one a whole new world, indeed I feel almost tempted to say, Alonzo is a romantic name, a fastidious name."

GieshÃ¼bler smiled with a very unusual degree of satisfaction and mustered up the courage to lay aside his silk hat, which up to this time he had been turning in his hand. "Yes, most gracious Lady, you hit the nail on the head that time."

Oh, I understand. I have heard about the consuls, of Kessin is said to have so many, and at the home of the Spanish consul your father presumably made the acquaintance of the daughter of a sea-captain, a beautiful Andalusian girl, I suppose; Andalusian girls are always beautiful."

"Precisely as you suppose, most gracious Lady. And my mother really was a beautiful woman, ill as it behooves me personally to undertake to prove it. But when your husband came here three years ago she was still alive and still had the same fiery eyes as in her youth. He will confirm my statement. I personally take more after the GieshÃ¼blers, who are people of little account, so far as external features are concerned, but otherwise tolerably well favored. We have been living here now for four generations, a full hundred years, and if there were an apothecary nobility--"

"You would have a right to claim it. And I, for my part, accept your claim as proved, and that beyond qstion. For us who come of old families it is a very easy matter, because we gladly recognize every sort of noble-mindedness, no matter from what source it may come. At least that is the way I was brought up by my father, as well as by my mother. I am a Briest by birth and am descended from the Briest, who, the day before the battle of Fehrbellin, led the sudden attack on Rathenow, of which you may perhaps have heard."

"Oh, certainly, most gracious Lady, that, you know, is my specialty."

"Well then I am a von Briest. And my father has said to me more than a hundred times: Effi,--for that is my name--Effi, here is our beginning, and here only. When Froben traded the horse, he was that moment a nobleman, and when Luther said, 'here I stand,' he was more than ever a nobleman. And I think, Mr. GieshÃ¼bler, Innstetten was quite right when he assured me you and I should be good friends."

GieshÃ¼bler would have liked nothing better than to make her a declaration of love then and there, and to ask that he might fight and die for her as a Cid or some other campeador. But as that was out of the qstion, and his heart could no longer endure the situation, he arose from his seat, looked for his hat, which he fortunately found at once, and, after again kissing the young wife's hand, withdrew quickly from her presence without saying another word.

CHAPTER IX

Such was Effi's first day in Kessin. Innstetten gave her half a week further time to become settled and write letters to her mother, Hulda, and the twins. Then the city calls began, some of which were made in a closed carriage, for the rains came just right to make this unusual procedure seem the sensible thing to do. When all the city calls had been made the country nobility came next in order. These took longer, as in most cases the distances were so great that it was not possible to make more than one visit on any one day. First they went to the Borckes' in Rothenmoor, then to Morgnitz, Dabergotz, and Kroschentin, where they made their duty call at the Ahlemanns', the Jatzkows', and the Grasenabbs'. Further down the list came, among other families, that of Baron von GÃ¼ldenklee in Papenhagen. The impression that Effi received was everywhere the same. Mediocre people, whose friendliness was for the most part of an uncertain character, and who, while pretending to speak of Bismarck and the Crown Princess, were in reality merely scrutinizing Effi's dress, which some considered too pretentious for so youthful a woman, while others looked upon it as too little suited to a lady of social position. Everything about her, they said, betrayed the Berlin school,--sense in external matters and a remarkable degree of uncertainty and embarrassment in the discussion of great problems. At the Borckes', and also at the homes in Morgnitz and Dabergotz, she had been declared "infected with rationalism," but at the Grasenabbs' she was pronounced point-blank an "atheist." To be sure, the elderly Mrs. Grasenabb, nÃ©e Stiefel, of Stiefelstein in South Germany, had made a weak attempt to save Effi at least for deism. But Sidonie von Grasenabb, an old maid of forty-three, had gruffly interjected the remark: "I tell you, mother, simply an atheist, and nothing short of an atheist, and that settles it." After this outburst the old woman, who was afraid of her own daughter, had observed discreet silence.

The whole round had taken just about two weeks, and at a late hour on the second day of December the Innstettens were returning home from their last visit. At the GÃ¼ldenklees' Innstetten had met with the inevitable fate of having to arg politics with old Mr. GÃ¼ldenklee. "Yes, dearest district councillor, when I consider how times have changed! A generation ago today, or about that long, there was, you know, another second of December, and good Louis, the nephew of Napoleon--*if* he was his nephew, and not in reality of entirely different extraction--was firing grape and canister at the Parisian mob. Oh well, let him be forgiven for that; he was just the man to do it, and I hold to the theory that every man fares exactly as well and as ill as he deserves. But when he later lost all appreciation and in the year seventy, without any provocation, was determined to have a bout with us, you see, Baron, that was--well, what shall I say?-- that was a piece of insolence. But he was repaid for it in his own coin. Our Ancient of Days up there is not to be trifled with and He is on our side."

"Yes," said Innstetten, who was wise enough to appear to be entering seriously into such Philistine discussions, "the hero and conqror of SaarbrÃ¼cken did not know what he was doing. But you must not be too strict in your judgment of him personally. After all, who is master in his own house? Nobody. I myself am already making preparations to put the reins of government into other hands, and Louis Napoleon, you know, was simply a piece of wax in the hands of his Catholic wife, or let us say, rather, of his Jesuit wife."

"Wax in the hands of his wife, who proceeded to bamboozle him. Certainly, Innstetten, that is just what he was. But you don't think, do you, that that is going to save him? He is forever condemned. Moreover it has never yet been shown conclusively"--at these words his glance sought rather timorously the eye of his better half--"that petticoat government is not really to be considered an advantage. Only, of course, it must be the right sort of a wife. But who was this wife? She was not a wife at all. The most charitable thing to call her is a 'dame,' and that tells the whole story. 'Dame' almost always leaves an after-taste. This Eugenie--whose relation to the Jewish banker I gladly ignore here, for I hate the 'I-am-holier-than-thou' attitude--had a streak of the *cafÃ©-chantant* in her, and, if the city in which she lived was a Babylon, she was a wife of Babylon. I don't care to express myself more plainly, for I know"--and he bowed toward Effi--"what I owe to German wives. Your pardon, most gracious Lady, that I have so much as touched upon these things within your hearing."

Such had been the trend of the conversation, after they had talked about the election, the assassin Nobiling, and the rape crop, and when Innstetten and Effi reached home they sat down to chat for half an hour. The two housemaids were already in bed, for it was nearly midnight.

Innstetten put on his short house coat and morocco slippers, and began to walk up and down in the room; Effi was still dressed in her society gown, and her fan and gloves lay beside her.

"Now," said Innstetten, standing still, "we really ought to celebrate this day, but I don't know as yet how. Shall I play you a triumphal march, or set the shark going out there, or carry you in triumph across the hall? Something must be done, for I would have you know, this visit today was the last one."

"Thank heaven, if it was," said Effi. "But the feeling that we now have peace and quiet is, I think, celebration enough in itself. Only you might give me a kiss. But that doesn't occur to you. On that whole long road not a touch, frosty as a snow-man. And never a thing but your cigar."

"Forget that, I am going to reform, but at present I merely want to know your attitude toward this whole qstion of friendly relations and social intercourse. Do you feel drawn to one or another of these new acquaintances? Have the Borckes won the victory over the Grasenabbs, or vice versa, or do you side with old Mr. GÃ¼ldenklee? What he said about Eugenie made a very noble and pure impression, don't you think so?"

"Aha, behold! Sir Geert von Innstetten is a gossip. I am learning to know you from an entirely new side."

"And if our nobility will not do," contind Innstetten, without allowing himself to be interrupted, "what do you think of the city officials of Kessin? What do you think of the club? After all, life and death depend upon your answer. Recently I saw you talking with our judge, who is a lieutenant of the reserves, a neat little man that one might perhaps get along with, if he could only rid himself of the notion that he accomplished the recapture of Le Bourget by attacking him on the flank. And his wife! She is considered our best Boston player and has, besides, the prettiest counters. So once more, Effi, how is it going to be in Kessin? Will you become accustomed to the place? Will you be popular and assure me a majority when I want to go to the Imperial Diet? Or do you favor a life of seclusion, holding yourself aloof from the people of Kessin, in the city as well as in the country?"

"I shall probably decide in favor of a secluded life, unless the Apothecary at the sign of the Moor draws me out. To be sure, that will make me fall still lower in Sidonie's estimation, but I shall have to take the risk. This fight will simply have to be fought. I shall stand or fall with GieshÃ¼bler. It sounds rather comical, but he is actually the only person with whom it is possible to carry on a conversation, the only real human being here."

"That he is," said Innstetten. "How well you choose!"

"Should I have *you* otherwise?" said Effi and leaned upon his arm.

That was on the 2d of December. A week later Bismarck was in Varzin, and Innstetten now knew that until Christmas, and perhaps even for a longer time, quiet days for him were not to be thought of. The Prince had cherished a fondness for him ever since the days in Versailles, and would often invite him to dinner, along with other gsts, but also alone, for the youthful district councillor, distinguished alike for his bearing and his wisdom, enjoyed the favor of the Princess also.

The first invitation came for the 14th. As there was snow on the ground Innstetten planned to take a sleigh for the two hours' drive to the station, from which he had another hour's ride by train. "Don't wait for me, Effi. I can't be back before midnight; it will probably be two o'clock or even later. But I'll not disturb you. Good-by, I'll see you in the morning." With that he climbed into the sleigh and away the Isabella-colored span flew through the city and across the country toward the station.

That was the first long separation, for almost twelve hours. Poor Effi! How was she to pass the evening? To go to bed early would be inadvisable, for she would wake up and not be able to go to sleep again, and would listen for every sound. No, it would be best to wait till she was very tired and then enjoy a sound sleep. She wrote a letter to her mother and then went to see Mrs. Kruse, whose condition aroused her sympathy. This poor woman had the habit of sitting till late at night with the black chicken in her lap. The friendliness the visit was meant to show was by no means returned by Mrs. Kruse, who sat in her overheated room quietly brooding away the time. So when Effi perceived that her coming was felt as a disturbance rather than a pleasure she went away, staying merely long enough to ask whether there was anything the invalid would like to have. But all offers of assistance were declined.

Meanwhile it had become evening and the lamp was already burning. Effi walked over to the window of her room and looked out at the grove, whose trees were covered with glistening snow. She was completely absorbed in the picture and took no notice of what was going on behind her in the room. When she turned around she observed that Frederick had quietly put the coffee tray on the table before the sofa and set a place for her. "Why, yes, supper. I must sit down, I suppose." But she could not make herself eat. So she got up from the table and reread the letter she had written to her mother. If she had had a feeling of loneliness before, it was doubly intense now. What would she not have given if the two sandy-haired Jahnkes had just stepped in, or even Hulda? The latter, to be sure, was always so sentimental and as a usual thing occupied solely with her own triumphs. But doubtful and insecure as these triumphs were, nevertheless Effi would be very happy to be told about them at this moment. Finally she opened the grand piano to play some music, but she could not play. "No, this will make me hopelessly melancholy; I will read, rather." She looked for a book, and the first to fall into her hands was a thick red tourist's handbook, an old edition, perhaps from the days when Innstetten was a lieutenant. "Yes, I will read in this book; there is nothing more quieting than books like this. Only the maps should always be avoided. But I shall guard against this source of sand in the eyes, which I hate."

She opened the book at random at page 153. In the adjoining room she heard the tick-tock of the clock, and out of doors Rollo, who at nightfall had left his place in the shed, as was his custom every evening, and had stretched himself out on the large woven mat just outside the bedroom door. The consciousness that he was near at hand decreased Effi's feeling that she was forsaken. In fact, it almost put her in a cheerful mood, and so she began, without further delay, to read. On the page lying open before her there was something about the "Hermitage," the well country-seat of the Margrave in the neighborhood of Beireuth. It attracted her attention. Beireuth, Richard Wagner. So she read: "Among the pictures in the 'Hermitage' let us mention one more, which not because of its beauty, but because of its age and the person it represents, may well claim our interest. It is a woman's portrait, which has grown dark with age. The head is small, the face has harsh, rather uncanny features, and she wears a ruff which seems to support her head. Some think it is an old margravine from the end of the 15th century, others are of the opinion that it is the Countess of Orlamunde. All are agreed that it is the picture of the Lady who since that time has achieved a certain notoriety in the history of the Hohenzollern dynasty under the name of the 'Lady in white.'"

"That was a lucky accident!" said Effi, as she shoved the book aside. "I seek to quiet my nerves, and the first thing I run into is the story of the 'Lady in white,' of whom I have been afraid as long as I can remember. But inasmuch as I already have a creepy feeling I might as well finish the story."

She opened the book again and read further: "This old portrait itself, the original of which plays such a rÃ´le in Hohenzollern history, has likewise a significance as a picture in the special history of the Hermitage. No doubt, one circumstance that has something to do with this is the fact that the picture hangs on a papered door, which is invisible to the stranger and behind which there is a stairway leading down into the cellar. It is said that when Napoleon spent the night here the 'Lady in white' stepped out of the frame and walked up to his bed. The Emperor, starting with fright, the story contins, called for his adjutant, and to the end of his life always spoke with exasperation of this 'cursed palace.'"

"I must give up trying to calm myself by reading," said Effi. "If I read further, I shall certainly come to a vaulted cellar that the devil once rode out of on a wine cask. There are several of these in Germany, I believe, and in a tourist's handbook all such things have to be collected; that goes without saying. So I will close my eyes, rather, and recall my wedding-eve celebration as well as I can,--how the twins could not get any farther because of their tears, and how, when everybody looked at everybody else with embarrassment, Cousin von Briest declared that such tears opened the gate to Paradise. He was truly charming and always in such exuberant spirits. And look at me now! Here, of all places! Oh, I am not at all suited to be a grand Lady. Now mama, she would have fitted this position, she would have sounded the key-note, as behooves the wife of a district councillor, and Sidonie Grasenabb would have been all homage toward her and would not have been greatly disturbed about her belief or unbelief. But I--I am a child and shall probably remain one, too. I once heard that it is a good fortune. But I don't know whether that is tr. Obviously a wife ought always to adapt herself to the position in which she is placed."

At this moment Frederick came to clear off the table.

"How late is it, Frederick?"

"It is going on nine, your Ladyship."

"Well, that is worth listening to. Send Johanna to me."

* * * * *

"Your Ladyship sent for me."

"Yes, Johanna; I want to go to bed. It is still early, to be sure, but I am so alone. Please go out first and post this letter, and when you come back it will surely be time. And even if it isn't."

Effi took the lamp and walked over to her bedroom. Just as she had expected, there lay Rollo on the rush mat. When he saw her coming he arose to make room for her to pass, and rubbed his ear against her hand. Then he lay down again.

Meanwhile Johanna had gone over to the office to post the letter. Over there she had been in no particular hurry; on the contrary, she had preferred to carry on a conversation with Mrs. Paaschen, the wife of the janitor of the building. About the young wife, of course.

"What kind of a woman is she anyhow?" asked Mrs. Paaschen.

"She is very young."

"Well, that is no misfortune, but rather the opposite. Young wives, and that is just the good thing about them, never do anything but stand before the mirror and pull at themselves and put on some ornament. They don't see much or hear much and have not yet formed the habit of counting the stubs of candles in the kitchen, and they don't begrudge a maid a kiss if she gets one, simply because she herself no longer gets any."

"Yes," said Johanna, "that was the way with my former madame, and wholly without occasion. But there is nothing of that kind about our mistress."

"Is he very affectionate?"

"Oh very. That you can easily imagine."

"But the fact that he leaves her thus alone--"

"Yes, dear Mrs. Paaschen, but you must not forget--the Prince. After all, you know, he is a district councillor, and perhaps he wants to rise still higher."

"Certainly he wants to, and he will, too. It's in him. Paaschen always says so and he knows."

This walk over to the office had consumed perhaps a quarter of an hour, and when Johanna returned, Effi was already sitting before the pier-glass, waiting.

"You were gone a long time, Johanna."

"Yes, your Ladyship--I beg your Ladyship's pardon--I met Mrs. Paaschen over there and was delayed a bit. It is so quiet here. One is always glad to meet a person with whom one can speak a word. Christel is a very good person, but she doesn't talk, and Frederick is such a sleepy-head. Besides, he is so cautious and never comes right out with what he has to say. Tr, one must be able to hold one's tong when necessary, and Mrs. Paaschen, who is so inquisitive, is really not at all according to my taste. Yet one likes to see and hear something once in a while."

Effi sighed. "Yes, Johanna, it is better so."

"Your Ladyship has such beautiful hair, so long, and soft as silk."

"Yes, it is very soft. But that is not a good thing, Johanna. As the hair is, so is the character."

"Certainly, your Ladyship. And a soft character is better than a hard one. I have soft hair, too."

"Yes, Johanna. And you have blonde hair, too. That the men like best."

"Oh, there is a great difference, your Ladyship. There are many who prefer black."

"To be sure," laughed Effi, "that has been my experience, too. But it must be because of something else entirely. Now, those who are blonde always have a white complexion. You have, too, Johanna, and I would wager my last pfennig that you have a good deal of attention paid to you. I am still very young, but I know that much. Besides, I have a girl friend, who was also so blonde, a regular flaxen blonde, even blonder than you, and she was a preacher's daughter."

"Oh, yes."

"I beg you, Johanna, what do you mean by 'oh yes?' It sounds very sarcastic and strange, and you have nothing against preachers' daughters, have you?--She was a very pretty girl, as even our officers thought, without exception, for we had officers, red hussars, too. At the same time she knew very well how to dress herself. A black velvet bodice and a flower, a rose or sometimes heliotrope, and if she had not had such large protruding eyes--Oh you ought to have seen them, Johanna, at least this large--" Effi laughingly pulled down her right eye-lid--"she would have been simply a beauty. Her name was Hulda, Hulda Niemeyer, and we were not even so very intimate. But if I had her here now, and she were sitting there, yonder in the corner of the little sofa, I would chat with her till midnight, or even longer. I am so homesick"--in saying this she drew Johanna's head close to her breast--"I am so much afraid."

"Oh, that will soon be overcome, your Ladyship, we were all that way."

"You were all that way? What does that mean, Johanna?"

"If your Ladyship is really so much afraid, why, I can make a bed for myself here. I can take the straw mattress and turn down a chair, so that I have something to lean my head against, and then I can sleep here till morning, or till his Lordship comes home."

"He doesn't intend to disturb me. He promised me that specially."

"Or I can merely sit down in the corner of the sofa."

"Yes, that might do perhaps. No, it will not, either. His Lordship must not know that I am afraid, he would not like it. He always wants me to be brave and determined, as he is. And I can't be. I was always somewhat easily inflnced.--But, of course, I see plainly, I must conqr myself and subject myself to his will in such particulars, as well as in general. And then I have Rollo, you know. He is lying just outside the threshold."

Johanna nodded at each statement and finally lit the candle on Effi's bedroom stand. Then she took the lamp. "Does your Ladyship wish anything more?"

"No, Johanna. The shutters are closed tight, are they not?"

"Merely drawn to, your Ladyship. Otherwise it would be so dark and stuffy."

"Very well."

Johanna withdrew, and Effi went to bed and wrapped herself up in the covers.

She left the candle burning, because she was determined not to go to sleep at once. On the contrary, she planned to recapitulate her wedding tour, as she had her wedding-eve celebration a short time before, and let everything pass before her mind's eye in review. But it turned out otherwise than she had expected, for when she had reached Verona and was looking for the house of Juliet Capulet, her eyes fell shut. The stub of candle in the little silver holder gradually burned down, flickered once or twice, and went out.

Effi had slept quite soundly for a while, when all of a sudden she started up out of her sleep with a loud scream, indeed, she was able to hear the scream, as she awoke, and she also noticed Rollo's barking outside. His "bow-wow" went echoing down the hall, muffled and almost terrifying. She felt as though her heart stood still, and was unable to call out. At this moment something whisked past her, and the door into the hall sprang open. But the moment of extreme fright was also the moment of her resc, for, instead of something terrible, Rollo now came up to her, sought her hand with his head, and, when he had found it, lay down upon the rug before her bed. With her other hand Effi had pressed three times on the button of the bell and in less than half a minute Johanna was there, in her bare feet, her skirt hanging over her arm and a large checkered cloth thrown over her head and shoulders.

"Thank heaven, Johanna, that you are here."

"What was the matter, your Ladyship? Your Ladyship has had a dream."

"Yes, a dream. It must have been something of the sort, but it was something else besides."

"Pray, what, your Ladyship?"

"I was sleeping quite soundly and suddenly I started up and screamed--perhaps it was a nightmare--they have nightmares in our family--My father has them, too, and frightens us with them. Mama always says he ought not to humor himself so--But that is easy to say--Well, I started up out of my sleep and screamed, and when I looked around, as well as I could in the dark, something slipped past my bed, right there where you are standing now, Johanna, and then it was gone. And if I ask myself seriously, what it was--"

"Well, your Ladyship?"

"And if I ask myself seriously--I don't like to say it, Johanna--but I believe it was the Chinaman."

"The one from upstairs?" said Johanna, trying to laugh, "our little Chinaman that we pasted on the back of the chair, Christel and I? Oh, your Ladyship has been dreaming, and even if your Ladyship was awake, it all came from a dream."

56

"I should believe that, if it had not been exactly the moment when Rollo began to bark outside. So he must have seen it too. Then the door flew open and the good faithful animal sprang toward me, as though he were coming to my resc. Oh, my dear Johanna, it was terrible. And I so alone and so young. Oh, if I only had some one here with whom I could weep. But so far from home--alas, from home."

"The master may come any hour."

"No, he shall not come. He shall not see me thus. He would probably laugh at me and I could never pardon him for that. For it was so fearful, Johanna--You must stay here now--But let Christel sleep and Frederick too. Nobody must know about it."

"Or perhaps I may fetch Mrs. Kruse to join us. She doesn't sleep anyhow; she sits there all night long."

"No, no, she is a kindred spirit. That black chicken has something to do with it, too. She must not come. No, Johanna, you just stay here yourself. And how fortunate that you merely drew the shutters to. Push them open, make a loud noise, so that I may hear a human sound, a human sound--I have to call it that, even if it seems qer--and then open the window a little bit, that I may have air and light."

Johanna did as ordered and Effi leaned back upon her pillows and soon thereafter fell into a lethargic sleep.

CHAPTER X

It was six o'clock in the morning when Innstetten returned home from Varzin. He made Rollo omit all demonstrations of affection and then retired as quietly as possible to his room. Here he lay down in a comfortable position, but would not allow Frederick to do more than cover him up with a traveling rug. "Wake me at nine." And at this hour he was wakened. He arose quickly and said: "Bring my breakfast."

"Her Ladyship is still asleep."

"But it is late. Has anything happened?"

"I don't know. I only know that Johanna had to sleep all night in her Ladyship's room."

"Well, send Johanna to me then."

She came. She had the same rosy complexion as ever, and so seemed not to have been specially upset by the events of the night.

"What is this I hear about her Ladyship? Frederick tells me something happened and you slept in her room."

"Yes, Sir Baron. Her Ladyship rang three times in very quick succession, and I thought at once it meant something. And it did, too. She probably had a dream, or it may perhaps have been the other thing."

"What other thing?"

"Oh, your Lordship knows, I believe."

"I know nothing. In any case we must put an end to it. And how did you find her Ladyship?"

"She was beside herself and clung to Rollo's collar with all her might. The dog was standing beside her Ladyship's bed and was frightened also."

"And what had she dreamed, or, if you prefer, what had she heard or seen? What did she say?"

"That it just slipped along close by her."

"What? Who?"

"The man from upstairs. The one from the social hall or from the small chamber."

"Nonsense, I say. Over and over that same silly stuff. I don't want to hear any more about it. And then you stayed with her Ladyship?"

"Yes, your Lordship. I made a bed on the floor close by her. And I had to hold her hand, and then she went to sleep."

"And she is still sleeping?"

"Very soundly."

"I am worried about that, Johanna. One can sleep one's self well, but also ill. We must waken her, cautiously, of course, so that she will not be startled again. And tell Frederick not to bring the breakfast. I will wait till her Ladyship is here. Now let me see how clever you can be."

Half an hour later Effi came. She looked charming, but quite pale, and was leaning on Johanna. The moment she caught sight of Innstetten she rushed up to him and embraced and kissed him, while the tears streamed down her face. "Oh, Geert, thank heaven, you are here. All is well again now. You must not go away again, you must not leave me alone again."

"My dear Effi--Just put it down, Frederick, I will do the rest--my dear Effi, I am not leaving you alone from lack of consideration or from caprice, but because it is necessary. I have no choice. I am a man in office and cannot say to the Prince, or even to the Princess: Your Highness, I cannot come; my wife is so alone, or, my wife is afraid. If I said that it would put us in a rather comical light, me certainly, and you, too. But first take a cup of coffee."

Effi drank her coffee and its stimulating effect was plainly to be seen. Then she took her husband's hand again and said: "You shall have your way. I see, it is impossible. And then, you know, we aspire to something higher. I say we, for I am really more eager for it than you."

"All wives are," laughed Innstetten.

"So it is settled. You will accept invitations as heretofore, and I will stay here and wait for my 'High Lord,' which reminds me of Hulda under the elder tree. I wonder how she is getting along?"

"Young ladies like Hulda always get along well. But what else were you going to say?"

"I was going to say, I will stay here, and even alone, if necessary. But not in this house. Let us move out. There are such handsome houses along the quay, one between Consul Martens and Consul GrÃ¼tzmacher, and one on the Market, just opposite GieshÃ¼bler. Why can't we live there? Why here, of all places? When we have had friends and relatives as gsts in our house I have often heard that in Berlin families move out on account of piano playing, or on account of cockroaches, or on account of an unfriendly concierge. If it is done on account of such a trifle--"

"Trifle? Concierge? Don't say that."

"If it is possible because of such things it must also be possible here, where you are district councillor and the people are obliged to do your bidding and many even owe you a debt of gratitude. GieshÃ¼bler would certainly help us, even if only for my sake, for he will sympathize with me. And now say, Geert, shall we give up this abominable house, this house with the--"

"Chinaman, you mean. You see, Effi, one can pronounce the fearful word without his appearing. What you saw or what, as you think, slipped past your bed, was the little Chinaman that the maids pasted on the back of the chair upstairs. I'll wager he had a bl coat on and a very flat-crowned hat, with a shining button on top."

She nodded.

"Now you see, a dream, a hallucination. And then, I presume, Johanna told you something last night, about the wedding upstairs."

"No."

"So much the better."

"She didn't tell me a word. But from all this I can see that there is something qer here. And then the crocodile; everything is so uncanny here."

"The first evening, when you saw the crocodile, you considered it fairy-like--"

"Yes, then."

"And then, Effi, I can't well leave here now, even if it were possible to sell the house or make an exchange. It is with this exactly as with declining an invitation to Varzin. I can't have the people here in the city saying that District Councillor Innstetten is selling his house because his wife saw the little pasted-up picture of a Chinaman as a ghost by her bed. I should be lost, Effi. One can never recover from such ridiculousness."

"But, Geert, are you so sure that there is nothing of the kind?"

"That I will not affirm. It is a thing that one can believe or, better, not believe. But supposing there were such things, what harm do they do? The fact that bacilli are flying around in the air, of which you have doubtless heard, is much worse and more dangerous than all this scurrying about of ghosts, assuming that they do scurry about, and that such a thing really exists. Then I am particularly surprised to see *you* show such fear and such an aversion, you a Briest. Why, it is as though you came from a low burgher family. Ghosts are a distinction, like the family tree and the like, and I know families that would as lief give up their coat of arms as their 'Lady in white,' who may even be in black, for that matter."

Effi remained silent.

"Well, Effi; no answer?"

"What do you expect me to answer? I have given in to you and shown myself docile, but I think you in turn might be more sympathetic. If you knew how I long for sympathy. I have suffered a great deal, really a very great deal, and when I saw you I thought I should now be rid of my fear. But you merely told me you had no desire to make yourself ridiculous in the eyes either of the Prince or of the city. That is small comfort. I consider it small, and so much the smaller, since, to cap the climax, you contradict yourself, and not only seem to believe in these things yourself, but even expect me to have a nobleman's pride in ghosts. Well, I haven't. When you talk about families that val their ghosts as highly as their coat of arms, all I have to say is, that is a matter of taste, and I count my coat of arms worth more. Thank heaven, we Briests have no ghosts. The Briests were always very good people and that probably accounts for it."

The dispute would doubtless have gone on longer and might perhaps have led to a first serious misunderstanding if Frederick had not entered to hand her Ladyship a letter. "From Mr. Gieshübler. The messenger is waiting for an answer."

All the ill-humor on Effi's countenance vanished immediately. It did her good merely to hear Gieshübler's name, and her cheerful feeling was further heightened when she examined the letter. In the first place it was not a letter at all, but a note, the address "Madame the Baroness von Innstetten, née Briest," in a beautiful court hand, and instead of a seal a little round picture pasted on, a lyre with a staff sticking in it. But the staff might also be an arrow. She handed the note to her husband, who likewise admired it.

"Now read it."

Effi broke open the wafer and read: "Most highly esteemed Lady, most gracious Baroness: Permit me to join to my most respectful forenoon greeting a most humble reqst. By the noon train a dear friend of mine for many years past, a daughter of our good city of Kessin, Miss Marietta Trippelli, will arrive here to sojourn in our midst till tomorrow morning. On the 17th she expects to be in St. Petersburg, where she will give concerts till the middle of January. Prince Kotschukoff is again opening his hospitable house to her. In her immutable kindness to me, Miss Trippelli has promised to spend this evening at my house and sing some songs, leaving the choice entirely to me, for she knows no such thing as difficulty. Could Madame the Baroness consent to attend this soirée musicale, at seven o'clock? Your husband, upon whose appearance I count with certainty, will support my most humble reqst. The only other gsts are Pastor Lindequist, who will accompany, and the widow Trippel, of course. Your most obedient servant. A. Gieshübler."

"Well," said Innstetten, "yes or no?"

"Yes, of course. That will pull me through. Besides, I cannot decline my dear GieshÃ¼bler's very first invitation."

"Agreed. So, Frederick, tell Mirambo, for I take it for granted he brought the letter, that we shall have the honor."

Frederick went out. When he was gone Effi asked: "Who is Mirambo?"

"The genuine Mirambo is a robber chief in Africa,--Lake Tanganyika, if your geography extends that far--but ours is merely GieshÃ¼bler's charcoal dispenser and factotum, and will this evening, in all probability, serve as a waiter in dress coat and cotton gloves."

It was quite apparent that the little incident had had a favorable effect on Effi and had restored to her a good share of her light-heartedness. But Innstetten wished to do what he could to hasten the convalescence. "I am glad you said yes, so quickly and without hesitation, and now I should like to make a further proposal to you to restore you entirely to your normal condition. I see plainly, you are still annoyed by something from last night foreign to my Effi and it must be got rid of absolutely. There is nothing better for that than fresh air. The weather is splendid, cool and mild at the same time, with hardly a breeze stirring. How should you like to take a drive with me? A long one, not merely out through the "Plantation." In the sleigh, of course, with the sleigh-bells on and the white snow blankets. Then if we are back by four you can take a rest, and at seven we shall be at GieshÃ¼bler's and hear Trippelli."

Effi took his hand. "How good you are, Geert, and how indulgent! For I must have seemed to you very childish, or at least very childlike, first in the episode of fright and then, later, when I asked you to sell the house, but worst of all in what I said about the Prince. I urged you to break off all connection with him, and that would be ridiculous. For after all he is the one man who has to decide our destiny. Mine, too. You don't know how ambitious I am. To tell the truth, it was only out of ambition that I married you. Oh, you must not put on such a serious expression. I love you, you know. What is it we say when we pluck a blossom and tear off the petals? 'With all my heart, with grief and pain, beyond compare.'" She burst out laughing. "And now tell me," she contind, as Innstetten still kept silent, "whither shall we go?"

"I thought, to the railway station, by a roundabout way, and then back by the turnpike. We can dine at the station or, better, at Golchowski's, at the Prince Bismarck Hotel, which we passed on the day of our return home, as you perhaps remember. Such a visit always has a good effect, and then I can have a political conversation with the Starost by the grace of Effi, and even if he does not amount to much personally he keeps his hotel in good condition and his cuisine in still better. The people here are connoisseurs when it comes to eating and drinking."

It was about eleven when they had this conversation. At twelve Kruse drove the sleigh up to the door and Effi got in. Johanna was going to bring a foot bag and furs, but Effi, after all that she had juat passed through, felt so strongly the need of fresh air that she took only a double blanket and refused everything else. Innstetten said to Kruse: "Now, Kruse, we want to drive to the station where you and I were this morning. The people will wonder at it, but that doesn't matter. Say, we drive here past the 'Plantation,' and then to the left toward the Kroschentin church tower. Make the horses fly. We must be at the station at one."

Thus began the drive. Over the white roofs of the city hung a bank of smoke, for there was little stir in the air. They flew past Utpatel's mill, which turned very slowly, and drove so close to the churchyard that the tips of the barberry bushes which hung out over the lattice brushed against Effi, and showered snow upon her blanket. On the other side of the road was a fenced-in plot, not much larger than a garden bed, and with nothing to be seen inside except a young pine tree, which rose out of the centre.

"Is anybody buried there?" asked Effi.

"Yes, the Chinaman."

Effi was startled; it came to her like a stab. But she had strength enough to control herself and ask with apparent composure: "Ours?"

"Yes, ours. Of course, he could not be accommodated in the community graveyard and so Captain Thomsen, who was what you might call his friend, bought this patch and had him buried here. There is also a stone with an inscription. It all happened before my time, of course, but it is still talked about."

"So there is something in it after all. A story. You said something of the kind this morning. And I suppose it would be best for me to hear what it is. So long as I don't know, I shall always be a victim of my imaginations, in spite of all my good resolutions. Tell me the real story. The reality cannot worry me so much as my fancy."

"Good for you, Effi. I didn't intend to speak about it. But now it comes in naturally, and that is well. Besides, to tell the truth, it is nothing at all."

"All the same to me: nothing at all or much or little. Only begin."

"Yes, that is easy to say. The beginning is always the hardest part, even with stories. Well, I think I shall begin with Captain Thomsen."

"Very well."

"Now Thomsen, whom I have already mentioned, was for many years a so-called China-voyager, always on the way between Shanghai and Singapore with a cargo of rice, and may have been about sixty when he arrived here. I don't know whether he was born here or whether he had other relations here. To make a long story short, now that he was here he sold his ship, an old tub that he disposed of for very little, and bought a house, the same that we are now living in. For out in the world he had become a wealthy man. This accounts for the crocodile and the shark and, of course, the ship. Thomsen was a very adroit man, as I have been told, and well liked, even by Mayor Kirstein, but above all by the man who was at that time the pastor in Kessin, a native of Berlin, who had come here shortly before Thomsen and had met with a great deal of opposition."

"I believe it. I notice the same thing. They are so strict and self-righteous here. I believe that is Pomeranian."

"Yes and no, depending. There are other regions where they are not at all strict and where things go topsy-turvy--But just see, Effi, there we have the Kroschentin church tower right close in front of us. Shall we not give up the station and drive over to see old Mrs. von Grasenabb? Sidonie, if I am rightly informed, is not at home. So we might risk it."

"I beg you, Geert, what are you thinking of? Why, it is heavenly to fly along thus, and I can simply feel myself being restored and all my fear falling from me. And now you ask me to sacrifice all that merely to pay these old people a flying visit and very likely cause them embarrassment. For heaven's sake let us not. And then I want above all to hear the story. We were talking about Captain Thomsen, whom I picture to myself as a Dane or an Englishman, very clean, with white stand-up collar, and perfectly white linen."

"Quite right. So he is said to have looked. And with him lived a young person of about twenty, whom some took for his niece, but most people for his grand-daughter. The latter, however, considering their ages, was hardly possible. Beside the grand-daughter or the niece, there was also a Chinaman living with him, the same one who lies there among the dunes and whose grave we have just passed."

"Fine, fine."

"This Chinaman was a servant at Thomsen's and Thomsen thought a great deal of him, so that he was really more a friend than a servant. And it remained so for over a year. Then suddenly it was rumored that Thomsen's grand-daughter, who, I believe, was called Nina, was to be married to a captain, in accordance with the old man's wish. And so indeed it came about. There was a grand wedding at the house, the Berlin pastor married them. The miller Utpatel, a Scottish Covenanter, and Gieshübler, a feeble light in church matters, were invited, but the more prominent gsts were a number of captains with their wives and daughters. And, as you can imagine, there was a lively time. In the evening there was dancing, and the bride danced with every man and finally with the Chinaman. Then all of a sudden the report spread that she had vanished. And she was really gone, somewhere, but nobody knew just what had happened. A fortnight later the Chinaman died. Thomsen bought the plot I have shown you and had him buried in it. The Berlin Pastor is said to have remarked: 'The Chinaman might just as well have been buried in the Christian churchyard, for he was a very good man and exactly as good as the rest.' Whom he really meant by the rest, GieshÃ¼bler says nobody quite knew."

"Well, in this matter I am absolutely against the pastor. Nobody ought to say such things, for they are dangerous and unbecoming. Even Niemeyer would not have said that."

"The poor pastor, whose name, by the way, was Trippel, was very seriously criticised for it, and it was truly a blessing that he soon afterward died, for he would have lost his position otherwise. The city was opposed to him, just as you are, in spite of the fact that they had called him, and the Consistory, of course, was even more antagonistic."

"Trippel, you say? Then, I presume, there is some connection between him and the pastor's widow, Mrs. Trippel, whom we are to see this evening."

"Certainly there is a connection. He was her husband, and the father of Miss Trippelli."

Effi laughed. "Of Miss Trippelli! At last I see the whole affair in a clear light. That she was born in Kessin, GieshÃ¼bler wrote me, you remember. But I thought she was the daughter of an Italian consul. We have so many foreign names here, you know. And now I find she is good German and a descendant of Trippel. Is she so superior that she could venture to Italianize her name in this fashion?"

"The daring shall inherit the earth. Moreover she is quite good. She spent a few years in Paris with the famous Madame Viardot, and there made the acquaintance of the Russian Prince. Russian Princes, you know, are very enlightened, are above petty class prejudices, and Kotschukoff and GieshÃ¼bler--whom she calls uncle, by the way, and one might almost call him a born uncle--it is, strictly speaking, these two who have made little Marie Trippel what she is. It was GieshÃ¼bler who induced her to go to Paris and Kotschukoff made her over into Marietta Trippelli."

"Ah, Geert, what a charming story this is and what a humdrum life I have led in Hohen-Cremmen! Never a thing out of the ordinary."

Innstetten took her hand and said: "You must not speak thus, Effi. With respect to ghosts one may take whatever attitude one likes. But beware of 'out of the ordinary' things, or what is loosely called out of the ordinary. That which appears to you so enticing, even a life such as Miss Trippelli leads, is as a rule bought at the price of

65

happiness. I know quite well how you love Hohen-Cremmen and are attached to it, but you often make sport of it, too, and have no conception of how much quiet days like those in Hohen-Cremmen mean."

"Yes I have," she said. "I know very well. Only I like to hear about something else once in a while, and then the desire comes over me to have a similar experience. But you are quite right, and, to tell the truth, I long for peace and quiet."

Innstetten shook his finger at her. "My dear, dear Effi, that again you only imagine. Always fancies, first one thing, then another."

CHAPTER XI

[Innstetten and Effi stopped at the Prince Bismarck Hotel for dinner and heard some of Golchowski's gossip. All three went out near the tracks, when they heard a fast express coming, and as it passed in the direction of Effi's old home, it filled her heart with longing. The soirÃ©e musicale at GieshÃ¼bler's was particularly enlivened by the bubbling humor of Miss Trippelli, whose singing was excellent, but did not overshadow her talent as a conversationalist. Effi admired her ability to sing dramatic pieces with composure. An uncanny ballad led to a discussion of haunted houses and ghosts, in both of which Miss Trippelli believed.]

CHAPTER XII

The gsts did not go home till late. Soon after ten Effi remarked to GieshÃ¼bler that it was about time to leave, as Miss Trippelli must not miss her train and would have to leave Kessin at six in order to catch it. But Miss Trippelli overheard the remark and, in her own peculiar unabashed way, protested against such thoughtful consideration. "Ah, most gracious Lady, you think that one following my career needs regular sleep, but you are mistaken. What we need regularly is applause and high prices. Oh, laugh if you like. Besides, I can sleep in my compartment on the train--for one learns to do such things--in any position and even on my left side, and I don't even need to unfasten my dress. To be sure, I am never laced tight; chest and lungs must always be free, and, above all, the heart. Yes, most gracious Lady, that is the prime essential. And then, speaking of sleep in general, it is not the quantity that tells; it is the quality. A good nap of five minutes is better than five hours of restless turning over and over, first one way, then the other. Besides, one sleeps marvelously in Russia, in spite of the strong tea. It must be the air that causes it, or late dinners, or because one is so pampered. There are no cares in Russia; in that regard Russia is better than America. In the matter of money the two are equal." After this explanation on the part of Miss Trippelli, Effi desisted from further warnings that it was time to go. When twelve o'clock came, the gsts, who had meanwhile developed a certain degree of intimacy, bade their host a merry and hearty good night.

* * * * *

Three days later GieshÃ¼bler's friend brought herself once more to Effi's attention by a telegram in French, from St. Petersburg: "Madame the Baroness von Innstetten, nÃ©e von Briest. Arrived safe. Prince K. at station. More taken with me than ever. Thousand thanks for your good reception. Kindest regards to Monsieur the Baron. Marietta Trippelli."

Innstetten was delighted and gave more enthusiastic expression to his delight than Effi was able to understand.

"I don't understand you, Geert."

"Because you don't understand Miss Trippelli. It's her tr self in the telegram, perfect to a dot."

"So you take it all as a bit of comedy."

"As what else could I take it, pray? All calculated for friends there and here, for Kotschukoff and GieshÃ¼bler. GieshÃ¼bler will probably found something for Miss Trippelli, or maybe just leave her a legacy."

GieshÃ¼bler's party had occurred in the middle of December. Immediately thereafter began the preparations for Christmas. Effi, who might otherwise have found it hard to live through these days, considered it a blessing to have a household with demands that had to be satisfied. It was a time for pondering, deciding, and buying, and this left no leisure for gloomy thoughts. The day before Christmas gifts arrived from her parents, and in the parcels were packed a variety of trifles from the precentor's family: beautiful qenings from a tree grafted by Effi and Jahnke several years ago, beside brown pulse-warmers and knee-warmers from Bertha and Hertha. Hulda only wrote a few lines, because, as she pretended, she had still to knit a traveling shawl for X. "That is simply not tr," said Effi, "I'll wager, there is no X in existence. What a pity she cannot cease surrounding herself with admirers who do not exist!"

When the evening came Innstetten himself arranged the presents for his young wife. The tree was lit, and a small angel hung at the top. On the tree was discovered a cradle with pretty transparencies and inscriptions, one of which referred to an event looked forward to in the Innstetten home the following year. Effi read it and blushed. Then she started toward Innstetten to thank him, but before she had time to carry out her design a Yule gift was thrown into the hall with a shout, in accordance with the old Pomeranian custom. It proved to be a box filled with a world of things. At the bottom they found the most important gift of all, a neat little lozenge box, with a number of Japanese pictures pasted on it, and inside of it a note, running,--

"Three kings once came on a Christmas eve, The king of the Moors was one, I believe;-- The druggist at the sign of the Moor Today with spices raps at your door; Regretting no incense or myrrh to have found, He throws pistachio and almonds around."

Effi read the note two or three times and was pleased. "The homage of a good man has something very comforting about it. Don't you think so, Geert?"

"Certainly I do. It is the only thing that can afford real pleasure, or at least ought to. Every one is otherwise so encumbered with stupid obligations--I am myself. But, after all, one is what one is."

The first holiday was church day, on the second they went to the Borckes'. Everybody was there, except the Grasenabbs, who declined to come, "because Sidonie was not at home." This excuse struck everybody as rather strange. Some even whispered: "On the contrary, this is the very reason they ought to have come."

New Year's eve there was to be a club ball, which Effi could not well miss, nor did she wish to, for it would give her an opportunity to see the cream of the city all at once. Johanna had her hands full with the preparation of the ball dress. Gieshübler, who, in addition to his other hobbies, owned a hothouse, had sent Effi some camelias. Innstetten, in spite of the little time at his disposal, had to drive in the afternoon to Papenhagen, where three barns had burned.

It became very quiet in the house. Christel, not having anything to do, sleepily shoved a footstool up to the stove, and Effi retired into her bedroom, where she sat down at a small writing desk between the mirror and the sofa, to write to her mother. She had already written a postal card, acknowledging receipt of the Christmas letter and presents, but had written no other news for weeks.

/# "Kessin, Dec. 31.

"*My dear mama*:

68

"This will probably be a long letter, as I have not let you hear from me for a long time. The card doesn't count. The last time I wrote, I was in the midst of Christmas preparations; now the Christmas holidays are past and gone. Innstetten and my good friend GieshÃ¼bler left nothing undone to make Holy Night as agreeable for me as possible, but I felt a little lonely and homesick for you. Generally speaking, much as I have cause to be grateful and happy, I cannot rid myself entirely of a feeling of loneliness, and if I formerly made more fun than necessary, perhaps, of Hulda's eternal tears of emotion, I am now being punished for it and have to fight against such tears myself, for Innstetten must not see them. However, I am sure that it will all be better when our household is more enlivened, which is soon to be the case, my dear mama. What I recently hinted at is now a certainty and Innstetten gives me daily proof of his joy on account of it. It is not necessary to assure you how happy I myself am when I think of it, for the simple reason that I shall then have life and entertainment at home, or, as Geert says, 'a dear little plaything.' This word of his is doubtless proper, but I wish he would not use it, because it always give me a little shock and reminds me how young I am and that I still half belong in the nursery. This notion never leaves me (Geert says it is pathological) and, as a result, the thing that should be my highest happiness is almost the contrary, a constant embarrassment for me. Recently, dear mama, when the good Flemming damsels plied me with all sorts of qstions imaginable, it seemed as though I were undergoing an examination poorly prepared, and I think I must have answered very stupidly. I was out of sorts, too, for often what looks like sympathy is mere inquisitiveness, and theirs impressed me as the more meddlesome, since I have a long while yet to wait for the happy event. Some time in the summer, early in July, I think. You must come then, or better still, so soon as I am at all able to get about, I'll take a vacation and set out for Hohen-Cremmen to see you. Oh, how happy it makes me to think of it and of the Havelland air! Here it is almost always cold and raw. There I shall drive out upon the marsh every day and see red and yellow flowers everywhere, and I can even now see the baby stretching out its hands for them, for I know it must feel really at home there. But I write this for you alone. Innstetten must not know about it and I should excuse myself even to you for wanting to come to Hohen-Cremmen with the baby, and for announcing my visit so early, instead of inviting you urgently and cordially to Kessin, which, you may know, has fifteen hundred summer gsts every year, and ships with all kinds of flags, and even a hotel among the dunes. But if I show so little hospitality it is not because I am inhospitable. I am not so degenerate as that. It is simply because our residence, with all its handsome and unusual features, is in reality not a suitable house at all; it is only a lodging for two people, and hardly that, for we haven't even a dining room, which, as you can well imagine, is embarrassing when people come to visit us. Tr, we have other rooms upstairs, a large social hall and four small rooms, but there is something uninviting about them, and I should call them lumber rooms, if there were any lumber in them. But they are entirely empty, except for a few rush-bottomed chairs, and leave a very qer impression, to say the least. You no doubt think this very easy to change, but the house we live in is--is haunted. Now it is out. I beseech you, however, not to make any reference to this in your answer, for I always show Innstetten your letters and he would be beside himself if he found out what I have written to you. I ought not to have done it either, especially as I have been undisturbed for a good many weeks and have ceased to be afraid; but Johanna tells me it will come back again, especially if some new person appears in the house. I couldn't think of exposing you to such a danger, or--if that is too harsh an expression--to such a peculiar and uncomfortable disturbance. I will not trouble you with the matter itself today, at least not in detail. They tell the story of an old captain, a so-called China-voyager, and his grand-daughter, who after a short engagement to a young captain here suddenly vanished on her wedding day. That might pass, but there is something of greater moment. A young Chinaman, whom her father had brought back from China and who was at first the servant and later the friend of the old man, died shortly afterward and was buried in a lonely spot near the churchyard. Not long ago I drove by there, but turned my face away quickly and looked in the other direction, because I believe I should otherwise have seen him sitting on the grave. For oh, my dear mama, I have really seen him once, or it at least seemed so, when I was sound asleep and Innstetten was away from home visiting the Prince. It was terrible. I should not like to experience anything like it again. I can't well invite you to such a house, handsome as it is otherwise, for, strange to say, it is both uncanny and cozy. Innstetten did not do exactly the right thing about it either, if you will allow me to say so, in spite of the fact that I finally agreed with him in many particulars. He expected me to consider it nothing but old wives' nonsense and laugh about it, but all of a sudden he himself seemed to believe in it, at the very time when he was making the qer demand of me to consider such hauntings a mark of bl blood and old nobility. But I can't do it and I won't, either. Kind as he is in other regards, in this particular he is not kind and considerate enough toward me. That there is something in it I know from Johanna and also from Mrs. Kruse. The latter is our coachman's wife and always sits holding a black chicken in an overheated room. This alone is enough to scare one. Now you know why *I* want to come when the time arrives. Oh, if it were only time now! There are so many reasons for this wish. Tonight we have a New Year's eve ball, and GieshÃ¼bler, the only amiable man here, in spite of the fact that he has one shoulder higher than the other, or, to tell the truth, has even a greater deformity--GieshÃ¼bler has sent me some camelias. Perhaps I shall dance after all. Our doctor says it would not hurt me; on the contrary. Innstetten has also given his consent, which almost surprised me. And now remember me to papa and kiss him for me, and all the other dear friends. Happy New Year!

Your Effi."

CHAPTER XIII

The New Year's eve ball lasted till the early morning and Effi was generously admired, not quite so unhesitatingly, to be sure, as the bouqt of camelias, which was known to have come from GieshÃ¼bler's greenhouse. After the ball everybody fell back into the same old routine, and hardly any attempt was made to establish closer social relations. Hence the winter seemed very long. Visits from the noble families of the neighborhood were rare, and when Effi was reminded of her duty to return the visits she always remarked in a half-sorrowful tone: "Yes, Geert, if it is absolutely necessary, but I shall be bored to death." Innstetten never disputed the statement. What was said, during these afternoon calls, about families, children, and agriculture, was bearable, but when church qstions were discussed and the pastors present were treated like little popes, even looked upon themselves as such, then Effi lost her patience and her mind wandered sadly back to Niemeyer, who was always modest and unpretentious, in spite of the fact that on every important occasion it was said he had the stuff in him to be called to the cathedral. Seemingly friendly as were the Borcke, Flemming, and Grasenabb families, with the exception of Sidonie Grasenabb, real friendship was out of the qstion, and often there would have been very little of pleasure and amusement, or even of reasonably agreeable association, if it had not been for GieshÄ¼bler.

He looked out for Effi as though he were a special Providence, and she was grateful to him for it. In addition to his many other interests he was a faithful and attentive reader of the newspapers. He was, in fact, the head of the Journal Club, and so scarcely a day passed that Mirambo did not bring to Effi a large white envelope full of separate sheets and whole papers, in which particular passages were marked, usually with a fine lead pencil, but occasionally with a heavy bl pencil and an exclamation or interrogation point. And that was not all. He also sent figs and dates, and chocolate drops done up in satin paper and tied with a little red ribbon. Whenever any specially beautiful flower was blooming in his greenhouse he would bring some of the blossoms himself and spend a happy hour chatting with his adored friend. He cherished in his heart, both separately and combined, all the beautiful emotions of love--that of a father and an uncle, a teacher and an admirer. Effi was affected by all these attentions and wrote to Hohen-Cremmen about them so often that her mother began to tease her about her "love for the alchymist." But this well-meant teasing failed of its purpose; it was almost painful to her, in fact, because it made her conscious, even though but dimly, of what was really lacking in her married life, viz., outspoken admiration, helpful suggestions, and little attentions.

Innstetten was kind and good, but he was not a lover. He felt that he loved Effi; hence his clear conscience did not require him to make any special effort to show it. It had almost become a rule with him to retire from his wife's room to his own when Frederick brought the lamp. "I have a difficult matter yet to attend to." With that he went. To be sure, the portiere was left thrown back, so that Effi could hear the turning of the pages of the document or the scratching of his pen, but that was all. Then Rollo would often come and lie down before her upon the fireplace rug, as much as to say: "Must just look after you again; nobody else does." Then she would stoop down and say softly: "Yes, Rollo, we are alone." At nine Innstetten would come back for tea, usually with the newspaper in his hand, and would talk about the Prince, who was having so much annoyance again, especially because of that Eugen Richter, whose conduct and language beggared all description. Then he would read over the list of appointments made and orders conferred, to the most of which he objected. Finally he would talk about the election and how fortunate it was to preside over a district in which there was still some feeling of respect. When he had finished with this he asked Effi to play something, either from *Lohengrin* or the *WalkÄ¼re*, for he was a Wagner enthusiast. What had won him over to this composer nobody quite knew. Some said, his nerves, for matter-of-fact as he seemed, he was in reality nervous. Others ascribed it to Wagner's position on the Jewish qstion. Probably both sides were right. At ten Innstetten relaxed and indulged in a few well-meant, but rather tired caresses, which Effi accepted, without genuinely returning them.

Thus passed the winter. April came and Effi was glad when the garden behind the court began to show green.

She could hardly wait for summer to come with its walks along the beach and its gsts at the baths. * * * The months had been so monotonous that she once wrote: "Can you imagine, mama, that I have almost become reconciled to our ghost? Of course, that terrible night, when Geert was away at the Prince's house, I should not like to live through again, no, certainly not; but this being always alone, with nothing whatever happening, is hard, too, and when I wake up in the night I occasionally listen to see if I can hear the shoes, shuffling up above, and when all is quiet I am almost disappointed and say to myself: If only it would come back, but not too bad and not too close!"

It was in February that Effi wrote these words and now it was almost May. The "Plantation" was beginning to take on new life again and one could hear the song of the finches. During this same week the storks returned, and one of them soared slowly over her house and alighted upon a barn near Utpatel's mill, its old resting place. Effi, who now wrote to her mother more freqntly than heretofore, reported this happening, and at the conclusion of her letter said: "I had almost forgotten one thing, my dear mama, viz., the new district commander of the landwehr, who has been here now for almost four weeks. But shall we really have him? That is the qstion, and a qstion of importance, too, much as my statement will make you laugh, because you do not know how we are suffering here from social famine. At least I am, for I am at a loss to know what to make of the nobility here. My fault, perhaps, but that is immaterial. The fact remains, there has been a famine, and for this reason I have looked forward, through all the winter months, to the new district commander as a bringer of comfort and deliverance. His predecessor was an abominable combination of bad manners and still worse morals and, as though that were not enough, was always in financial straits. We have suffered under him all this time, Innstetten more than I, and when we heard early in April that Major von Crampas was here--for that is the name of the new man--we rushed into each other's arms, as though no further harm could befall us in our dear Kessin. But, as already mentioned, it seems as though there will be nothing going on, now that he is here. He is married, has two children, one eight, the other ten years old, and his wife is a year older than he--say, forty-five. That of itself would make little difference, and why shouldn't I find a motherly friend delightfully entertaining? Miss Trippelli was nearly thirty, and I got along with her quite well. But Mrs. Crampas, who by the way was not a von, is impossible. She is always out of sorts, almost melancholy, much like our Mrs. Kruse, of whom she reminds me not a little, and it all comes from jealousy. Crampas himself is said to be a man of many 'relations,' a ladies' man, which always sounds ridiculous to me and would in this case, if he had not had a dl with a comrade on account of just such a thing. His left arm was shattered just below the shoulder and it is noticeable at first sight, in spite of the operation, which was heralded abroad as a masterpiece of surgical art. It was performed by Wilms and I believe they call it resection.

"Both Mr. and Mrs. Crampas were at our house a fortnight ago to pay us a visit. The situation was painful, for Mrs. Crampas watched her husband so closely that he became half-embarrassed, and I wholly. That he can be different, even jaunty and in high spirits, I was convinced three days ago, when, he sat alone with Innstetten, and I was able to follow their conversation from my room. I afterward talked with him myself and found him a perfect gentleman and extraordinarily clever. Innstetten was in the same brigade with him during the war and they often saw each other at Count GrÄ¶ben's to the north of Paris. Yes, my dear mama, he is just the man to instill new life into Kessin. Besides, he has none of the Pomeranian prejudices, even though he is said to have come from Swedish Pomerania. But his wife! Nothing can be done without her, of course, and still less with her."

Effi was quite right. As a matter of fact no close friendship was established with the Crampas family. They met once at the Borckes', again quite casually at the station, and a few days later on a steamer excursion up the "Broad" to a large beech and oak forest called "The Chatter-man." But they merely exchanged short greetings, and Effi was glad when the bathing season opened early in June. To be sure, there was still a lack of summer visitors, who as a rule did not come in numbers before St. John's Day. But even the preparations afforded entertainment. In the "Plantation" a merry-go-round and targets were set up, the boatmen calked and painted their boats, every little apartment put up new curtains, and rooms with damp exposure and subject to dry-rot were fumigated and aired.

In Effi's own home everybody was also more or less excited, not because of summer visitors, however, but of another expected arrival. Even Mrs. Kruse wished to help as much as she could. But Effi was alarmed at the thought of it and said: "Geert, don't let Mrs. Kruse touch anything. It would do no good, and I have enough to worry about without that." Innstetten promised all she asked, adding that Christel and Johanna would have plenty of time, anyhow.

* * * * *

[An elderly widow and her maid arrived and took rooms for the season opposite the Innstetten house. The widow died and was buried in the cemetery. After watching the funeral from her window Effi walked out to the hotel among the dunes and on her way home turned into the cemetery, where she found the widow's maid sitting in the burning sun.]

* * * * *

"It is a hot place you have picked out," said Effi, "much too hot. And if you are not cautious you may have a sun-stroke."

"That would be a blessing."

"How so?"

"Then I should be out of the world."

"I don't think you ought to say that, even if you had bad luck or lost a dear friend. I presume you loved her very dearly?"

"I? Her? Oh, heaven forbid!"

"You are very sad, however, and there must be some cause."

"There is, too, your Ladyship."

"Do you know me?"

"Yes. You are the wife of the district councillor across the street from us. I was always talking with the old woman about you. But the time came when she could talk no more, because she could not draw a good breath. There was something the matter with her here, dropsy, perhaps. But so long as she could speak she spoke incessantly. She was a genuine Berlin--"

"Good woman?"

"No. If I said that it would be a lie. She is in her grave now and we ought not to say anything bad about the dead, especially as even they hardly have peace. Oh well, I suppose she has found peace. But she was good for nothing and was quarrelsome and stingy and made no provision for me. The relatives who came yesterday from Berlin * * * were very rude and unkind to me and raised all sorts of objections when they paid me my wages, merely because they had to and because there are only six more days before the beginning of a new quarter. Otherwise I should have received nothing, or only half, or only a quarter--nothing with their good will. And they gave me a torn five-mark note to pay my fare back to Berlin. Well, it is just enough for a fourth-class ticket and I suppose I shall have to sit on my luggage. But I won't do it. I will sit here and wait till I die--Heavens, I thought I should have peace here and I could have stood it with the old woman, too. But now this has come to nothing and I shall have to be knocked around again. Besides, I am a Catholic. Oh, I have had enough of it and I wish I lay where the old woman lies. She might go on living for all of me. * * *"

74

Rollo, who had accompanied Effi, had meanwhile sat down before the maid, with his tong away out, and looked at her. When she stopped talking he arose, stepped forward, and laid his head upon her knees. Suddenly she was transformed. "My, this means something for me. Why, here is a creature that can endure me, that looks at me like a friend and lays its head on my knees. My, it has been a long time since anything like that has happened to me. Well, old boy, what's your name? My, but you are a splendid fellow!"

"Rollo," said Effi.

"Rollo; that is strange. But the name makes no difference. I have a strange name, too, that is, forename. And the likes of me have no other, you know."

"What is your name?"

"I am called Roswitha."

"Yes, that is strange; why, that is--"

"Yes, quite right, your Ladyship, it is a Catholic name. And that is another trouble, that I am a Catholic. From Eichsfeld. Being a Catholic makes it harder and more disagreeable for me. Many won't have Catholics, because they run to the church so much. * * *"

"Roswitha," said Effi, sitting down by her on the bench. "What are you going to do now?"

"Ah, your Ladyship, what could I be going to do? Nothing. Honestly and truly, I should like to sit here and wait till I fall over dead. * * *"

"I want to ask you something, Roswitha. Are you fond of children? Have you ever taken care of little children?"

"Indeed I have. That is the best and finest thing about me. * * * When a dear little thing stands up in one's lap, a darling little creature like a doll, and looks at one with its little peepers, that, I tell you, is something that opens up one's heart. * * *"

"Now let me tell you, Roswitha, you are a good tr person; I can tell it by your looks. A little bit unceremonious, but that doesn't hurt; it is often tr of the best people, and I have had confidence in you from the beginning. Will you come along to my house? It seems as though God had sent you to me. I am expecting a little one soon, and may God help me at the time. When the child comes it must be cared for and waited upon and perhaps even fed from a bottle, though I hope not. But one can never tell. What do you say? Will you come?"

75

Roswitha sprang up, seized the hand of the young wife and kissed it fervently. "Oh, there is indeed a God in heaven, and when our need is greatest help is nearest. Your Ladyship shall see, I can do it. I am an orderly person and have good references. You can see for yourself when I bring you my book. The very first time I saw your Ladyship I thought: 'Oh, if I only had such a mistress!' And now I am to have her. O, dear God, O, holy Virgin Mary, who would have thought it possible, when we had put the old woman in her grave and the relatives made haste to get away and left me sitting here?"

"Yes, it is the unexpected that often happens, Roswitha, and occasionally for our good. Let us go now. Rollo is getting impatient and keeps running down to the gate."

Roswitha was ready at once, but went back to the grave, mumbled a few words and crossed herself. Then they walked down the shady path and back to the churchyard gate.
* * *

CHAPTER XIV

In less than a quarter of an hour the house was reached. As they stepped into the cool hall * * * Effi said: "Now, Roswitha, you go in there. That is our bedroom. I am going over to the district councillor's office to tell my husband that I should like to have you as a nurse for the baby. He will doubtless agree to it, but I must have his consent. Then when I have it we must find other quarters for him and you will sleep with me in the alcove * * *"

When Innstetten learned the situation he said with alacrity: "You did the right thing, Effi, and if her testimonials are not too bad we will take her on her good face * * *"

Effi was very happy to have encountered so little difficulty, and said: "Now it will be all right. Now I am no longer afraid * * *"

That same hour Roswitha moved into the house with her few possessions and established herself in the little alcove. When the day was over she went to bed early and, tired as she was, fell asleep instantly.

The next morning Effi inquired how she had slept and whether she had heard anything.

"What?" asked Roswitha.

"Oh, nothing. I just meant some sound as though a broom were sweeping or some one were sliding over the floor."

Roswitha laughed and that made an especially good impression upon her young mistress. Effi had been brought up a Protestant and would have been very much alarmed if any Catholic traits had been discovered in her. And yet she believed that Catholicism affords the better protection against such things as "that upstairs" * * *

All soon began to feel at home with one another, for Effi, like most country noblewomen of Brandenburg, had the amiable characteristic of liking to listen to such little stories as those for which the deceased widow, with her avarice, her nephews and their wives, afforded Roswitha an inexhaustible fund of material. Johanna was also an appreciative listener.

Often, when Effi laughed aloud at the drastic passages, Johanna would deign to smile, but inwardly she was surprised that her Ladyship found pleasure in such stupid stuff. This feeling of surprise, along with her sense of superiority, proved on the whole very fortunate and helped to avoid quarrels with Johanna about their relative positions. Roswitha was simply the comic figure, and for Johanna to be jealous of her would have been as bad as to envy Rollo his position of friendship.

Thus passed a week, chatty and almost jolly, for Effi looked forward with less anxiety than heretofore to the important coming event. Nor did she think that it was so near. On the ninth day the chattering and jollity came to an end. Running and hurrying took their place, and Innstetten himself laid aside his customary reserve entirely. On the morning of the 3d of July a cradle was standing by Effi's bed. Dr. Hannemann joyously grasped the young mother's hand and said: "We have today the anniversary of KÃ¶niggrÃ¤tz; a pity, that it is a girl. But the other may come yet, and the Prussians have many anniversaries of victories." Roswitha doubtless had some similar idea, but for the present her joy over the new arrival knew no bounds. Without further ado she called the child "little Annie," which the young mother took as a sign. "It must have been an inspiration," she said, "that Roswitha hit upon this particular name." Even Innstetten had nothing to say against it, and so they began to talk about "little Annie" long before the christening day arrived.

Effi, who expected to be with her parents in Hohen-Cremmen from the middle of August on, would have liked to postpone the baptism till then. But it was not feasible. Innstetten could not take a vacation and so the 15th of August * * * was set for the ceremony, which of course was to take place in the church. The accompanying banqt was held in the large clubhouse on the quay, because the district councillor's house had no dining hall. All the nobles of the neighborhood were invited and all came. Pastor Lindequist delivered the toast to the mother and the child in a charming way that was admired on all sides. But Sidonie von Grasenabb took occasion to remark to her neighbor, an assessor of the strict type: "Yes, his occasional addresses will pass. But he cannot justify his sermons before God or man. He is a half-way man, one of those who

are rejected because they are lukewarm. I don't care to quote the Bible here literally."
Immediately thereafter old Mr. von Borcke took the floor to drink to the health of
Innstetten: "Ladies and Gentlemen: These are hard times in which we live; rebellion,
defiance, lack of discipline, whithersoever we look. But * * * so long as we still have
men like Baron von Innstetten, whom I am proud to call my friend, just so long we can
endure it, and our old Prussia will hold out. Indeed, my friends, with Pomerania and
Brandenburg we can conqr this foe and set our foot upon the head of the poisonous
dragon of revolution. Firm and tr, thus shall we gain the victory. The Catholics, our
brethren, whom we must respect, even though we fight them, have the 'rock of Peter,'
but our rock is of bronze. Three cheers for Baron Innstetten!" Innstetten thanked him
briefly. Effi said to Major von Crampas, who sat beside her, that the 'rock of Peter' was
probably a compliment to Roswitha, and she would later approach old Councillor of
Justice Gadebusch and ask him if he were not of her opinion. For some unaccountable
reason Crampas took this remark seriously and advised her not to ask the Councillor's
opinion, which amused Effi exceedingly. "Why, I thought you were a better mind-
reader."

"Ah, your Ladyship, in the case of beautiful young women who are not yet eighteen the
art of mind-reading fails utterly."

"You are defeating your cause completely, Major. You may call me a grandmother, but
you can never be pardoned for alluding to the fact that I am not yet eighteen."

When they left the table the late afternoon steamer came down the Kessine and called at
the landing opposite the clubhouse. Effi sat by an open window with Crampas and
GieshÃ¼bler, drinking coffee and watching the scene below. "Tomorrow morning at
nine the same boat will take me up the river, and at noon I shall be in Berlin, and in the
evening I shall be in Hohen-Cremmen, and Roswitha will walk beside me and carry the
child in her arms. I hope it will not cry. Ah, what a feeling it gives me even today! Dear
GieshÃ¼bler, were you ever so happy to see again your parental home?"

[Illustation: *Permission F. Bruckmann A.-G. Munich* PROCESSION AT GASTEIN
Adolph von Menzel] "Yes, the feeling is not new to me, most gracious Lady, excepting
only that I have never taken any little Annie with me, for I have none to take."

CHAPTER XV

Effi left home in the middle of August and was back in Kessin at the end of September.
During the six weeks' visit she had often longed to return, but when she now reached
the house and entered the dark hall into which no light could enter except the little from

the stairway, she had a sudden feeling of fear and said to herself: "There is no such pale, yellow light in Hohen-Cremmen."

A few times during the days in Hohen-Cremmen she had longed for the "Haunted house," but on the whole her life there had been full of happiness and contentment. To be sure, she had not known what to make of Hulda, who was not taking kindly to her rÃ´le of waiting for a husband or fiancÃ© to turn up. With the twins, however, she got along much better, and more than once when she played ball or croqt with them she entirely forgot that she was married. Those were happy moments. Her chief delight was, as in former days, to stand on the swing board as it flew through the air and gave her a tingling sensation, a shudder of sweet danger, when she felt she would surely fall the next moment. When she finally sprang out of the swing, she went with the two girls to sit on the bench in front of the schoolhouse and there told old Mr. Jahnke, who joined them, about her life in Kessin, which she said was half-hanseatic and half-Scandinavian, and anything but a replica of Schwantikow and Hohen-Cremmen.

Such were the little daily amusements, to which were added occasional drives into the summery marsh, usually in the dog-cart. But Effi liked above everything else the chats she had almost every morning with her mother, as they sat upstairs in the large airy room, while Roswitha rocked the baby and sang lullabies in a Thuringian dialect which nobody fully understood, perhaps not even Roswitha. Effi and her mother would move over to the open window and look out upon the park, the sundial, or the pond with the dragon flies hovering almost motionless above it, or the tile walk, where von Briest sat beside the porch steps reading the newspapers. Every time he turned a page he took off his nose glasses and greeted his wife and daughter. When he came to his last paper, usually the *Havelland Advertiser*, Effi went down either to sit beside him or stroll with him through the garden and park. On one such occasion they stepped from the gravel walk over to a little monument standing to one side, which Briest's grandfather had erected in memory of the battle of Waterloo. It was a rusty pyramid with a bronze cast of BlÃ¼cher in front and one of Wellington in the rear.

"Have you any such walks in Kessin?" said von Briest, "and does Innstetten accompany you and tell you stories?"

"No, papa, I have no such walks. It is out of the qstion, for we have only a small garden behind the house, in reality hardly a garden at all, just a few box-bordered plots and vegetable beds with three or four fruit trees. Innstetten has no appreciation of such things and, I fancy, does not expect to stay much longer in Kessin."

"But, child, you must have exercise and fresh air, for you are accustomed to them."

"Oh, I have both. Our house is situated near a grove, which they call the 'Plantation,' and I walk there a great deal and Rollo with me."

"Always Rollo," laughed von Briest. "If I didn't know better, I should be tempted to think that you cared more for Rollo than for your husband and child."

"Ah, papa, that would be terrible, even if I am forced to admit that there was a time when I could not have gotten along without Rollo. That was--oh, you know when--On that occasion he virtually saved my life, or I at least fancied he did, and since then he has been my good friend and my chief dependence. But he is only a dog, and of course human beings come first."

"Yes, that is what they always say, but I have my doubts. There is something peculiar about brute creatures and a correct understanding of them has not yet been arrived at. Believe me, Effi, this is another wide field. When I think how a person has an accident on the water or on the slippery ice, and some dog, say, one like your Rollo, is at hand, he will not rest till he has brought the unfortunate person to the shore. And if the victim is already dead, the dog will lie down beside him and bark and whine till somebody comes, and if nobody comes he will stay by the corpse till he himself is dead. That is what such an animal always does. And now take mankind on the other hand. God forgive me for saying it, but it sometimes seems to me as though the brute creature were better than man."

"But, papa, if I said that to Innstetten--"

"No, Effi, you would better not."

"Rollo would resc me, of course, but Innstetten would, too. He is a man of honor, you know."

"That he is."

"And loves me."

"That goes without saying. And where there is love it is reciprocated. That is the way of the world. I am only surprised that he didn't take a vacation and flit over here. When one has such a young wife--"

Effi blushed, for she thought exactly the same thing. But she did not care to admit it. "Innstetten is so conscientious and he desires to be thought well of, I believe, and has his own plans for the future. Kessin, you know, is only a stepping stone. And, after all, I am not going to run away from him. He has me, you see. If he were too affectionate-- beside the difference between our ages--people would merely smile."

"Yes, they would, Effi. But one must not mind that. Now, don't say anything about it, not even to mama. It is so hard to say what to do and what not. That is also a wide field."

More than once during Effi's visit with her parents such conversations as the above had occurred, but fortunately their effect had not lasted long. Likewise the melancholy impression made upon her by the Kessin house at the moment of her return quickly faded away. Innstetten was full of little attentions, and when tea had been taken and the news of the city and the gossip about lovers had been talked over in a merry mood Effi took his arm affectionately and went into the other room with him to contin their chat and hear some anecdotes about Miss Trippelli, who had recently had another lively correspondence with GieshÃ¼bler. This always meant a new debit on her never settled account. During this conversation Effi was very jolly, enjoying to the full the emotions of a young wife, and was glad to be rid of Roswitha, who had been transferred to the servants' quarters for an indefinite period.

The next morning she said: "The weather is beautiful and mild and I hope the veranda on the side toward the 'Plantation' is in good order, so that we can move out of doors and take breakfast there. We shall be shut up in our rooms soon enough, at best, for the Kessin winters are really four weeks too long."

Innstetten agreed heartily. The veranda Effi spoke of, which might perhaps better be called a tent, had been put up in the summer, three or four weeks before Effi's departure for Hohen-Cremmen. It consisted of a large platform, with the side in front open, an immense awning overhead, while to the right and left there were broad canvas curtains, which could be shoved back and forth by means of rings on an iron rod. It was a charming spot and all summer long was admired by the visitors who passed by on their way to the baths.

Effi had leaned back in a rocking chair and said, as she pushed the coffee tray toward her husband: "Geert, you might play the amiable host today. I for my part find this rocker so comfortable that I do not care to get up. So exert yourself and if you are right glad to have me back again I shall easily find some way to get even." As she said this she straightened out the white damask cloth and laid her hand upon it. Innstetten took her hand and kissed it.

"Well, how did you get on without me?"

"Badly enough, Effi."

"You just say so and try to look gloomy, but in reality there is not a word of truth in it."

"Why, Effi--"

"As I will prove to you, If you had had the least bit of longing for your child--I will not speak of myself, for, after all, what is a woman to such a high lord, who was a bachelor for so many years and was in no hurry--"

"Well?"

"Yes, Geert, if you had had just the least bit of longing, you would not have left me for six weeks to enjoy widow-like my own sweet society in Hohen-Cremmen, with nobody about but Niemeyer and Jahnke, and now and then our friends in Schwantikow. Nobody at all came from Rathenow, which looked as though they were afraid of me, or I had grown too old."

"Ah, Effi, how you do talk! Do you know that you are a little coqtte?"

"Thank heaven that you say so. You men consider a coqtte the best thing a woman can be. And you yourself are not different from the rest, even if you do put on such a solemn and honorable air. I know very well, Geert--To tell the truth, you are--"

"Well, what?"

"Well, I prefer not to say. But I know you very well. To tell the truth, you are, as my Schwantikow uncle once said, an affectionate man, and were born under the star of love, and Uncle Belling was quite right when he said so. You merely do not like to show it and think it is not proper and spoils one's career. Have I struck it?"

Innstetten laughed. "You have struck it a little bit. And let me tell you, Effi, you seem to me entirely changed. Before little Annie came you were a child, but all of a sudden--"

"Well?"

"All of a sudden you are like another person. But it is becoming to you and I like you very much. Shall I tell you further?"

"What?"

"There is something alluring about you."

"Oh, my only Geert, why, what you say is glorious. Now my heart is gladder than ever-- Give me another half a cup--Do you know that that is what I have always desired? We women must be alluring, or we are nothing whatever."

"Is that your own idea?"

82

"I might have originated it, but I got it from Niemeyer."

"From Niemeyer! My, oh my, what a fine pastor he is! Well, I just tell you, there are none like him here. But how did he come by it? Why, it seems as though some Don Juan, some regular heart smasher had said it."

"Ah, who knows?" laughed Effi. "But isn't that Crampas coming there? And from the beach! You don't suppose he has been swimming? On the 27th of September!"

"He often does such things, purely to make an impression."

Crampas had meanwhile come up quite near and greeted them.

"Good morning," cried Innstetten. "Come closer, come closer."

Crampas, in civilian dress, approached and kissed Effi's hand. She went on rocking, and Innstetten said: "Excuse me, Major, for doing the honors of the house so poorly; but the veranda is not a house and, strictly speaking, ten o'clock in the morning is no time. At this hour we omit formalities, or, if you like, we all make ourselves at home. So sit down and give an account of your actions. For by your hair,--I wish for your sake there were more of it--I see plainly you have been swimming."

He nodded.

"Inexcusable," said Innstetten, half in earnest and half joking. "Only four weeks ago you yourself witnessed Banker Heinersdorf's calamity. He too thought the sea and the magnificent waves would respect him on account of his millions. But the gods are jealous of each other, and Neptune, without any apparent cause, took sides against Pluto, or at least against Heinersdorf."

Crampas laughed. "Yes, a million marks! If I had that much, my dear Innstetten, I should not have risked it, I presume; for beautiful as the weather is, the water was only 9Â° centigrade. But a man like me, with his million deficit,--permit me this little bit of boasting--a man like me can take such liberties without fearing the jealousy of the gods. Besides, there is comfort in the proverb, 'Whoever is born for the noose cannot perish in the water.'"

"Why, Major," said Effi, "you don't mean to talk your neck into--excuse me!--such an unprosaic predicament, do you? To be sure, many believe--I refer to what you just said-- that every man more or less deserves to be hanged. And yet, Major--for a major--"

"It is not the traditional way of dying. I admit it, your Ladyship. Not traditional and, in my case, not even very probable. So it was merely a quotation, or, to be more accurate,

83

a common expression. Still, there is some sincerity back of it when I say the sea will not harm me, for I firmly expect to die a regular, and I hope honorable, soldier's death. Originally it was only a gypsy's prophesy, but with an echo in my own conscience."

Innstetten laughed. "There will be a few obstacles, Crampas, unless you plan to serve under the Sublime Porte or the Chinese dragon. There the soldiers are knocking each other around now. Take my word for it, that kind of business is all over here for the next thirty years, and if anybody has the desire to meet his death as a soldier--"

"He must first order a war of Bismarck. I know all about it, Innstetten. But that is a mere bagatelle for you. It is now the end of September. In ten weeks at the latest the Prince will be in Varzin again, and as he has a liking for you--I will refrain from using the more vulgar term, to avoid facing the barrel of your pistol--you will be able, won't you, to provide a little war for an old Vionville comrade? The Prince is only a human being, like the rest of us, and a kind word never comes amiss."

During this conversation Effi had been wadding bread and tossing it on the table, then making figures out of the little balls, to indicate that a change of topic was desirable. But Innstetten seemed bent on answering Crampas's joking remarks, for which reason Effi decided it would be better for her simply to interrupt. "I can't see, Major, why we should trouble ourselves about your way of dying. Life lies nearer to us and is for the time being a more serious matter."

Crampas nodded.

"I am glad you agree with me. How are we to live here? That is the qstion right now. That is more important than anything else. GieshÃ¼bler has written me a letter on the subject and I would show it to you if it did not seem indiscreet or vain, for there are a lot of other things besides in the letter. Innstetten doesn't need to read it; he has no appreciation of such things. Incidentally, the handwriting is like engraving, and the style is what one would expect if our Kessin friend had been brought up at an Old French court. The fact that he is humpbacked and wears white jabots such as no other human being wears--I can't imagine where he has them ironed--all this fits so well. Now GieshÃ¼bler has written to me about plans for the evenings at the club, and about a manager by the name of Crampas. You see, Major, I like that better than the soldier's death, let alone the other."

"And I, personally, no less than you. It will surely be a splendid winter if we may feel assured of the support of your Ladyship. Miss Trippelli is coming--"

"Trippelli? Then I am superfluous."

84

"By no means, your Ladyship. Miss Trippelli cannot sing from one Sunday till the next; it would be too much for her and for us. Variety is the spice of life, a truth which, to be sure, every happy marriage seems to controvert."

"If there are any happy marriages, mine excepted," and she held out her hand to Innstetten.

"Variety then," contind Crampas. "To secure it for ourselves and our club, of which for the time being I have the honor to be the vice-president, we need the help of everybody who can be depended upon. If we put our heads together we can turn this whole place upside down. The theatrical pieces have already been selected--*War in Peace, Mr. Hercules, Youthful Love,* by Wilbrandt, and perhaps *Euphrosyne*, by Gensichen. You as Euphrosyne and I middle-aged Goethe. You will be astonished to see how well I can act the prince of poets, if act is the right word."

"No doubt. In the meantime I have learned from the letter of my alchemistic correspondent that, in addition to your other accomplishments, you are an occasional poet. At first I was surprised."

"You couldn't see that I looked the part."

"No. But since I have found out that you go swimming at 9° I have changed my mind. Nine degrees in the Baltic Sea beats the Castalian Fountain."

"The temperature of which is unknown."

"Not to me; at least nobody will contradict me. But now I must get up. There comes Roswitha with little Annie."

She arose and went toward Roswitha, took the child, and tossed it up with pride and joy.

CHAPTER XVI

[For the next few weeks Crampas came regularly every morning to gossip a while with Effi on the veranda and then ride horseback with her husband. Finally she desired to ride with them and, although Innstetten did not approve of the idea, Crampas secured a horse for her. On one of their rides Crampas let fall a remark about how it bored him to have to observe such a multitude of petty laws. Effi applauded the sentiment. Innstetten

85

took the Major to task and reminded him that one of his frivolous escapades had cost him an arm. When the election campaign began Innstetten; could no longer take the time for the horseback rides, and so Effi went out with Crampas, accompanied by two lackeys. One day, while riding slowly through the woods, Crampas spoke at length of Innstetten's character, telling how in earlier life the councillor was more respected than loved, how he had a mystical tendency and was inclined to make sport of his comrades. He referred also to Innstetten's fondness for ghost stories, which led Effi to tell her experience with the Chinaman. Crampas said that because of an unusual ambition Innstetten had to have an unusual residence; hence the haunted house. He further poisoned Effi's mind by telling her that her husband was a born pedagog and in the education of his wife was employing the haunted house in accordance with a definite pedagogical plan.]

CHAPTER XVII

The clock struck two as they reached the house. Crampas bade Effi adieu, rode into the city, and dismounted at his residence on the market square. Effi changed her dress and tried to take a nap, but could not go to sleep, for she was less weary than out of humor. That Innstetten should keep his ghosts, in order to live in an extraordinary house, that she could endure; it harmonized with his inclination to be different from the great mass. But the other thing, that he should use his ghosts for pedagogical purposes, that was annoying, almost insulting. It was clear to her mind that "pedagogical purposes" told less than half the story. What Crampas had meant was far, far worse, was a kind of instrument designed to instill fear. It was wholly lacking in goodness of heart and bordered almost on crlty. The blood rushed to her head, she clenched her little fist, and was on the point of laying plans, but suddenly she had to laugh. "What a child I am!" she exclaimed. "Who can assure me that Crampas is right? Crampas is entertaining, because he is a gossip, but he is unreliable, a mere braggart, and cannot hold a candle to Innstetten."

At this moment Innstetten drove up, having decided to come home earlier today than usual. Effi sprang from her seat to greet him in the hall and was the more affectionate, the more she felt she had something to make amends for. But she could not entirely ignore what Crampas had said, and in the midst of her caresses, while she was listening with apparent interest, there was the ever recurring echo within: "So the ghost is part of a design, a ghost to keep me in my place."

Finally she forgot it, however, and listened artlessly to what he had to tell her.

* * * * *

86

About the middle of November the north wind blew up a gale, which for a day and a half swept over the moles so violently that the Kessine, more and more dammed back, finally overflowed the quay and ran into the streets. But after the storm had spent its rage the weather cleared and a few sunny autumn days followed. "Who knows how long they will last," said Effi to Crampas, and they decided to ride out once more on the following morning. Innstetten, who had a free day, was to go too. They planned to ride to the mole and dismount there, then take a little walk along the beach and finally have luncheon at a sheltered spot behind the dunes.

At the appointed hour Crampas rode up before the house. Kruse was holding the horse for her Ladyship, who quickly lifted herself into the saddle, saying that Innstetten had been prevented from going and wished to be excused. There had been another big fire in Morgenitz the night before, the third in three weeks, pointing to incendiarism, and he had been obliged to go there, much to his sorrow, for he had looked forward with real pleasure to this ride, thinking it would probably be the last of the season.

Crampas expressed his regret, perhaps just to say something, but perhaps with sincerity, for inconsiderate as he was in chivalrous love affairs, he was, on the other hand, equally a hale fellow well met. To be sure, only superficially. To help a friend and five minutes later deceive him were things that harmonized very well with his sense of honor. He could do both with incredible bonhomie.

The ride followed the usual route through the "Plantation." Rollo went ahead, then came Crampas and Effi, and Kruse followed. Crampas's lackey was not along.

"Where did you leave Knut?"

"He has the mumps."

"Remarkable," laughed Effi. "To tell the truth, he always looked as though he had something of the sort."

"Quite right. But you ought to see him now. Or rather not, for you can take the mumps from merely seeing a case."

"I don't believe it."

"There is a great deal that young wives don't believe."

"And again they believe many things they would better not believe."

"Do you say that for my benefit?"

"No."

"Sorry."

"How becoming this 'sorry' is to you! I really believe, Major, you would consider it entirely proper, if I were to make a declaration of love to you."

"I will not go quite that far. But I should like to see the fellow who would not desire such a thing. Thoughts and wishes go free of duty."

"There is some qstion about that. Besides, there is a difference between thoughts and wishes. Thoughts, as a rule, keep in the background, but wishes, for the most part, hover on the lips."

"I wish you wouldn't say that."

"Ah, Crampas, you are--you are--"

"A fool."

"No. That is another exaggeration. But you are something else. In Hohen-Cremmen we always said, I along with the rest, that the most conceited person in the world was a hussar ensign at eighteen."

"And now?"

"Now I say, the most conceited person in the world is a district major of the landwehr at forty-two."

"Incidentally, my other two years that you most graciously ignore make amends for the remark. Kiss the hand" (--My respects to you).

"Yes, 'kiss the hand.' That is just the expression that fits you. It is Viennese. And the Viennese--I made their acquaintance four years ago in Carlsbad, where they courted me, a fourteen-year-old slip of a girl. What a lot of things I had to listen to!"

"Certainly nothing more than was right."

"If that were tr, the intended compliment would be rather rude--But see the buoys yonder, how they swim and dance. The little red flags are hauled in. Every time I have seen the red flags this summer, the few times that I have ventured to go down to the beach, I have said to myself: there lies Vineta, it must lie there, those are the tops of the towers."

"That is because you know Heine's poem."

"Which one?"

"Why, the one about Vineta."

"No, I don't know that one; indeed I know very few, to my sorrow."

"And yet you have GieshÃ¼bler and the Journal Club. However, Heine gave the poem a different name, 'Sea Ghosts,' I believe, or something of the sort. But he meant Vineta. As he himself--pardon me, if I proceed to tell you here the contents of the poem--as the poet, I was about to say, is passing the place, he is lying on the ship's deck and looking down into the water, and there he sees narrow, medieval streets, and women tripping along in hoodlike hats. All have songbooks in their hands and are going to church, and all the bells are ringing. When he hears the bells he is seized with a longing to go to church himself, even though only for the sake of the hoodlike hats, and in the heat of desire he screams aloud and is about to plunge in. But at that moment the captain seizes him by the leg and exclaims: 'Doctor, are you crazy?'"

"Why, that is delicious! I'd like to read it. Is it long?"

"No, it is really short, somewhat longer than 'Thou hast diamonds and pearls,' or 'Thy soft lily fingers,'" and he gently touched her hand. "But long or short, what descriptive power, what objectivity! He is my favorite poet and I know him by heart, little as I care in general for this poetry business, in spite of the jingles I occasionally perpetrate myself. But with Heine's poetry it is different. It is all life, and above everything else he is a connoisseur of love, which, you know, is the highest good. Moreover, he is not one-sided."

"What do you mean?"

"I mean he is not all for love."

"Well, even if he had this one-sidedness it would not be the worst thing in the world. What else does he favor?"

"He is also very much in favor of romance, which, to be sure, follows closely after love and, in the opinion of some people, coincides with it. But I don't believe it does. In his later poems, which have been called 'romantic'--as a matter of fact, he called them that himself--in these romantic poems there is no end of killing. Often on account of love, to be sure, but usually for other, more vulgar reasons, among which I include politics, which is almost always vulgar. Charles Stuart, for example, carries his head under his arm in one of these romances, and still more grsome is the story of Vitzliputzli."

"Of whom?"

"Vitzliputzli. He is a Mexican god, and when the Mexicans had taken twenty or thirty Spaniards prisoners, these twenty or thirty had to be sacrificed to Vitzliputzli. There was no help for it, it was a national custom, a cult, and it all took place in the turn of a hand--belly open, heart out--"

"Stop, Crampas, no more of that. It is indecent, and disgusting besides. And all this when we are just about on the point of eating lunch!"

"I for my part am not affected by it, as I make it my rule to let my appetite depend only upon the menu."

During this conversation they had come from the beach, according to program, to a bench built in the lee of the dunes, with an extremely primitive table in front of it, simply a board on top of two posts. Kruse, who had ridden ahead, had the lunch already served--tea rolls, slices of cold roast meat, and red wine, and beside the bottle stood two pretty little gold-rimmed glasses, such as one buys in watering places or takes home as souvenirs from glass works.

They dismounted. Kruse, who had tied the reins of his own horse around a stunted pine, walked up and down with the other two horses, while Crampas and Effi sat down at the table and enjoyed the clear view of beach and mole afforded by a narrow cut through the dunes.

The half-wintery November sun shed its fallow light upon the still agitated sea and the high-running surf. Now and then a puff of wind came and carried the spray clear up to the table. There was lyme grass all around, and the bright yellow of the immortelles stood out sharply against the yellow sand they were growing in, despite the kinship of colors. Effi played the hostess. "I am sorry, Major, to have to pass you the rolls in a basket lid."

"I don't mind the platter, so long as it holds a favor."

"But this is Kruse's arrangement--Why, there you are too, Rollo. But our lunch does not take you into account. What shall we do with Rollo?"

"I say, give him everything--I for my part out of gratitude. For, you see, dearest Effi--"

Effi looked at him.

"For, you see, most gracious Lady, Rollo reminds me of what I was about to tell you as a continuation or counterpart of the Vitzliputzli story, only much more racy, because a love story. Have you ever heard of a certain Pedro the Crl?"

"I have a faint recollection."

"A kind of Blbeard king."

"That is fine. That is the kind girls like best to hear about, and I still remember we always said of my friend Hulda Niemeyer, whose name you have heard, I believe, that she knew no history, except the six wives of Henry the Eighth, that English Blbeard, if the word is strong enough for him. And, really, she knew these six by heart. You ought to have heard her when she pronounced the names, especially that of the mother of qen Elizabeth,--so terribly embarrassed, as though it were her turn next--But now, please, the story of Don Pedro."

"Very well. At Don Pedro's court there was a handsome black Spanish knight, who wore on his breast the cross of Calatrava, which is about the equivalent of the Black Eagle and the *Pour le Mérite* together. This cross was essential, they always had to wear it, and this Calatrava knight, whom the qen secretly loved, of course--"

"Why of course?"

"Because we are in Spain."

"So we are."

"And this Calatrava knight, I say, had a very beautiful dog, a Newfoundland dog, although there were none as yet, for it was just a hundred years before the discovery of America. A very beautiful dog, let us call him Rollo."

When Rollo heard his name he barked and wagged his tail.

"It went on thus for many a day. But the secret love, which probably did not remain entirely secret, soon became too much for the king, who cared very little for the Calatrava knight anyhow; for he was not only a crl king, but also a jealous old wether-- or, if that word is not just suited for a king, and still less for my amiable listener, Mrs. Effi, call him at least a jealous creature. Well, he resolved to have the Calatrava knight secretly beheaded for his secret love."

91

"I can't blame him."

"I don't know, most gracious Lady. You must hear further. In part it was all right, but it was too much. The king, in my judgment, went altogether too far. He pretended he was going to arrange a feast for the knight in honor of his deeds as a warrior and hero, and there was a long table and all the grandees of the realm sat at this table, and in the middle sat the king, and opposite him was the place of honor for the Calatrava knight. But the knight failed to appear, and when they had waited a long while for him, they finally had to begin the feast without him, and his place remained vacant. A vacant place just opposite the king!"

"And then?"

"And then, fancy, most gracious Lady, as the king, this Pedro, is about to rise in order dissemblingly to express his regret that his 'dear gst' has not yet appeared, the horrified servants are heard screaming on the stairway, and before anybody knows what has happened, something flies along the table, springs upon the chair, and places a severed head upon the empty plate. Over this very head Rollo stares at the one sitting face to face with him, viz., the king. Rollo had accompanied his master on his last journey, and the moment the ax fell the faithful animal snatched the falling head, and here he was now, our friend Rollo, at the long festal board, accusing the royal murderer."

Effi was rapt with attention. After a few moments she said: "Crampas, that is in its way very beautiful, and because it is very beautiful I will forgive you. But you might do better, and please me more, if you would tell stories of another kind, even from Heine. Certainly Heine has not written exclusively of Vitzliputzli and Don Pedro and *your* Rollo. I say *your*, for mine would not have done such a thing. Come, Rollo. Poor creature, I can't look at you any more without thinking of the Calatrava knight, whom the qen secretly loved--Call Kruse, please, that he may put these things back in the saddle bag, and, as we ride home, you must tell me something different, something entirely different."

Kruse came. As he was about to take the glasses Crampas said: "Kruse, leave the one glass, this one here. I'll take it myself."

"Your servant, Major."

Effi, who had overheard this, shook her head. Then she laughed. "Crampas, what in the world are you thinking of? Kruse is stupid enough not to think a second time about anything, and even if he did he fortunately would arrive at no conclusion. But that does not justify you in keeping this thirty-pfennig glass from the Joseph Glass Works."

"Your scornful reference to its price makes me feel its val all the more deeply."

"Always the same story. You are such a humorist, but a very qer one. If I understand you rightly you are going to--it is ridiculous and I almost hesitate to say it--you are going to perform now the act of the King of Thule."

He nodded with a touch of roguishness.

"Very well, for all I care. Everybody wears his right cap; you know which one. But I must be permitted to say that the rÃ´le you are assigning to me in this connection is far from flattering. I don't care to figure as a rhyme to your King of Thule. Keep the glass, but please draw no conclusions that would compromise me. I shall tell Innstetten about it."

"That you will not do, most gracious Lady."

"Why not?"

"Innstetten is not the man to see such things in their proper light."

She eyed him sharply for a moment, then lowered her eyes confused and almost embarrassed.

CHAPTER XVIII

[Effi's peace was disturbed, but the prospect of a quiet winter, with few occasions to meet Crampas, reassured her. She and her husband began to spend their evenings reviewing their Italian journey. GieshÃ¼bler joined them and soon announced that Crampas was planning an amateur performance of *A Step out of the Way*, with Effi as the heroine. She felt the danger, but was eager to act, as Crampas was only the coach. Her playing won enthusiastic applause and Innstetten raved over his captivating wife. A casual remark about Mrs. Crampas led him to assert that she was insanely jealous of Effi, and to tell how Crampas had wheedled her into agreeing to stay at home the second day after Christmas, while he himself joined the Innstettens and others on a sleighing party. Innstetten then said, in a way suggesting the strict pedagog, that Crampas was not to be trusted, particularly in his relations to women. On Christmas day Effi was happy till she discovered she had received no greeting from Crampas. That put her out of sorts and made her conscious that all was not well. Innstetten noticed her troubled state and, when she told him she felt unworthy of the kindness showered upon her, he said that people get only what they deserve, but she was not sure of his meaning. The proposed sleighing party was carried out. After coffee at Forester Ring's lodge all went out for a walk. Crampas remarked to Effi that they were in danger of being snowed in. She replied with the story of a poem entitled *God's Wall*, which she had learned from her pastor. During a war an aged widow prayed God to build a wall to protect her from the enemy. God caused her cottage to be snowed under, and the enemy passed by. Crampas changed the subject.]

CHAPTER XIX

[At seven o'clock dinner was served. At the table Sidonie Grasenabb had much to say against the loose modern way of bringing up girls, with particular reference to the Forester's frivolous daughters. After a toast to Ring, in which GÃ¼ldenklee indulged in various puns on the name, the Prussian song was sung and the company made ready to start home. GieshÃ¼bler's coachman had meanwhile been kicked in the shin by one of the horses and the doctor ordered him to stay at the Forester's for the present. Innstetten undertook to drive home in his place. Sidonie Grasenabb rode part of the way with Effi and Crampas, till a small stream with a quicksand bottom was encountered, when she left the sleigh and joined her family in their carriage. Crampas who had been sent by Innstetten to look after the ladies in his sleigh, was now alone with Effi. When she saw that the roundabout way was bringing them to a dark forest, through which they would have to pass, she sought to steady her nerves by clasping her hands together with all her might. Then she recalled the poem about *God's Wall* and tried two or three times to repeat the widow's prayer for protection, but was conscious that her words were dead. She was afraid, and yet felt as though she were under a spell, which she did not care to cast off. When the sleigh entered the dark woods Crampas spoke her name softly, with trembling voice, took her hand, loosened the clenched fingers, and covered them with fervent kisses. She felt herself fainting. When she again opened her eyes the sleigh had passed out of the woods and it soon drove up before her home in Kessin.]

CHAPTER XX

Innstetten, who had observed Effi sharply as he lifted her from the sleigh, but had avoided speaking to her in private about the strange drive, arose early the following morning and sought to overcome his ill-humor, from the effects of which he still suffered.

94

"Did you sleep well?" he asked, as Effi came to breakfast.

"Yes."

"How fortunate! I can't say the same of myself. I dreamed you met with an accident in the sleigh, in the quicksand, and Crampas tried to resc you--I must call it that--, but he sank out of sight with you."

"You say all this so qerly, Geert. Your words contain a covert reproach, and I can gss why."

"Very remarkable."

"You do not approve of Crampas's coming and offering us his assistance."

"Us?"

"Yes, us. Sidonie and me. You seem to have forgotten entirely that the Major came at your reqst. At first he sat opposite me, and I may say, incidentally, that it was indeed an uncomfortable seat on that miserable narrow strip, but when the Grasenabbs came up and took Sidonie, and our sleigh suddenly drove on, I suppose you expected that I should ask him to get out? That would have made a laughing stock of me, and you know how sensitive you are on that point. Remember, we have ridden horseback many times together, with your consent, and now you don't think I should ride in the same vehicle with him. It is wrong, we used to say at home, to mistrust a nobleman."

"A nobleman," said Innstetten with emphasis.

"Isn't he one? You yourself called him a cavalier, a perfect cavalier, in fact."

"Yes," contind Innstetten, his tone growing more friendly, though it still betrayed a slight shade of sarcasm. "A cavalier he is, and a perfect cavalier, that is beyond dispute. But nobleman? My dear Effi, a nobleman has a different look. Have you ever noticed anything noble about him? Not I."

Effi stared at the ground and kept silent.

"It seems we are of the same opinion. But, as you said, I myself am to blame. I don't care to speak of a *faux pas*; it is not the right word in this connection. I assume the blame, and it shall not occur again, if I can prevent it. But you will be on your guard, too, if you heed my advice. He is coarse and has designs of his own on young women. I knew him of old."

95

"I shall remember what you say. But just one thing--I believe you misunderstand him."

"I do *not* misunderstand him."

"Or me," she said, with all the force at her command, and attempted to meet his gaze.

"Nor you either, my dear Effi. You are a charming little woman, but persistence is not exactly your specialty."

He arose to go. When he had got as far as the door Frederick entered to deliver a note from GieshÃ¼bler, addressed, of course, to her Ladyship.

Effi took it. "A secret correspondence with GieshÃ¼bler," she said. "Material for another fit of jealousy on the part of my austere Lord. Or isn't it?"

"No, not quite, my dear Effi. I am so foolish as to make a distinction between Crampas and GieshÃ¼bler. They are not the same number of carats fine, so to speak. You know, the val of gold is estimated by carats, in certain circumstances that of men also. And I must add that I personally have a considerably higher regard for GieshÃ¼bler's white jabot, in spite of the fact that jabots are no longer worn, than I have for Crampas's red sapper whiskers. But I doubt if that is feminine taste."

"You think we are weaker than we are."

"A consolation of extraordinarily little practical application. But enough of that. Read your note."

Effi read: "May I inquire about the health of my gracious Lady? I know only that you luckily escaped the quicksand. But there was still plenty of danger lurking along the road through the woods. Dr. Hannemann has just returned and reassures me concerning Mirambo, saying that yesterday he considered the case more serious than he cared to let us know, but not so today. It was a charming sleigh-ride.--In three days we shall celebrate New Year's eve. We shall have to forego a festivity like last year's, but we shall have a ball, of course, and to see you present would delight the dancers and, by no means least, Yours most respectfully, Alonzo G."

Effi laughed. "Well, what do you say?"

"The same as before, simply that I should rather see you with GieshÃ¼bler than with Crampas."

"Because you take Crampas too seriously and GieshÃ¼bler too lightly."

Innstetten jokingly shook his finger at her.

Three days later was New Year's eve. Effi appeared in a charming ball gown, a gift that the Christmas table had brought her. But she did not dance. She took her seat among the elderly dames, for whom easy chairs were placed near the orchestra gallery. Of the particular noble families with which the Innstettens associated there was nobody present, because, shortly before, there had occurred a slight disagreement with the city faction in the management of the club, which had been accused of "destructive tendencies," especially by old Mr. Güldenklee. However, three or four other noble families from over the Kessine, who were not members of the club, but only invited gsts, had crossed over the ice on the river, some of them from a great distance, and were happy to take part in the festivity. Effi sat between the elderly wife of baronial councillor von Padden and a somewhat younger Mrs. von Titzewitz. The former, an excellent old lady, was in every way an original, and sought by means of orthodox German Christianity to counteract the tendency toward Wendish heathenism, with which nature had endowed her, especially in the prominent structure of her cheek bones. In her orthodoxy she went so far that even Sidonie von Grasenabb was in comparison a sort of *esprit fort*. The elderly dame, having sprung from a union of the Radegast and the Schwantikow branches of the family, had inherited the old Padden humor, which had for years rested like a blessing upon the family and had heartily rejoiced everybody who came into touch with them, even though enemies in politics or religion.

"Well, child," said the baronial councillor's wife, "how are you getting on, anyhow?"

"Quite well, most gracious Lady. I have a very excellent husband."

"I know. But that does not always suffice. I, too, had an excellent husband. How do matters actually stand? No temptations?"

Effi was startled and touched at the same time. There was something uncommonly refreshing about the free and natural tone in which the old lady spoke, and the fact that she was such a pious woman made it even more refreshing.

"Ah, most gracious Lady--"

"There it comes. Nothing new, the same old story. Time makes no change here, and perhaps it is just as well. The essential thing, my dear young woman, is struggle. One must always wrestle with the natural man. And when one has conqred self and feels almost like screaming out, because it hurts so, then the dear angels shout for joy."

"Ah, most gracious Lady, it is often very hard."

"To be sure, it is hard. But the harder the better. You must be glad of that. The weakness of the flesh is lasting. I have grandsons and granddaughters and see it every day. But the conqring of self in the faith, my dear Lady, that is the essential thing, that is the tr way. This was brought to our knowledge by our old man of God, Martin Luther. Do you know his *Table Talks*?"

"No, most gracious Lady."

"I am going to send them to you."

At this moment Major von Crampas stepped up to Effi and inquired about her health. Effi was red as blood. Before she had time to reply he said: "May I ask you, most gracious Lady, to present me to these Ladies?"

Effi introduced Crampas, who had already got his bearings perfectly and in the course of his small talk mentioned all the von Paddens and von Titzewitzes he had ever heard of. At the same time he excused himself for not yet having made his call and presented his wife to the people beyond the Kessine. "But it is strange what a separating power water has. It is the same way with the English Channel."

"How?" asked old Mrs. von Titzewitz.

Crampas, considering it inadvisable to give explanations which would have been to no purpose, contind: "To twenty Germans who go to France there is not one who goes to England. That is because of the water. I repeat, water has a dividing power."

Mrs. von Padden, whose fine instinct scented some insinuation in this remark, was about to take up the cudgels for water, but Crampas spoke on with increasing flncy and turned the attention of the ladies to a beautiful Miss von Stojentin, "without qstion the qen of the ball," he said, incidentally casting an admiring glance at Effi. Then he bowed quickly to the three ladies and walked away.

"Handsome man," said Mrs. von Padden. "Does he ever come to your house?"

"Casually."

"Truly a handsome man," repeated Mrs. von Padden. "A little bit too self-assured. Pride will have a fall. But just see, there he is, taking his place with Grete Stojentin. Why, really, he is too old, he is at least in the middle of the forties."

"He is going on forty-four."

"Aha, you seem to be well acquainted with him."

* * * * *

It was very opportune for Effi that the new year, from the very beginning, brought a variety of diversions. New Year's eve a sharp northeast wind began to blow and during the next few days it increased in velocity till it amounted almost to a hurricane. On the 3d of January in the afternoon it was reported that a ship which had not been able to make its way into port had been wrecked a hundred yards from the mole. It was said to be an English ship from Sunderland and, so far as could be ascertained, had seven men on board. In spite of strenuous efforts the pilots were unable to row around the mole, and the launching of a boat from the beach was out of the qstion, as the surf was too heavy. That sounded sad enough. But Johanna, who brought the news, had a word of comfort. Consul Eschrich, she said, was hastening to the scene with the life-saving apparatus and the rocket battery, and success was certain. The distance was not quite as great as in the year '75, and that time all lives had been saved; even the poodle had been rescd. "It was very touching to see how the dog rejoiced and again and again licked with his red tong both the Captain's wife and the dear little child, not much larger than little Annie."

"Geert, I must go there, I must see it," Effi declared, and both set out at once in order not to be too late. They chose just the right moment, for as they reached the beach beyond the "Plantation" the first shot was fired and they saw plainly how the rocket with the life line sailed beneath the storm cloud and fell down beyond the ship. Immediately all hands were astir on board and they used the small line to haul in the heavier hawser with the basket. Before long the basket returned and one of the sailors, a very handsome, slender man, with an oilcloth hood, was safe on land. He was plied with qstions by the inquisitive spectators, while the basket made another trip to fetch the second man, then the third, and so on. All were rescd, and as Effi walked home with her husband a half hour later she felt like throwing herself on the sand and having a good cry. A beautiful emotion had again found lodgment in her heart and she was immeasurably happy that it was so.

This occurred on the 3d. On the 5th a new excitement was experienced, of an entirely different kind, to be sure. On his way out of the council house Innstetten had met Gieshübler, who, by the way, was an alderman and a member of the magistracy. In conversation with him Innstetten had learned that the ministry of war had inquired what attitude the city authorities would assume in case the qstion of a garrison were raised. If they showed their willingness to meet the necessary conditions, viz., to build stables and barracks, they might be granted two squadrons of hussars. "Well, Effi, what do you say about it?" Effi looked as though struck dumb. All the innocent happiness of her childhood years was suddenly brought back to her and for a moment it seemed as though red hussars--for these were to be red hussars, like those at home in Hohen-Cremmen--were the tr guardians of Paradise and innocence. Still she remained silent.

"Why, you aren't saying anything, Effi."

"Strangely, I'm not, Geert. But it makes me so happy that I cannot speak for joy. Is it really going to be? Are they truly going to come?"

"It is a long way off yet. In fact, GieshÃ¼bler said the city fathers, his colleags, didn't deserve it at all. Instead of simply being unanimous and happy over the honor, or if not over the honor, at least over the advantage, they had brought forward all sorts of 'ifs' and 'buts,' and had been niggardly about the buildings. In fact, Confectioner Michelsen had gone so far as to say it would corrupt the morals of the city, and whoever had a daughter would better be forehanded and secure iron grills for his windows."

"That is incredible. I have never seen more mannerly people than our hussars. Really, Geert. Well, you know so yourself. And so this Michelsen wants to protect everything with iron bars. Has he any daughters?"

"Certainly. Three, in fact. But they are all out of the race."

Effi laughed more heartily than she had for a long time. But the mood was of short duration and when Innstetten went away and left her alone she sat down by the baby's cradle, and tears fell on the pillows. The old feeling came over her again that she was a prisoner without hope of escape.

She suffered intensely from the feeling and longed more than ever for liberty. But while she was capable of strong emotions she had not a strong character. She lacked steadfastness and her good desires soon passed away. Thus she drifted on, one day, because she could not help it, the next, because she did not care to try to help it. She seemed to be in the power of the forbidden and the mysterious.

So it came about that she, who by nature was frank and open, accustomed herself more and more to play an underhand part. At times she was startled at the ease with which she could do it. Only in one respect she remained unchanged--she saw everything clearly and glossed nothing. Late one evening she stepped before the mirror in her bedroom. The lights and shadows flitted to and fro and Rollo began to bark outside. That moment it seemed to her as though somebody were looking over her shoulder. But she quickly bethought herself. "I know well enough what it is. It was not *he*," and she pointed her finger toward the haunted room upstairs. "It was something else--my conscience--Effi, you are lost."

Yet things contind on this course; the ball was rolling, and what happened one day made the actions of the next a necessity.

About the middle of the month there came invitations from the four families with which the Innstettens associated most. They had agreed upon the order in which they would entertain. The Borckes were to begin, the Flemmings and Grasenabbs followed, the GÃ¼ldenklees came last. Each time a week intervened. All four invitations came on the same day. They were evidently intended to leave an impression of orderliness and careful planning, and probably also of special friendliness and congeniality.

"I shall not go, Geert, and you must excuse me in advance on the ground of the treatment which I have been undergoing for weeks past."

Innstetten laughed. "Treatment. I am to blame it on the treatment. That is the pretext. The real reason is you don't care to."

"No, I am more honest than you are willing to admit. It was your own suggestion that I consult the doctor. I did so and now I must follow his advice. The good doctor thinks I am anÃ¦mic, strangely enough, and you know that I drink chalybeate water every day. If you combine this in imagination with a dinner at the Borckes', with, say, brawn and eel aspic, you can't help feeling that it would be the death of me. And certainly you would not think of asking such a thing of your Effi. To be sure, I feel at times--"

"I beg you, Effi."

"However, the one good thing about it is that I can look forward with pleasure to accompanying you each time a part of the way in the carriage, as far as the mill, certainly, or the churchyard, or even to the corner of the forest, where the crossroad to Morgnitz comes in. Then I can alight and saunter back. It is always very beautiful among the dunes."

Innstetten was agreed, and when the carriage drove up three days later Effi got in with her husband and accompanied him to the corner of the forest. "Stop here, Geert. You drive on to the left now, but I am going to the right, down to the beach and back through the 'Plantation.' It is rather far, but not too far. Dr. Hannemann tells me every day that exercise is everything, exercise and fresh air. And I almost believe he is right. Give my regards to all the company, only you needn't say anything to Sidonie."

The drives on which Effi accompanied her husband as far as the corner of the forest were repeated every week, but even on the intervening days she insisted that she should strictly observe the doctor's orders. Not a day passed that she did not take her prescribed walk, usually in the afternoon, when Innstetten began to become absorbed in his newspapers. The weather was beautiful, the air soft and fresh, the sky cloudy. As a rule she went out alone, after saying to Roswitha: "Roswitha, I am going down the turnpike now and then to the right to the place with the merrygo-round. There I shall wait for you, meet me there. Then we can walk back by the aven of birches or through the ropewalk. But do not come unless Annie is asleep. If she is not asleep send Johanna. Or, rather, just let it go. It is not necessary; I can easily find the way."

The first day they met as planned. Effi sat on a bench by a long shed, looking over at a low yellow plaster house with exposed timbers painted black, an inn at which the lower middle classes drank their glass of beer or played at ombre. It was hardly dusk, but the windows were already bright, and their gleams of light fell upon the piles of snow and the few trees standing at one side. "See, Roswitha, how beautiful that looks."

This was repeated for a few days. But usually, when Roswitha reached the merry-go-round and the shed, nobody was there, and when she came back home and entered the hall Effi came to meet her, saying: "Where in the world have you been, Roswitha? I have been back a long time."

Thus it went on for weeks. The matter of the hussars was about given up, on account of objections made by the citizens. But as the negotiations were not yet definitely closed and had recently been referred to the office of the commander in chief, Crampas was called to Stettin to give his opinion to the authorities.

From there he wrote the second day to Innstetten: "Pardon me, Innstetten, for taking French leave. It all came so quickly. Here, however, I shall seek to draw the matter out long, for it is a pleasure to be out in the world again. My regards to your gracious wife, my amiable patroness."

He read it to Effi, who remained silent. Finally she said:

"It is very well thus."

"What do you mean by that?"

"That he is gone. To tell the truth, he always says the same things. When he is back he will at least for a time have something new to say."

Innstetten gave her a sharp scrutinizing glance, but he saw nothing, and his suspicion was allayed. "I am going away, too," he said after a while, "and to Berlin at that. Perhaps I, too, can bring back something new, as well as Crampas. My dear Effi always wants to hear something new. She is bored to death in our good Kessin. I shall be away about a week, perhaps a day or two longer. But don't be alarmed--I don't think it will come back--You know, that thing upstairs--But even if it should, you have Rollo and Roswitha."

Effi smiled to herself and felt at the same time a mingling of sadness. She could not help recalling the day when Crampas had told her for the first time that her husband was acting out a play with the ghost and her fear. The great pedagog! But was he not right? Was not the play in place? All kinds of contradicting thoughts, good and bad, shot through her head.

The third day Innstetten went away. He had not said anything about his business in Berlin.

CHAPTER XXI

Innstetten had been gone but four days when Crampas returned from Stettin with the news that the higher authorities had definitely dropped the plan of detailing two squadrons to Kessin. There were so many small cities that were applying for a garrison of cavalry, particularly for Blücher hussars, that as a rule, he said, an offer of such troops met with a hearty reception, and not a halting one. When Crampas made this report the magistracy looked quite badly embarrassed. Only Gieshübler was triumphant, because he thought the discomfiture served his narrow-minded colleags exactly right. When the news reached the common people a certain amount of depression spread among them, indeed even some of the consuls with eligible daughters were for the time being dissatisfied. But on the whole they soon forgot about it, perhaps because the qstion of the day, "What was Innstetten's business in Berlin?" was more interesting to the people of Kessin, or at least to the dignitaries of the city. They did not care to lose their unusually popular district councillor, and yet very exaggerated rumors about him were in circulation, rumors which, if not started by Gieshübler, were at least supported and further spread by him. Among other things it was said that Innstetten would go to Morocco as an ambassador with a suite, bearing gifts, including not only the traditional vase with a picture of Sans Souci and the New Palace, but above all a large refrigerator. The latter seemed so probable in view of the temperature in Morocco, that the whole story was believed.

In time Effi heard about it. The days when the news would have cheered her were not yet so very far distant. But in the frame of mind in which she had been since the end of the year she was no longer capable of laughing artlessly and merrily. Her face had taken on an entirely new expression, and her half-pathetic, half-roguish childishness, which she had preserved as a woman, was gone. The walks to the beach and the "Plantation," which she had given up while Crampas was in Stettin, she resumed after his return and would not allow them to be interfered with by unfavorable weather. It was arranged as formerly that Roswitha should come to meet her at the end of the ropewalk, or near the churchyard, but they missed each other oftener than before. "I could scold you, Roswitha, for never finding me. But it doesn't matter; I am no longer afraid, not even by the churchyard, and in the forest I have never yet met a human soul."

It was on the day before Innstetten's return from Berlin that Effi said this. Roswitha paid little attention to the remarks, as she was absorbed in hanging up garlands over the doors. Even the shark was decorated with a fir bough and looked more remarkable than usual. Effi said: "That is right, Roswitha. He will be pleased with all the green when he comes back tomorrow. I wonder whether I should go out again today? Dr. Hannemann insists upon it and is continually saying I do not take it seriously enough, otherwise I should certainly be looking better. But I have no real desire today; it is drizzling and the sky is so gray."

"I will fetch her Ladyship's raincoat."

"Do so, but don't come for me today; we should not meet anyhow," and she laughed. "Really, Roswitha, you are not a bit good at finding. And I don't want to have you catch a cold all for nothing."

So Roswitha remained at home and, as Annie was sleeping, went over to chat with Mrs. Kruse. "Dear Mrs. Kruse," she said, "you were going to tell me about the Chinaman. Yesterday Johanna interrupted you. She always puts on such airs, and such a story would not interest her. But I believe there was, after all, something in it, I mean the story of the Chinaman and Thomsen's niece, if she was not his granddaughter."

Mrs. Kruse nodded.

Roswitha contind: "Either it was an unhappy love"--Mrs. Kruse nodded again--"or it may have been a happy one, and the Chinaman was simply unable to endure the sudden termination of it. For the Chinese are human, like the rest of us, and everything is doubtless the same with them as with us."

"Everything," assured Mrs. Kruse, who was about to corroborate it by her story, when her husband entered and said: "Mother, you might give me the bottle of leather varnish. I must have the harness shining when his Lordship comes home tomorrow. He sees everything, and even if he says nothing, one can tell that he has seen it all."

"I'll bring it out to you, Kruse," said Roswitha. "Your wife is just going to tell me something more; but it will soon be finished and then I'll come and bring it."

A few minutes later Roswitha came out into the yard with the bottle of varnish in her hand and stood by the harness which Kruse had just hung over the garden fence. "By George!" he said, as he took the bottle from her hand, "it will not do much good; it keeps drizzling all the time and the shine will come off. But I am one of those who think everything must be kept in order."

"Indeed it must. Besides, Kruse, that is good varnish, as I can see at a glance, and first-class varnish doesn't stay sticky very long, it must dry immediately. Even if it is foggy tomorrow, or dewy, it will be too late then to hurt it. But, I must say, that is a remarkable story about the Chinaman."

Kruse laughed. "It is nonsense, Roswitha. My wife, instead of paying attention to proper things, is always telling such tales, and when I go to put on a clean shirt there is a button off. It has been so ever since we came here. She always had just such stories in her head and the black hen besides. And the black hen doesn't even lay eggs. After all, what can she be expected to lay eggs out of? She never goes out, and such things as eggs can't come from mere cock-a-doodle-dooing. It is not to be expected of any hen."

"See here, Kruse, I am going to repeat that to your wife. I have always considered you a respectable man and now you say things like that about the cock-a-doodle-dooing. Men are always worse than we think. Really I ought to take this brush right now and paint a black moustache on your face."

"Well, Roswitha, one could put up with that from you," and Kruse, who was usually on his dignity, seemed about to change to a more flirting tone, when he suddenly caught sight of her Ladyship, who today came from the other side of the "Plantation" and just at this moment was passing along the garden fence.

"Good day, Roswitha, my, but you are merry. What is Annie doing?"

"She is asleep, your Ladyship."

As Roswitha said this she turned red and quickly breaking off the conversation, started toward the house to help her Ladyship change her clothes. For it was doubtful whether Johanna was there. She hung around a good deal over at the "office" nowadays, because there was less to do at home and Frederick and Christel were too tedious for her and never knew anything.

Annie was still asleep. Effi leaned over the cradle, then had her hat and raincoat taken off and sat down upon the little sofa in her bedroom. She slowly stroked back her moist hair, laid her feet on a stool, which Roswitha drew up to her, and said, as she evidently enjoyed the comfort of resting after a rather long walk: "Roswitha, I must remind you that Kruse is married."

"I know it, your Ladyship."

"Yes, what all doesn't one know, and yet one acts as though one did *not* know. Nothing can ever come of this."

"Nothing is supposed to come of it, your Ladyship."

"If you think she is an invalid you are reckoning without your host. Invalids live the longest. Besides she has the black chicken. Beware of it. It knows everything and tattles everything. I don't know, it makes me shudder. And I'll wager all that business upstairs has some connection with this chicken."

"Oh, I don't believe it. But it is terrible just the same, and Kruse, who always sides himself against his wife, cannot talk me out of it."

"What did he say?"

"He said it was nothing but mice."

"Well, mice are quite bad enough. I can't bear mice. But, to change the subject, I saw you chatting with Kruse, plainly, also your familiar actions, and in fact I think you were going to paint a moustache on his lip. That I call pretty far advanced. A little later you will be jilted. You are still a smug person and have your charms. But beware, that is all I have to say to you. Just what was your experience the first time? Was it such that you can tell me about it?"

"Oh, I can tell you. But it was terrible. And because it was so terrible, your Ladyship's mind can be perfectly easy with regard to Kruse. A girl who has gone through what I did has enough of it and takes care. I still dream of it occasionally and then I am all knocked to pieces the next day. Such awful fright."

Effi sat up and leaned her head on her arm. "Tell me about it, and how it came about. I know from my observations at home that it is always the same story with you girls."

"Yes, no doubt it is always the same at first, and I am determined not to think that there was anything special about my case. But when the time came that they threw it into my face and I was suddenly forced to say: 'yes, it is so,' oh, *that* was terrible. Mother--well, I could get along with her, but father, who had the village blacksmith's shop, he was severe and quick to fly into a rage. When he heard it, he came at me with a pair of tongs which he had just taken from the fire and was going to kill me. I screamed and ran up to the attic and hid myself and there I lay and trembled, and did not come down till they called me and told me to come. Besides, I had a younger sister, who always pointed at me and said: 'Ugh!' Then when the child was about to come I went into a barn near by, because I was afraid to stay in the house. There strangers found me half dead and carried me into the house and laid me in my bed. The third day they took the child away and when I asked where it was they said it was well taken care of. Oh, your Ladyship, may the holy mother of God protect you from such distress!"

Effi was startled and stared at Roswitha with wide-opened eyes. But she was more frightened than vexed. "The things you do say! Why, I am a married woman. You must not say such things; it is improper, it is not fitting."

"Oh, your Ladyship."

106

"Tell me rather what became of you. They had robbed you of your baby. You told me that."

"And then, a few days later, somebody from Erfurt drove up to the mayor's office and asked whether there was not a wet nurse there, and the mayor said 'yes,' God bless him! So the strange gentleman took me away with him and from that day I was better off. Even with the old widow my life was tolerable, and finally I came to your Ladyship. That was the best, the best of all." As she said this she stepped to the sofa and kissed Effi's hand.

"Roswitha, you must not always be kissing my hand, I don't like it. And do beware of Kruse. Otherwise you are a good and sensible person--With a married man--it is never well."

"Ah, your Ladyship, God and his saints lead us wondrously, and the bad fortune that befalls us has also its good side. If one is not made better by it there is no help for him-- Really, I like the men."

"You see, Roswitha, you see."

"But if the same feeling should come over me again--the affair with Kruse, there is nothing in that--and I could not control myself, I should run straight into the water. It was too terrible. Everything. And I wonder what ever became of the poor baby? I don't think it is still living; they had it killed, but I am to blame." She threw herself down by Annie's cradle, and rocked the child and sang her favorite lullaby over and over again without stopping.

"Stop," said Effi, "don't sing any more; I have a headache. Bring in the newspapers. Or has Gieshübler sent the journals?"

"He did, and the fashion paper was on top. We were turning over the leaves, Johanna and I, before she went across the street. Johanna always gets angry that she cannot have such things. Shall I fetch the fashion paper?"

"Yes, fetch it and bring me the lamp, too."

Roswitha went out and when Effi was alone she said: "What things they do have to help one out! One pretty woman with a muff and another with a half veil--fashion puppets. But it is the best thing for turning my thoughts in some other direction."

In the course of the following morning a telegram came from Innstetten, in which he said he would come by the second train, which meant that he would not arrive in Kessin before evening. The day proved one of never ending restlessness. Fortunately

GieshÃ¼bler came in the afternoon and helped pass an hour. Finally, at seven o'clock, the carriage drove up. Effi went out and greeted her husband. Innstetten was in a state of excitement that was unusual for him and so it came about that he did not notice the embarrassment mingled with Effi's heartiness. In the hall the lamps and candles were burning, and the tea service, which Frederick had placed on one of the tables between the cabinets, reflected the brilliant light.

"Why, this looks exactly as it did when we first arrived here. Do you remember, Effi?"

She nodded.

"Only the shark with his fir bough behaves more calmly today, and even Rollo pretends to be reticent and does not put his paws on my shoulders. What is the matter with you, Rollo?"

Rollo rubbed past his master and wagged his tail.

"He is not exactly satisfied; either it is with me or with others. Well, I'll assume, with me. At all events let us go in." He entered his room and as he sat down on the sofa asked Effi to take a seat beside him. "It was so fine in Berlin, beyond expectation, but in the midst of all my pleasure I always felt a longing to be back. And how well you look! A little bit pale and also a little bit changed, but it is all becoming to you."

Effi turned red.

"And now you even turn red. But it is as I tell you. You used to have something of the spoiled child about you; now all of a sudden you look like a wife."

"I like to hear that, Geert, but I think you are just saying it."

"No, no, you can credit yourself with it, if it is something creditable."

"I should say it is."

"Now gss who sent you his regards."

"That is not hard, Geert. Besides, we wives, for I can count myself one since you are back"--and she reached out her hand and laughed--"we wives gss easily. We are not so obtuse as you."

"Well, who was it?"

"Why, Cousin von Briest, of course. He is the only person I know in Berlin, not counting my aunts, whom you no doubt failed to look up, and who are far too envious to send me their regards. Haven't you found, too, that all old aunts are envious?"

"Yes, Effi, that is tr. And to hear you say it reminds me that you are my same old Effi. For you must know that the old Effi, who looked like a child, also suited my taste. Just exactly as does your Ladyship at present."

"Do you think so? And if you had to decide between the two"--

"That is a qstion for scholars; I shall not talk about it. But there comes Frederick with the tea. How I have longed for this hour! And I said so, too, even to your Cousin Briest, as we were sitting at Dressel's and drinking Champagne to your health--Your ears must have rung--And do you know what your cousin said?"

"Something silly, certainly. He is great at that."

"That is the blackest ingratitude I have ever heard of in all my life. 'Let us drink to the health of Effi,' he said, 'my beautiful cousin--Do you know, Innstetten, that I should like nothing better than to challenge you and shoot you dead? For Effi is an angel, and you robbed me of this angel.' And he looked so serious and sad, as he said it, that one might almost have believed him."

"Oh, I know that mood of his. The how-manieth were you drinking?"

"I don't recall now and perhaps could not have told you then. But this I do believe, that he was wholly in earnest. And perhaps it would have been the right match. Don't you think you could have lived with him?"

"Could have lived? That is little, Geert. But I might almost say, I could not even have lived with him."

"Why not? He is really a fine amiable fellow and quite sensible, besides."

"Yes, he is that."

"But--"

"But he is a tomfool. And that is not the kind of a man we women love, not even when we are still half children, as you have always thought me and perhaps still do, in spite of my progress. Tomfoolery is not what we want. Men must be men."

109

"It's well you say so. My, a man surely has to mind his p's and q's. Fortunately I can say I have just had an experience that looks as though I had minded my p's and q's, or at least I shall be expected to in the future--Tell me, what is your idea of a ministry?"

"A ministry? Well, it may be one of two things. It may be people, wise men of high rank, who rule the state; and it may be merely a house, a palace, a Palazzo Strozzi or Pitti, or, if these are not fitting, any other. You see I have not taken my Italian journey in vain."

"And could you make up your mind to live in such a palace? I mean in such a ministry?"

"For heaven's sake, Geert, they have not made you a minister, have they? GieshÃ¼bler said something of the sort. And the Prince is all-powerful. Heavens, he has accomplished it at last and I am only eighteen."

Innstetten laughed. "No, Effi, not a minister; we have not risen to that yet. But perhaps I may yet develop a variety of gifts that would make such a thing not impossible."

"So not just yet, not yet a minister?"

"No. And, to tell the truth, we are not even to live in the ministry, but I shall go daily to the ministry, as I now go to our district council office, and I shall make reports to the minister and travel with him, when he inspects the provincial offices. And you will be the wife of a head clerk of a ministerial department and live in Berlin, and in six months you will hardly remember that you have been here in Kessin, where you have had nothing but GieshÃ¼bler and the dunes and the 'Plantation.'"

Effi did not say a word, but her eyes kept getting larger and larger. About the corners of her mouth there was a nervous twitching and her whole slender body trembled. Suddenly she slid from her seat down to Innstetten's feet, clasped her arms around his knees and said in a tone, as though she were praying: "Thank God!"

Innstetten turned pale. What was that? Something that had come over him weeks before, but had swiftly passed away, only to come back from time to time, returned again now and spoke so plainly out of his eyes that it startled Effi. She had allowed herself to be carried away by a beautiful feeling, differing but little from a confession of her guilt, and had told more than she dared. She must offset it, must find some way of escape, at whatever cost.

"Get up, Effi. What is the matter with you?"

Effi arose quickly. However, she did not sit down on the sofa again, but drew up a high-backed chair, apparently because she did not feel strong enough to hold herself up without support.

"What is the matter with you?" repeated Innstetten. "I thought you had spent happy days here. And now you cry out, 'Thank God!' as though your whole life here had been one prolonged horror. Have I been a horror to you? Or is it something else? Speak!"

"To think that you can ask such a qstion!" said Effi, seeking by a supreme effort to suppress the trembling of her voice. "Happy days! Yes, certainly, happy days, but others, too. Never have I been entirely free from fear here, never. Never yet a fortnight that it did not look over my shoulder again, that same face, the same sallow complexion. And these last nights while you were away, it came back again, not the face, but there was shuffling of feet again, and Rollo set up his barking again, and Roswitha, who also heard it, came to my bed and sat down by me and we did not go to sleep till day began to dawn. This is a haunted house and I was expected to believe in the ghost, for you are a pedagog. Yes, Geert, that you are. But be that as it may, thus much I know, I have been afraid in this house for a whole year and longer, and when I go away from here the fear will leave me, I think, and I shall be free again."

Innstetten had not taken his eyes off her and had followed every word. What could be the meaning of "You are a pedagog," and the other statement that preceded, "And I was expected to believe in the ghost?" What was all that about? Where did it come from? And he felt a slight suspicion arising and becoming more firmly fixed. But he had lived long enough to know that all signs deceive, and that in our jealousy, in spite of its hundred eyes, we often go farther astray than in the blindness of our trust. Possibly it was as she said, and, if it was, why should she not cry out: "Thank God!"

And so, quickly looking at the matter from all possible sides, he overcame his suspicion and held out his hand to her across the table: "Pardon me, Effi, but I was so much surprised by it all. I suppose, of course, it is my fault. I have always been too much occupied with myself. We men are all egoists. But it shall be different from now on. There is one good thing about Berlin, that is certain: there are no haunted houses there. How could there be! Now let us go into the other room and see Annie; otherwise Roswitha will accuse me of being an unaffectionate father."

During these words Effi had gradually become more composed, and the consciousness of having made a felicitous escape from a danger of her own creation restored her countenance and buoyancy.

CHAPTER XXII

The next morning the two took their rather late breakfast together. Innstetten had overcome his ill-humor and something worse, and Effi was so completely taken up with her feeling of liberation that not only had her power of feigning a certain amount of good humor returned, but she had almost regained her former artlessness. She was still in Kessin, and yet she already felt as though it lay far behind her.

"I have been thinking it over, Effi," said Innstetten, "you are not entirely wrong in all you have said against our house here. For Captain Thomsen it was quite good enough, but not for a spoiled young wife. Everything old-fashioned and no room. You shall have a better house in Berlin, with a dining hall, but different from the one here, and in the hall and on the stairway colored-glass windows, Emperor William with sceptre and crown, or some religious picture, a St. Elizabeth or a Virgin Mary. Let us say a Virgin Mary; we owe that to Roswitha."

Effi laughed. "So shall it be. But who will select an apartment for us? I couldn't think of sending Cousin von Briest to look for one, to say nothing of my aunts. They would consider anything good enough."

"When it comes to selecting an apartment, nobody can do that to the satisfaction of any one else. I think you will have to go yourself."

"And when do you think?"

"The middle of March."

"Oh, that is much too late, Geert; everything will be gone then. The good apartments will hardly wait for us."

"All right. But it was only yesterday that I came home and I can't well say: 'go tomorrow.' That would not look right and it would not suit me very well either. I am happy to have you with me once more."

"No," she said, as she gathered together the breakfast dishes rather noisily to hide a rising embarrassment, "no, and it shall not be either, neither today nor tomorrow, but before very long, however. And if I find anything I shall soon be back again. But one thing more, Roswitha and Annie must go with me. It would please me most if you went too. But, I see, that is out of the qstion. And I think the separation will not last long. I already know, too, where I shall rent."

"Where?"

"That must remain my secret. I want to have a secret myself. I want to surprise you later."

At this point Frederick entered to bring the mail. The most of the pieces were official and newspapers. "Ah, there is also a letter for you," said Innstetten. "And, if I am not mistaken, mama's handwriting."

Effi took the letter. "Yes, from mama. But that is not the Friesack postmark. Just see, why, it is plainly Berlin."

"Certainly," laughed Innstetten. "You act as though it were a miracle. Mama is doubtless in Berlin and has written her darling a letter from her hotel."

"Yes," said Effi, "that is probably it. But I almost have fears, and can find no real consolation in what Hulda Niemeyer always said: that when one has fears it is better than when one has hopes. What do you think about it?"

"For a pastor's daughter not quite up to the standard. But now read the letter. Here is a paper knife."

Effi cut open the envelope and read: "My dear Effi: For the last twenty-four hours I have been here in Berlin--Consultations with Schweigger. As soon as he saw me he congratulated me, and when I asked him, astonished, what occasion there was, I learned that a director of a ministerial department by the name of Wüllersdorf had just been at his office and told him that Innstetten had been called to a position with the ministry. I am a little vexed to have to learn a thing like that from a third person. But in my pride and joy I forgive you. Moreover, I always knew, even when I was at Rathenow, that he would make something of himself. Now you are to profit by it. Of course you must have an apartment and new furniture. If, my dear Effi, you think you can make use of my advice, come as soon as your time will permit. I shall remain here a week for treatment, and if it is not effective, perhaps somewhat longer. Schweigger is rather indefinite on the subject. I have taken a private room on Schadow St. Adjoining my room there are others vacant. What the matter is with my eye I will tell you when I see you. The thing that occupies me at present is your future. Briest will be unspeakably happy. He always pretends to be so indifferent about such things, but in reality he thinks more of them than I do. My regards to Innstetten, and a kiss for Annie, whom you will perhaps bring along. As ever your tenderly loving mother, Louise von B."

Effi laid the letter on the table and said nothing. Her mind was firmly made up as to what she should do, but she did not want to say it herself. She wanted Innstetten to speak the first word and then she would hesitatingly say, "yes."

Innstetten actually fell into the trap. "Well, Effi, you remain so calm."

"Ah, Geert, everything has its two sides. On the one hand I shall be happy to see mother again, and maybe even in a few days. But there are so many reasons for delaying."

"What are they?"

"Mama, as you know, is very determined and recognizes only her own will. With papa she has been able to have her way in everything. But I should like to have an apartment to suit *my* taste, and new furniture that *I* like."

Innstetten laughed. "Is that all?"

"Well, that is enough, I should think. But it is not all." Then she summoned up her courage, looked at him, and said: "And then, Geert, I should not like to be separated from you again so soon."

"You rog, you just say that because you know my weakness. But we are all vain, and I will believe it. I will believe it and yet, at the same time, play the hero who foregoes his own desires. Go as soon as you think it necessary and can justify it before your own heart."

"You must not talk like that, Geert. What do you mean by 'justifying it before my own heart?' By saying that you force me, half tyrannically, to assume a role of affection, and I am compelled to say from sheer coqtry: 'Ah, Geert, then I shall never go.' Or something of the sort."

Innstetten shook his finger at her. "Effi, you are too clever for me. I always thought you were a child, and now I see that you are on a par with all the rest. But enough of that, or, as your papa always said, 'that is too wide a field.' Say, rather, when you are going?"

"Today is Tsday. Let us say, then, Friday noon by the boat. Then I shall be in Berlin in the evening."

"Settled. And when will you be back?"

"Well, let us gay Monday evening. That will make three days."

"Impossible. That is too soon. You can't accomplish everything in three days. Your mama will not let you go so soon, either."

"Then leave it to my discretion."

"All right," and Innstetten arose from his seat to go over to the district councillor's office.

* * * * *

The days before Effi's departure flew by quickly. Roswitha was very happy. "Ah, your Ladyship, Kessin, oh yes--but it is not Berlin. And the street cars. And then when the gong rings and one does not know whether to turn to the right or the left, and it has sometimes seemed to me as though everything would run right over me. Oh, there is nothing like that here. Many a day I doubt if we see six people, and never anything else but the dunes and the sea outside. And it roars and roars, but that is all."

"Yes, Roswitha, you are right. It roars and roars all the time, but this is not the right kind of life. Besides, one has all sorts of stupid ideas. That you cannot deny, and your conduct with Kruse was not in accord with propriety."

"Ah, your Ladyship--"

"Well, I will not make any further inquiries. You would not admit anything, of course. Only be sure not to take too few things with you. In fact, you may take all your things along, and Annie's too."

"I thought we were coming back."

"Yes, I am. It is his Lordship's desire. But you may perhaps stay there, with my mother. Only see to it that she does not spoil little Annie too badly. She was often strict with me, but a grandchild--"

"And then, too, you know, little Annie is so sweet, one is tempted to take a bite of her. Nobody can help being fond of her."

That was on Thursday, the day before the departure. Innstetten had driven into the country and was not expected home till toward evening. In the afternoon Effi went down town, as far as the market square, and there entered the apothecary's shop and asked for a bottle of *sal volatile*. "One never knows with whom one is to travel," she said to the old clerk, with whom she was accustomed to chat, and who adored her as much as GieshÃ¼bler himself.

"Is the doctor in?" she asked further, when she had put the little bottle in her pocket.

"Certainly, your Ladyship, he is in the adjoining room reading the papers."

115

"I shall not disturb him, shall I?"

"Oh, never."

Effi stepped in. It was a small room with a high ceiling and shelves around the walls, on which stood alembics and retorts. Along one wall were filing cases arranged alphabetically and provided with iron rings on the front ends. They contained the prescriptions.

Gieshübler was delighted and embarrassed. "What an honor! Here among my retorts! May I invite her Ladyship to be seated for a moment?"

"Certainly, dear Gieshübler. But really only for a moment. I want to bid you farewell."

"But, most gracious Lady, you are coming back, aren't you? I heard it was only for three or four days."

"Yes, dear friend, I am supposed to come back, and it is even arranged that I shall be back in Kessin in a week at the latest. But it is possible that I may *not* come back. I don't need to tell you all the thousand possibilities--I see you are about to tell me I am still too young to--but young people sometimes die. And then there are so many other things. So I prefer to take leave of you as though it were for ever."

"But, most gracious Lady--"

"As though it were for ever. And I want to thank you, dear Gieshübler. For you were the best thing here; naturally, because you were the best man. If I live to be a hundred years old I shall not forget you. I have felt lonely here at times, and at times my heart was so heavy, heavier than you can ever know. I have not always managed rightly. But whenever I have seen you, from the very first day, I have always felt happier, and better, too."

"Oh, most gracious Lady."

"And I wished to thank you for it. I have just bought a small bottle of *sal volatile*. There are often such remarkable people in the compartment, who will not even permit a window to be opened. If I shed any tears--for, you know, it goes right up into one's head, the salts, I mean--then I will think of you. Adieu, dear friend, and give my regards to your friend, Miss Trippelli. During these last weeks I have often thought of her and of Prince Kotschukoff. After all is said and done it remains a peculiar relation. But I can understand it--and let me hear from you some day. Or I shall write."

116

With these words Effi went out. GieshÃ¼bler accompanied her out upon the square. He was dumbfounded, so completely that he entirely overlooked many enigmatical things she said.

Effi went back home. "Bring me the lamp, Johanna," she said, "but into my bedroom. And then a cup of tea. I am so cold and cannot wait till his Lordship returns."

The lamp and the tea came. Effi was already sitting at her little writing desk, with a sheet of letter paper before her and the pen in her hand. "Please, Johanna, put the tea on the table there."

When Johanna had left the room Effi locked her door, looked into the mirror for a moment and then sat down again, and wrote: "I leave tomorrow by the boat, and these are farewell lines. Innstetten expects me back in a few days, but I am *not* coming back-- why I am not coming back, you know--it would have been better if I had never seen this corner of the earth. I implore you not to take this as a reproach. All the fault is mine. If I look at your house--*your* conduct may be excusable, not mine. My fault is very grievous, but perhaps I can overcome it. The fact that we were called away from here is to me, so to speak, a sign that I may yet be restored to favor. Forget the past, forget me. Your Effi."

She ran hastily over the lines once more. The strangest thing to her was the avoidance of the familiar "Du," but that had to be. It was meant to convey the idea that there was no bridge left. Then she put the letter into an envelope and walked toward a house between the churchyard and the corner of the forest. A thin column of smoke arose from the half tumbled down chimney. There she delivered the letter.

When she reached home Innstetten was already there and she sat down by him and told him about GieshÃ¼bler and the *sal volatile*. Innstetten laughed. "Where did you get your Latin, Effi?"

The boat, a light sailing vessel (the steamers ran only in the summer) left at twelve. A quarter of an hour before, Effi and Innstetten were on board; likewise Roswitha and Annie.

The baggage was bulkier than seemed necessary for a journey of so few days. Innstetten talked with the captain. Effi, in a raincoat and light gray traveling hat, stood on the after deck, near the tiller, and looked out upon the quay and the pretty row of houses that followed the line of the quay. Just opposite the landing stood the Hoppensack Hotel, a three-story building, from whose gable a yellow flag, with a cross and a crown on it, hung down limp in the quiet foggy air. Effi looked up at the flag for a while, then let her eyes sink slowly until they finally rested on a number of people who stood about inquisitively on the quay. At this moment the bell rang. Effi had a very peculiar sensation. The boat slowly began to move, and as she once more looked closely at the

117

landing bridge she saw that Crampas was standing in the front row. She was startled to see him, but at the same time was glad. He, on the other hand, with his whole bearing changed, was obviously agitated, and waved an earnest adieu to her. She returned his greeting in like spirit, but also with great friendliness, and there was pleading in her eyes. Then she walked quickly to the cabin, where Roswitha had already made herself at home with Annie. She remained here in the rather close rooms till they reached the point where the river spreads out into a sheet of water called the "Broad." Then Innstetten came and called to her to come up on deck and enjoy the glorious landscape. She went up. Over the surface of the water hung gray clouds and only now and then could one catch a half-veiled glimpse of the sun through a rift in the dense mass. Effi thought of the day, just a year and a quarter ago, when she had driven in an open carriage along the shore of this same "Broad." A brief span, and life often so quiet and lonely. Yet how much had happened since then!

Thus they sailed up the fairway and at two o'clock were at the station or very near it. As they, a moment later, passed the Prince Bismarck Hotel, Golchowski, who was again standing at the door, joined them and accompanied them to the steps leading up the embankment. At the station they found the train was not yet signaled, so they walked up and down on the platform. Their conversation turned about the qstion of an apartment. They agreed on the quarter of the city, that it must be between the Tiergarten and the Zoological Garden. "I want to hear the finches sing and the parrots scream," said Innstetten, and Effi was willing.

Then they heard the signal and the train ran into the station. The station master was full of attentions and Effi received a compartment to herself.

Another handshake, a wave of her handkerchief, and the train began again to move.

CHAPTER XXIII

[Effi was met at the Berlin station by her mother and Cousin von Briest. While drinking tea in the mother's room Cousin von Briest was asked to tell a joke, and propounded a Bible conundrum, which Effi took as an omen that no more sorrow was to befall her. The following day began the search for an apartment, and one was found on Keith street, which exactly suited, except that the house was not finished and the walls not yet dried out. Effi kept it in mind, however, and looked further, being as long about it as possible. After two weeks Innstetten began to insist on her return and to make pointed allusions. She saw there was nothing left but to sham illness. Then she rented the apartment on Keith street, wrote a card saying she would be home the next day, and had the trunks packed. The next morning she stayed in bed and feigned illness, but preferred not to call a doctor. She telegraphed about her delay to her husband. After three days of the farce she yielded to her mother and called an old ladies' doctor by the name of RummschÃ¼ttel ('Shake 'em around'). After a few qstions he prescribed a mixture of bitter almond water and orange blossom syrup and told her to keep quiet. Later he called every third day, noticing that his calls embarrassed her. She felt he had seen through her from the start, but the farce had to be kept up till Innstetten had closed his house and shipped his things. Four days before he was d in Berlin she suddenly got well and wrote him she could now travel, but thought it best to await him in Berlin. As soon as she received his favorable telegram she hastened to the new apartment, where she raised her eyes, folded her hands, and said: "Now, with God's help, a new life, and a different one!"]

CHAPTER XXIV

Three days later, at nine o 'clock in the evening, Innstetten arrived in Berlin. Effi, her mother, and Cousin Briest were at the station. The reception was hearty, particularly on the part of Effi, and a world of things had been talked about when the carriage they had taken stopped before their new residence on Keith street. "Well, you have made a good choice, Effi," said Innstetten, as he entered the vestibule; "no shark, no crocodile, and, I hope, no spooks."

"No, Geert, that is all past. A new era has dawned and I am no longer afraid. I am also going to be better than heretofore and live more according to your will." This she whispered to him as they climbed the carpeted stairs to the third story. Cousin von Briest escorted the mother.

In their apartment there was still a great deal to be done, but enough had been accomplished to make a homelike impression and Innstetten exclaimed out of the joy of his heart: "Effi, you are a little genius." But she declined the praise, pointing to her mother, saying she really deserved the credit. Her mother had issd inexorable commands, such as, "It must stand here," and had always been right, with the natural result that much time had been saved and their good humor had never been disturbed. Finally Roswitha came in to welcome her master. She took advantage of the opportunity to say: "Miss Annie begs to be excused for today,"--a little joke, of which she was proud, and which accomplished her purpose perfectly.

They took seats around the table, already set, and when Innstetten had poured himself a glass of wine and all had joined him in a toast to "happy days," he took Effi's hand and said: "Now tell me, Effi, what was the nature of your illness?"

119

"Oh, let us not talk about that; it would be a waste of breath--A little painful and a real disturbance, because it cancelled our plans. But that was all, and now it is past. RummschÃ¼ttel justified his reputation; he is a fine, amiable old man, as I believe I wrote you. He is said not to be a particularly brilliant scholar, but mama says that is an advantage. And she is doubtless right, as usual. Our good Dr. Hannemann was no luminary either, and yet he was always successful. Now tell me, how are GieshÃ¼bler and all the others?"

"Let me see, who are all the others? Crampas sends his regards to her Ladyship."

"Ah, very polite."

"And the pastor also wishes to be remembered to you. But the people in the country were rather cool and seemed inclined to hold me responsible for your departure without formally taking leave. Our friend Sidonie spoke quite pointedly, but good Mrs. von Padden, whom I called on specially the day before yesterday, was genuinely pleased to receive your regards and your declaration of love for her. She said you were a charming woman, but I ought to guard you well. When I replied that you considered me more of a pedagog than a husband, she said in an undertone and almost as though speaking from another world: 'A young lamb as white as snow!' Then she stopped."

Cousin von Briest laughed. "'A young lamb as white as snow.' Hear that, cousin?" He was going to contin teasing her, but gave it up when he saw that she turned pale.

The conversation dragged on a while longer, dealing chiefly with former relations, and Effi finally learned, from various things Innstetten said, that of all their Kessin household Johanna alone had declared a willingness to move with them to Berlin. She had remained behind, to be sure, but would arrive in two or three days with the rest of the things. Innstetten was glad of her decision, for she had always been their most useful servant and possessed an unusual amount of the style demanded in a large city, perhaps a bit too much. Both Christel and Frederick had said they were too old, and Kruse had not even been asked. "What do we want with a coachman here?" concluded Innstetten, "private horses and carriages are things of the past; that luxury is seen no more in Berlin. We could not even have found a place for the black chicken. Or do I underestimate the apartment?"

Effi shook her head, and as a short pause ensd the mother arose, saying it was half past ten and she had still a long way to go, but nobody should accompany her, as the carriage stand was quite near. Cousin Briest declined, of course, to accede to this reqst. Thereupon they bade each other good night, after arranging to meet the following morning.

Effi was up rather early and, as the air was almost as warm as in the summer, had ordered the breakfast table moved close to the open balcony door. When Innstetten appeared she stepped out upon the balcony with him and said: "Well, what do you say? You wished to hear the finches singing in the Tiergarten and the parrots calling in the Zoological Garden. I don't know whether both will do you the favor, but it is possible. Do you hear that? It came from the little park over yonder. It is not the real Tiergarten, but near it."

Innstetten was delighted and as grateful as though Effi herself had conjured up all these things for him. Then they sat down and Annie came in. Roswitha expected Innstetten to find a great change in the child, and he did. They went on chatting, first about the people of Kessin, then about the visits to be made in Berlin, and finally about a summer journey. They had to stop in the middle of their conversation in order to be at the rendezvous on time.

They met, as agreed, at Helms's, opposite the Red Palace, went to various stores, lunched at Hiller's, and were home again in good season. It was a capital day together, and Innstetten was very glad to be able once more to share in the life of a great city and feel its inflnce upon him. The following day, the 1st of April, he went to the Chancellor's Palace to register, considerably foregoing a personal call, and then went to the Ministry to report for duty. He was received, in spite of the rush of business and social obligations, in fact he was favored with a particularly friendly reception by his chief, who said: "I know what a valuable man you are and am certain nothing can ever disturb our harmony."

Likewise at home everything assumed a good aspect. Effi truly regretted to see her mother return to Hohen-Cremmen, even after her treatment had been prolonged to nearly six weeks, as she had predicted in the beginning. But the loss was partly offset by Johanna's arrival in Berlin on the same day. That was at least something, and even if the pretty blonde was not so near to Effi's heart as the wholly unselfish and infinitely good-natured Roswitha, nevertheless she was treated on an equality with her, both by Innstetten and her young mistress, because she was very clever and useful and showed a decided, self-conscious reserve toward the men. According to a Kessin rumor the roots of her existence could be traced to a long-retired officer of the Pasewalk garrison, which was said to explain her aristocratic temperament, her beautiful blonde hair, and the special shapeliness of her appearance. Johanna shared the joy displayed on all hands at her arrival and was perfectly willing to resume her former duties as house servant and lady's maid, whereas Roswitha, who after an experience of nearly a year had acquired about all of Christel's cookery art, was to superintend the culinary department. The care and nurture of Annie fell to Effi herself, at which Roswitha naturally laughed, for she knew young wives.

Innstetten was wholly devoted to his office and his home. He was happier than formerly in Kessin, because he could not fail to observe that Effi manifested more artlessness and cheerfulness. She could do so because she felt freer. Tr, the past still cast a shadow over her life, but it no longer worried her, or at least much more rarely and transiently, and all such after-effects served but to give her bearing a peculiar charm. In everything she did there was an element of sadness, of confession, so to speak, and it would have made her happy if she could have shown it still more plainly. But, of course, she dared not.

When they made their calls, during the first weeks of April, the social season of the great city was not yet past, but it was about to end, so they were unable to share in it to any great extent. During the latter half of May it expired completely and they were more than ever happy to be able to meet at the noon hour in the Tiergarten, when Innstetten came from his office, or to take a walk in the afternoon to the garden of the Palace in Charlottenburg. As Effi walked up and down the long front, between the Palace and the orange trees, she studied time and again the many Roman emperors standing there, found a remarkable resemblance between Nero and Titus, gathered pine cones that had fallen from the trees, and then walked arm in arm with her husband toward the Spree till they came to the lonely Belvedere Palace.

"They say this palace was also once haunted," she remarked.

"No, merely ghostly apparitions."

"That is the same thing."

"Yes, sometimes," said Innstetten. "As a matter of fact, however, there is a difference. Ghostly apparitions are always artificial, or at least that is said to have been the case in the Belvedere, as Cousin von Briest told me only yesterday, but hauntings are never artificial; hauntings are natural."

"So you do believe in them?"

"Certainly I believe in them. There are such things. But I don't quite believe in those we had in Kessin. Has Johanna shown you her Chinaman yet?"

"What Chinaman?"

"Why, ours. Before she left our old house she pulled him off the back of the chair upstairs and put him in her purse. I caught a glimpse of him not long ago when she was changing a mark for me. She was embarrassed, but confessed."

"Oh, Geert, you ought not to have told me that. Now there is such a thing in our house again."

"Tell her to burn it up."

"No, I don't want to; it would not do any good anyhow. But I will ask Roswitha--"

122

"What? Oh, I understand, I can imagine what you are thinking of. You will ask her to buy a picture of a saint and put it also in the purse. Is that about it?"

Effi nodded.

"Well, do what you like, but do not tell anybody."

* * * * *

Effi finally said she would rather not do it, and they went on talking about all sorts of little things, till the plans for their summer journey gradually crowded out other interests. They rode back to the "Great Star" and then walked home by the Korso Boulevard and the broad Frederick William Street.

They planned to take their vacation at the end of July and go to the Bavarian Alps, as the Passion Play was to be given again this year at Oberammergau. But it could not be done, as Privy Councillor von WÃ¼llersdorf, whom Innstetten had known for some time and who was now his special colleag, fell sick suddenly and Innstetten had to stay and take his place. Not until the middle of August was everything again running smoothly and a vacation journey possible. It was too late then to go to Oberammergau, so they fixed upon a sojourn on the island of RÃ¼gen. "First, of course, Stralsund, with Schill, whom you know, and with Scheele, whom you don't know. Scheele discovered oxygen, but you don't need to know that. Then from Stralsund to Bergen and the Rugard, where WÃ¼llersdorf said one can get a good view of the whole island, and thence between the Big and the Little Jasmund Bodden to Sassnitz. Going to RÃ¼gen means going to Sassnitz. Binz might perhaps be possible, too, but, to quote WÃ¼llersdorf again, there are so many small pebbles and shells on the beach, and we want to go bathing."

Effi agreed to everything planned by Innstetten, especially that the whole household should be broken up for four weeks, Roswitha going with Annie to Hohen-Cremmen, and Johanna visiting her younger half-brother, who had a sawmill near Pasewalk. Thus everybody was well provided for.

At the beginning of the following week they set out and the same evening were in Sassnitz. Over the hostelry was the sign, "Hotel Fahrenheit." "I hope the prices are according to RÃ©aumur," added Innstetten, as he read the name, and the two took an evening walk along the beach cliffs in the best of humor. From a projecting rock they looked out upon the bay quivering in the moonlight. Effi was entranced. "Ah, Geert, why, this is Capri, it is Sorrento. Yes, let us stay here, but not in the hotel, of course. The waiters are too aristocratic for me and I feel ashamed to ask for a bottle of soda water."

"Yes, everybody is an employee. But, I think, we can find private quarters."

123

"I think so too. And we will look for them the first thing in the morning."

The next morning was as beautiful as the evening had been, and they took coffee out of doors. Innstetten received a few letters, which had to be attended to promptly, and so Effi decided at once to employ the hour thus left free for her in looking for quarters. She first walked past an inclosed meadow, then past groups of houses and fields of oats, finally turning into a road which ran through a kind of gully to the sea. Where this gully road struck the beach there stood an inn shaded by tall beech trees, not so aristocratic as the "Fahrenheit," a mere restaurant, in fact, which because of the early hour was entirely empty. Effi sat down at a point with a good view and hardly had she taken a sip of the sherry she had ordered when the inn-keeper stepped up to engage her in conversation, half out of curiosity and half out of politeness.

"We like it very well here," she said, "my husband and I. What a splendid view of the bay! Our only worry is about a place to stay."

"Well, most gracious Lady, that will be hard."

"Why, it is already late in the season."

"In spite of that. Here in Sassnitz there is surely nothing to be found, I can guarantee you. But farther along the shore, where the next village begins--you can see the shining roofs from here--there you might perhaps find something."

"What is the name of the village?"

"Crampas."

Effi thought she had misunderstood him. "Crampas," she repeated, with an effort. "I never heard the word as the name of a place. Nothing else in the neighborhood?"

"No, most gracious Lady, nothing around here. But farther up, toward the north, you will come to other villages, and in the hotel near Stubbenkammer they will surely be able to give you information. Addresses are always left there by people who would be willing to rent rooms."

Effi was glad to have had the conversation alone and when she reported it a few moments later to her husband, keeping back only the name of the village adjoining Sassnitz, he said: "Well, if there is nothing around here the best thing will be to take a carriage, which, incidentally, is always the way to take leave of a hotel, and without any ado move farther up toward Stubbenkammer. We can doubtless find there some idyllic spot with a honeysuckle arbor, and, if we find nothing, there is still left the hotel, and they are all alike."

Effi was willing, and about noon they reached the hotel near Stubbenkammer, of which Innstetten had just spoken, and there ordered a lunch. "But not until half an hour from now. We intend to take a walk first and view the Hertha Lake. I presume you have a guide?"

Following the affirmative answer a middle-aged man approached our travelers. He looked as important and solemn as though he had been at least an adjunct of the ancient Hertha worship.

The lake, which was only a short distance away, had a border of tall trees and a hem of rushes, while on its quiet black surface there swam hundreds of water lilies.

"It really looks like something of the sort," said Effi, "like Hertha worship."

"Yes, your Ladyship, and the stones are further evidences of it."

"What stones?"

"The sacrificial stones."

While the conversation contind in this way they stepped from the lake to a perpendicular wall of gravel and clay, against which leaned a few smooth polished stones, with a shallow hollow in each drained by a few grooves.

"What is the purpose of these?"

"To make it drain better, your Ladyship."

"Let us go," said Effi, and, taking her husband's arm, she walked back with him to the hotel, where the breakfast already ordered was served at a table with a view far out upon the sea. Before them lay the bay in the sunshine, with sail boats here and there gliding across its surface and sea gulls pursuing each other about the neighboring cliffs. It was very beautiful and Effi said so; but, when she looked across the glittering surface, she saw again, toward the south, the brightly shining roofs of the long-stretched-out village, whose name had given her such a start earlier in the morning.

Even without any knowledge or suspicion of what was occupying her, Innstetten saw clearly that she was having no joy or satisfaction. "I am sorry, Effi, that you derive no real pleasure from these things here. You cannot forget the Hertha Lake, and still less the stones."

She nodded. "It is as you say, and I must confess that I have seen nothing in my life that made me feel so sad. Let us give up entirely our search for rooms. I can't stay here."

"And yesterday it seemed to you a Gulf of Naples and everything beautiful you could think of."

"Yes, yesterday."

"And today? No longer a trace of Sorrento?"

"Still one trace, but only one. It is Sorrento on the point of dying."

"Very well, then, Effi," said Innstetten, reaching her his hand. "I do not want to worry you with Rügen and so let us give it up. Settled. It is not necessary for us to tie ourselves up to Stubbenkammer or Sassnitz or farther down that way. But whither?"

"I suggest that we stay a day longer and wait for the steamer that comes from Stettin tomorrow on its way to Copenhagen. It is said to be so pleasurable there and I can't tell you how I long for something pleasurable. Here I feel as though I could never laugh again in all my life and had never laughed at all, and you know how I like to laugh."

Innstetten showed himself full of sympathy with her state, the more readily, as he considered her right in many regards. Really everything, though beautiful, was melancholy.

They waited for the Stettin boat and in the very early morning of the third day they landed in Copenhagen. Two hours later they were in the Thorwaldsen Museum, and Effi said: "Yes, Geert, this is beautiful and I am glad we set out for here." Soon thereafter they went to dinner and at the table made the acquaintance of a Jutland family, opposite them, whose daughter, Thora von Penz, was as pretty as a picture and attracted immediately the attention and admiration of both Innstetten and Effi. Effi could not stop looking at her large bl eyes and flaxen blonde hair, and when they left the table an hour and a half later the Penz family, who unfortunately had to leave Copenhagen the same day, expressed the hope that they might have the privilege of entertaining the young Prussian couple in the near future at Aggerhuus Castle, some two miles from the Lym-Fiord. The invitation was accepted by the Innstettens with little hesitation.

Thus passed the hours in the hotel. But that was not yet enough of a good thing for this memorable day, which Effi enthusiastically declared ought to be a red-letter day in the calendar. To fill her measure of happiness to the full the evening brought a performance at the Tivoli Theatre, an Italian pantomime, *Arlequin and Columbine*. She was completely captivated by the little roguish tricks, and when they returned to their hotel late in the evening she said: "Do you know, Geert, I now feel that I am gradually coming to again. I will not even mention beautiful Thora, but when I consider that this morning Thorwaldsen and this evening Columbine--"

"Whom at bottom you liked better than Thorwaldsen--"

"To be frank, yes. I have a natural appreciation of such things. Our good Kessin was a misfortune for me. Everything got on my nerves there. RÃ¼gen too, almost. I suggest we stay here in Copenhagen a few days longer, including an excursion to Fredericksborg and Helsingor, of course, and then go over to Jutland. I anticipate real pleasure from seeing beautiful Thora again, and if I were a man I should fall in love with her."

Innstetten laughed. "You don't know what I am going to do."

"I shouldn't object. That will create a rivalry and I shall show you that I still have my powers, too."

"You don't need to assure me of that."

The journey was made according to this plan. Over in Jutland they went up the Lym-Fiord as far as Aggerhuus Castle, where they spent three days with the Penz family, and then returned home, making many stops on the way, for sojourns of various lengths, in Viborg, Flensburg, Kiel, and Hamburg. From Hamburg, which they liked uncommonly well, they did not go direct to Keith St. in Berlin, but first to Hohen-Cremmen, where they wished to enjoy a well-earned rest. For Innstetten it meant but a few days, as his leave of absence expired, but Effi remained a week longer and declared her desire not to arrive at home till the 3d of October, their wedding anniversary.

Annie had flourished splendidly in the country air and Roswitha's plan of having her walk to meet her mother succeeded perfectly. Briest proved himself an affectionate grandfather, warned them against too much love, and even more strongly against too much severity, and was in every way the same as always. But in reality all his affection was bestowed upon Effi, who occupied his emotional nature continually, particularly when he was alone with his wife.

"How do you find Effi?"

"Dear and good as ever. We cannot thank God enough that we have such a lovely daughter. How thankful she is for everything, and always so happy to be under our rooftree again."

"Yes," said Briest, "she has more of this virt than I like. To tell the truth, it seems as though this were still her home. Yet she has her husband and child, and her husband is a

127

jewel and her child an angel, and still she acts as though Hohen-Cremmen were her favorite abode, and her husband and child were nothing in comparison with you and me. She is a splendid daughter, but she is too much of a daughter to suit me. It worries me a little bit. She is also unjust to Innstetten. How do matters really stand between them?"

"Why, Briest, what do you mean?"

"Well, I mean what I mean and you know what, too. Is she happy? Or is there something or other in the way? From the very beginning it has seemed to me as though she esteemed him more than she loved him, and that to my mind is a bad thing. Even love may not last forever, and esteem will certainly not. In fact women become angry when they have to esteem a man; first they become angry, then bored, and in the end they laugh."

"Have you had any such experience?"

"I will not say that I have. I did not stand high enough in esteem. But let us not get wrought up any further. Tell me how matters stand."

"Pshaw! Briest, you always come back to the same things. We have talked about and exchanged our views on this qstion more than a dozen times, and yet you always come back and, in spite of your pretended omniscience, ask me about it with the most dreadful naÃ¯vetÃ©, as though my eyes could penetrate any depth. What kind of notions have you, anyhow, of a young wife, and more especially of your daughter? Do you think that the whole situation is so plain? Or that I am an oracle--I can't just recall the name of the person--or that I hold the truth cut and dried in my hands, when Effi has poured out her heart to me?--at least what is so designated. For what does pouring out one's heart mean? After all, the real thing is kept back. She will take care not to initiate me into her secrets. Besides, I don't know from whom she inherited it, but she is--well, she is a very sly little person and this slyness in her is the more dangerous because she is so very lovable."

"So you do admit that--lovable. And good, too?"

"Good, too. That is, full of goodness of heart. I am not quite certain about anything further. I believe she has an inclination to let matters take their course and to console herself with the hope that God will not call her to a very strict account."

"Do you think so?"

"Yes, I do. Furthermore I think she has improved in many ways. Her character is what it is, but the conditions since she moved to Berlin are much more favorable and they are becoming more and more devoted to each other. She told me something to that effect and, what is more convincing to me, I found it confirmed by what I saw with my own eyes."

"Well, what did she say?"

"She said: 'Mama, things are going better now. Innstetten was always an excellent husband, and there are not many like him, but I couldn't approach him easily, there was something distant about him. He was reserved even in his affectionate moments, in fact, more reserved then than ever. There have been times when I feared him.'"

"I know, I know."

"What do you mean, Briest? That I have feared you, or that you have feared me? I consider the one as ridiculous as the other."

"You were going to tell me about Effi."

"Well, then, she confessed to me that this feeling of strangeness had left her and that had made her very happy. Kessin had not been the right place for her, the haunted house and the people there, some too pious, others too dull; but since she had moved to Berlin she felt entirely in her place. He was the best man in the world, somewhat too old for her and too good for her, but she was now 'over the mountain.' She used this expression, which, I admit, astonished me."

"How so? It is not quite up to par, I mean the expression. But--"

"There is something behind it, and she wanted to give me an inkling."

"Do you think so?"

"Yes, Briest. You always seem to think she could never be anything but innocent. But you are mistaken. She likes to drift with the waves, and if the wave is good she is good, too. Fighting and resisting are not her affair."

Roswitha came in with Annie and interrupted the conversation.

This conversation occurred on the day that Innstetten departed from Hohen-Cremmen for Berlin, leaving Effi behind for at least a week. He knew she liked nothing better than whiling away her time, care-free, with sweet dreams, always hearing friendly words and assurances of her loveliness. Indeed that was the thing which pleased her above everything else, and here she enjoyed it again to the full and most gratefully, even though diversions were utterly lacking. Visitors seldom came, because after her marriage there was no real attraction, at least for the young people. * * *

On her wedding anniversary, the 3d of October, Effi was to be back in Berlin. On the evening before, under the pretext of desiring to pack her things and prepare for the journey, she retired to her room comparatively early. As a matter of fact, her only desire was to be alone. Much as she liked to chat, there were times when she longed for repose.

Her rooms were in the upper story on the side toward the garden. In the smaller one Roswitha was sleeping with Annie and their door was standing ajar. She herself walked to and fro in the larger one, which she occupied. The lower casements of the windows were open and the little white curtains were blown by the draft and slowly fell over the back of the chair, till another puff of wind came and raised them again. It was so light that she could read plainly the titles of the pictures hanging in narrow gilt frames over the sofa: "The Storming of DÃ¼ppel, Fort No. 5," and "King William and Count Bismarck on the Heights of Lipa." Effi shook her head and smiled. "When I come back again I am going to ask for different pictures; I don't like such warlike sights." Then she closed one window and sat down by the other, which she left open. How she enjoyed the whole scene! Almost behind the church tower was the moon, which shed its light upon the grassy plot with the sundial and the heliotrope beds. Everything was covered with a silvery sheen. Beside the strips of shadow lay white strips of light, as white as linen on the bleaching ground. Farther on stood the tall rhubarb plants with their leaves an autumnal yellow, and she thought of the day, only a little over two years before, when she had played there with Hulda and the Jahnke girls. On that occasion, when the visitor came she ascended the little stone steps by the bench and an hour later was betrothed.

She arose, went toward the door, and listened. Roswitha was asleep and Annie also.

Suddenly, as the child lay there before her, a throng of pictures of the days in Kessin came back to her unbidden. There was the district councillor's dwelling with its gable, and the veranda with the view of the "Plantation," and she was sitting in the rocking chair, rocking. Soon Crampas stepped up to her to greet her, and then came Roswitha with the child, and she took it, held it up, and kissed it.

"That was the first day, there is where it began." In the midst of her revery she left the room the two were sleeping in and sat down again at the open window and gazed out into the quiet night.

"I cannot get rid of it," she said. "But worst of all, and the thing that makes me lose faith in myself--" Just then the tower clock began to strike and Effi counted the strokes. "Ten--Tomorrow at this time I shall be in Berlin. We shall speak about our wedding anniversary and he will say pleasing and friendly things to me and perhaps words of affection. I shall sit there and listen and have a sense of guilt in my heart." She leaned her head upon her hand and stared silently into the night.

"And have a sense of guilt in my heart," she repeated. "Yes, the sense is there. But is it a burden upon my heart? No. That is why I am alarmed at myself. The burden there is quite a different thing--dread, mortal dread, and eternal fear that it may some day be found out. And, besides the dread, shame. I am ashamed of myself. But as I do not feel tr repentance, neither do I tr shame. I am ashamed only on account of my continual lying and deceiving. It was always my pride that I could not lie and did not need to-- lying is so mean, and now I have had to lie all the time, to him and to everybody, big lies and little lies. Even RummschÃ¼ttel noticed it and shrugged his shoulders, and who knows what he thinks of me? Certainly not the best things. Yes, dread tortures me, and shame on account of my life of lies. But not shame on account of my guilt--that I do not feel, or at least not truly, or not enough, and the knowledge that I do not is killing me. If all women are like this it is terrible, if they are not--which I hope--then *I* am in a bad predicament; there is something out of order in my heart, I lack proper feeling. Old Mr. Niemeyer once told me, in his best days, when I was still half a child, that proper feeling is the essential thing, and if we have that the worst cannot befall us, but if we have it not, we are in eternal danger, and what is called the Devil has sure power over us. For the mercy of God, is this my state?"

She laid her head upon her arms and wept bitterly. When she straightened up again, calmed, she gazed out into the garden. All was so still, and her ear could detect a low sweet sound, as of falling rain, coming from the plane trees. This contind for a while. Then from the village street came the sound of a human voice. The old nightwatchman Kulicke was calling out the hour. When at last he was silent she heard in the distance the rattling of the passing train, some two miles away. This noise gradually became fainter and finally died away entirely--Still the moonlight lay upon the grass plot and there was still the low sound, as of falling rain upon the plane trees. But it was only the gentle playing of the night air.

CHAPTER XXV

[The following evening Innstetten met Effi at the station in Berlin and said he had thought she would not keep her word, as she had not when she came to Berlin to select their apartment. In a short time he began to bestir himself to make a place for his wife in Berlin society. At a small party early in the season he tactlessly twitted her about Crampas and for days thereafter she felt haunted by the Major's spirit. But once the Empress had selected her to be a lady of honor at an important function, and the Emperor had addressed a few gracious remarks to her at a court ball, the past began to seem to her a mere dream, and her cheerfulness was restored. After about seven years in

Berlin Dr. Rummschüttel was one day called to see her for various reasons and prescribed treatment at Schwalbach and Ems. She was to be accompanied by the wife of Privy Councillor Zwicker, who in spite of her forty odd years seemed to need a protectress more than Effi did. While Roswitha was helping with the preparations for the journey Effi called her to account for never going, as a good Catholic should, to a priest to confess her sins, particularly her great sin, and promised to talk the matter over with her seriously after returning from Ems.]

CHAPTER XXVI

[Innstetten could see by Effi's letters from Ems that Mrs. Zwicker was not the right kind of a companion for her and he longed for her to come back to him. As the end of her sojourn at the watering place approached, preparations were made to welcome her on her return home. A "W," made of forget-me-nots, was to be hung up and some verses composed by a friend of the family were to be spoken by Annie. One day when Annie was returning from school Roswitha went out to meet her and was challenged by her to a race up the stairs. When Annie reached the top she stumbled and fell upon a scraper, cutting an ugly gash in her forehead. Roswitha and Johanna washed the wound with cold water and decided to tie it up with the long bandage once used to bind the mother's sprained ankle. In their search for the bandage they broke open the lock to the sewing table drawers, which they began to empty of their contents. Among other things they took out a small package of letters tied up with a red silk cord. Before they had ended the search Innstetten came home. He examined the wound and sent for Dr. Rummschüttel. After scolding Annie and telling her what she must do till her mother came home, he sat down with her to dine and promised to read her a letter just received from her mother.]

CHAPTER XXVII

For a while Innstetten sat at the table with Annie in silence. Finally, when the stillness became painful to him, he asked her a few qstions about the school superintendent and which teacher she liked best. She answered rather listlessly, because she felt he was not paying much attention. The situation was not improved till Johanna whispered to little Annie, after the second course, that there was something else to come. And surely enough, good Roswitha, who felt under obligation to her pet on this unlucky day, had prepared something extra. She had risen to an omelet with sliced apple filling.

132

The sight of it made Annie somewhat more talkative. Innstetten's frame of mind was likewise bettered when the doorbell rang a moment later and Dr. RummschÃ¼ttel entered, quite accidentally. He had just dropped in, without any suspicion that he had been sent for. He approved of the compresses. "Send for some Goulard water and keep Annie at home tomorrow. Quiet is the best remedy." Then he asked further about her Ladyship and what kind of news had been received from Ems, and said he would come again the next day to see the patient.

When they got up from the table and went into the adjoining room, where the bandage had been searched for so zealously, albeit in vain, Annie was again laid upon the sofa. Johanna came and sat down beside her, while Innstetten began to put back into the sewing table the countless things that still lay in gay confusion upon the window sill. Now and then he was at a loss to know what to do and was obliged to ask.

"Where do these letters belong, Johanna?"

"Clear at the bottom," said she, "here in this drawer."

During the qstion and answer Innstetten examined more closely than before the little package tied up with a red cord. It seemed to consist of a number of notes, rather than letters. Bending it between his thumb and forefinger, like a pack of cards, he slowly let the edges slip off one at a time, and a few lines, in reality only disconnected words, darted past his eyes. It was impossible to distinguish them clearly, yet it seemed to him as though he had somewhere seen the handwriting before. Should he look into the matter?

"Johanna, you might bring us the coffee. Annie will also take half a cup. The doctor has not forbidden it, and what is not forbidden is allowed."

As he said this he untied the red cord, and while Johanna was going to the kitchen he quickly ran over the whole contents of the package. Only two or three letters were addressed to Mrs. District Councillor von Innstetten. He now recognized the handwriting; it was that of the Major. Innstetten had known nothing about a correspondence between Crampas and Effi. His brain began to grow dizzy. He put the package in his pocket and returned to his room. A few moments later Johanna rapped softly on his door to let him know that the coffee was served. He answered, but that was all. Otherwise the silence was complete. Not until a quarter of an hour later was he heard walking to and fro on the rug. "I wonder what ails papa?" said Johanna to Annie. "The doctor said it was nothing, didn't he?"

The walking to and fro in the adjoining room showed no signs of ending, but Innstetten finally came out and said: "Johanna, keep an eye on Annie and make her remain quiet on the sofa. I am going out to walk for an hour or two." Then he gazed fixedly at the child and left the room.

133

"Did you notice, Johanna, how papa looked?"

"Yes, Annie. He must have had a great vexation. He was all pale. I never saw him like that."

Hours passed. The sun was already down and only a red glow was visible above the roofs across the street, when Innstetten came back. He took Annie's hand and asked her how she was. Then he ordered Johanna to bring the lamp into his room. The lamp came. In its green shade were half-transparent ovals with photographs, various pictures of his wife that had been made in Kessin for the other members of the cast when they played Wichert's *A Step out of the Way*. Innstetten turned the shade slowly from left to right and studied each individual picture. Then he gave that up and, as the air was so sultry, opened the balcony door and finally took up the package of letters again. He seemed to have picked out a few and laid them on top the first time he looked them over. These he now read once more in a half audible voice:

"Come again this afternoon to the dunes behind the mill. At old Mrs. Adermann's we can see each other without fear, as the house is far enough off the road. You must not worry so much about everything. We have our rights, too. If you will say that to yourself emphatically, I think all fear will depart from you. Life would not be worth the living if everything that applies in certain specific cases should be made to apply in all. All the best things lie beyond that. Learn to enjoy them."

"'Away from here,' you write, 'flight.' Impossible. I cannot leave my wife in the lurch, in poverty, along with everything else. It is out of the qstion, and we must take life lightly, otherwise we are poor and lost. Light-heartedness is our best possession. All is fate; it was not so to be. And would you have it otherwise--that we had never seen each other?"

Then came the third letter:

"Be at the old place again today. How are my days to be spent without you here in this dreary hole? I am beside myself, and yet thus much of what you say is right; it is salvation, and we must in the end bless the hand that inflicts this separation on us."

Innstetten had hardly shoved the letters aside when the doorbell rang. In a moment Johanna announced Privy Councillor Wüllersdorf. Wüllersdorf entered and saw at a glance that something must have happened.

"Pardon me, Wüllersdorf," said Innstetten, receiving him, "for having asked you to come at once to see me. I dislike to disturb anybody in his evening's repose, most of all a hard-worked department chief. But it could not be helped. I beg you, make yourself comfortable, and here is a cigar."

134

WÃ¼llersdorf sat down. Innstetten again walked to and fro and would gladly have gone on walking, because of his consuming restlessness, but he saw it would not do. So he took a cigar himself, sat down face to face with WÃ¼llersdorf, and tried to be calm.

"It is for two reasons," he began, "that I have sent for you. Firstly, to deliver a challenge, and, secondly, to be my second in the encounter itself. The first is not agreeable and the second still less. And now your answer?"

"You know, Innstetten, I am at your disposal. But before I know about the case, pardon me the naÃ¯ve qstion, must it be? We are beyond the age, you know--you to take a pistol in your hand, and I to have a share in it. However, do not misunderstand me; this is not meant to be a refusal. How could I refuse you anything? But tell me now what it is."

"It is a qstion of a gallant of my wife, who at the same time was my friend, or almost a friend."

WÃ¼llersdorf looked at Innstetten. "Instetten, that is not possible."

"It is more than possible, it is certain. Read."

WÃ¼llersdorf ran over the letters hastily. "These are addressed to your wife?"

"Yes. I found them today in her sewing table."

"And who wrote them?"

"Major von Crampas."

"So, things that occurred when you were still in Kessin?"

Innstetten nodded.

"So, it was six years ago, or half a year longer?"

"Yes."

WÃ¼llersdorf kept silent. After a while Innstetten said: "It almost looks, WÃ¼llersdorf, as though the six or seven years made an impression on you. There is a theory of limitation, of course, but I don't know whether we have here a case to which the theory can be applied."

135

"I don't know, either," said WÃ¼llersdorf. "And I confess frankly, the whole case seems to turn upon that qstion."

Innstetten looked at him amazed. "You say that in all seriousness?"

"In all seriousness. It is no time for trying one's skill at pleasantry or dialectic hair-splitting."

"I am curious to know what you mean. Tell me frankly what you think about it."

"Innstetten, your situation is awful and your happiness in life is destroyed. But if you kill the lover your happiness in life is, so to speak, doubly destroyed, and to your sorrow over a wrong suffered will be added the sorrow over a wrong done. Everything hinges on the qstion, do you feel absolutely compelled to do it? Do you feel so injured, insulted, so indignant that one of you must go, either he or you? Is that the way the matter stands?"

"I don't know."

"You must know."

Innstetten sprang up, walked to the window, and tapped on the panes, full of nervous excitement. Then he turned quickly, stepped toward WÃ¼llersdorf and said: "No, that is not the way the matter stands."

"How does it stand then?"

"It amounts to this--that I am unspeakably unhappy. I am mortified, infamously deceived, and yet I have no feeling of hatred or even of thirst for revenge. If I ask myself 'why not?' on the spur of the moment, I am unable to assign any other reason than the intervening years. People are always talking about inexpiable guilt. That is undeniably wrong in the sight of God, but I say it is also in the sight of man. I never should have believed that time, purely as time, could so affect one. Then, in the second place, I love my wife, yes, strange to say, I love her still, and dreadful as I consider all that has happened, I am so completely under the spell of her loveliness, the bright charm peculiarly her own, that in spite of myself I feel in the innermost recesses of my heart inclined to forgive."

WÃ¼llersdorf nodded. "I fully understand your attitude, Innstetten, I should probably feel the same way about it. But if that is your feeling and you say to me: 'I love this woman so much that I can forgive her everything,' and if we consider, further, that it all happened so long, long ago that it seems like an event in some other world, why, if that is the situation, Innstetten, I feel like asking, wherefore all this fuss?"

"Because it must be, nevertheless. I have thought it over from every point of view. We are not merely individuals, we belong to a whole, and have always to take the whole into consideration. We are absolutely dependent. If it were possible to live in solitude I could let it pass. I should then bear the burden heaped upon me, though real happiness would be gone. But so many people are forced to live without real happiness, and I should have to do it too, and I could. We don't need to be happy, least of all have we any claim on happiness, and it is not absolutely necessary to put out of existence the one who has taken our happiness away. We can let him go, if we desire to live on apart from the world. But in the social life of the world a certain something has been worked out that is now in force, and in accordance with the principles of which we have been accustomed to judge everybody, ourselves as well as others. It would never do to run counter to it. Society would despise us and in the end we should despise ourselves and, not being able to bear the strain, we should fire a bullet into our brains. Pardon me for delivering such a discourse, which after all is only a repetition of what every man has said to himself a hundred times. But who can say anything now? Once more then, no hatred or anything of the kind, and I do not care to have blood on my hands for the sake of the happiness taken away from me. But that social something, let us say, which tyrannizes us, takes no account of charm, or love, or limitation. I have no choice. I must."

"I don't know, Innstetten."

Innstetten smiled. "You shall decide yourself, WÃ¼llersdorf. It is now ten o 'clock. Six hours ago, I will concede, I still had control of the situation, I could do the one thing or the other, there was still a way out. Not so now; now I am in a blind alley. You may say, I have nobody to blame but myself; I ought to have guarded and controlled myself better, ought to have hid it all in my own heart and fought it out there. But it came upon me too suddenly, with too much force, and so I can hardly reproach myself for not having held my nerves in check more successfully. I went to your room and wrote you a note and thereby lost the control of events. From that very moment the secret of my unhappiness and, what is of greater moment, the smirch on my honor was half revealed to another, and after the first words we exchanged here it was wholly revealed. Now, inasmuch as there is another who knows my secret, I can no longer turn back."

"I don't know," repeated WÃ¼llersdorf. "I don't like to resort to the old worn-out phrase, but still I can do no better than to say: Innstetten, it will all rest in my bosom as in a grave."

"Yes, WÃ¼llersdorf, that is what they all say. But there is no such thing as secrecy. Even if you remain tr to your word and are secrecy personified toward others, still *you* know it and I shall not be saved from your judgment by the fact that you have just expressed to me your approval and have even said you fully understood my attitude. It is unalterably settled that from this moment on I should be an object of your sympathy, which in itself is not very agreeable, and every word you might hear me exchange with my wife would be subject to your check, whether you would or no, and if my wife should speak of fidelity or should pronounce judgment upon another woman, as women have a way of doing, I should not know which way to look. Moreover, if it came to pass that I counseled charitable consideration in some wholly commonplace affair of honor, 'because of the apparent lack of deception,' or something of the sort, a smile would pass over your countenance, or at least a twitch would be noticeable, and in your heart you would say: 'poor Innstetten, he has a real passion for analyzing all insults chemically, in order to determine their insulting contents, and he *never* finds the proper quantity of the suffocating element. He has never yet been suffocated by an affair.' Am I right, Wüllersdorf, or not?"

Wüllersdorf had risen to his feet. "I think it is awful that you should be right, but you *are* right. I shall no longer trouble you with my 'must it be.' The world is simply as it is, and things do not take the course *we* desire, but the one *others* desire. This talk about the 'ordeal,' with which many pompous orators seek to assure us, is sheer nonsense, there is nothing in it. On the contrary, our cult of honor is idolatry, but we must submit to it so long as the idol is honored."

Innstetten nodded.

They remained together a quarter of an hour longer and it was decided that Wüllersdorf should set out that same evening. A night train left at twelve. They parted with a brief "Till we meet again in Kessin."

CHAPTER XXVIII

According to the agreement Innstetten set out the following evening. He took the same train Wüllersdorf had taken the day before and shortly after five o'clock in the morning was at the station, from which the road branched off to the left for Kessin. The steamer referred to several times before was scheduled to leave daily, during the season, immediately after the arrival of this train, and Innstetten heard its first signal for departure as he reached the bottom step of the stairway leading down the embankment. The walk to the landing took less than three minutes. After greeting the captain, who was somewhat embarrassed and hence must have heard of the whole affair the day before, he took a seat near the tiller. In a moment the boat pulled away from the foot bridge; the weather was glorious, the morning sun bright, and but few passengers on board. Innstetten thought of the day when, returning here from his wedding tour, he had driven along the shore of the Kessine with Effi in an open carriage. That was a gray November day, but his heart was serene. Now it was the reverse: all was serene without, and the November day was within. Many, many a time had he come this way afterward, and the peace hovering over the fields, the horses in harness pricking up their ears as he drove by, the men at work, the fertility of the soil--all these things had done his soul good, and now, in harsh contrast with that, he was glad when clouds came up and began slightly to overcast the laughing bl sky. They steamed down the river and soon after they had passed the splendid sheet of water called the "Broad" the Kessin church tower hove in sight and a moment later the quay and the long row of houses with ships and boats in front of them. Soon they were at the landing. Innstetten bade the captain goodbye and approached the bridge that had been rolled out to facilitate the disembarkation. WÃ¼llersdorf was there. The two greeted each other, without speaking a word at first, and then walked across the levee to the Hoppensack Hotel, where they sat down under an awning.

"I took a room here yesterday," said WÃ¼llersdorf, who did not wish to begin with the essentials. "When we consider what a miserable hole Kessin is, it is astonishing to find such a good hotel here. I have no doubt that my friend the head waiter speaks three languages. Judging by the parting of his hair and his low-cut vest we can safely count on four--Jean, please bring us some coffee and cognac."

Innstetten understood perfectly why WÃ¼llersdorf assumed this tone, and approved of it, but he could not quite master his restlessness and kept taking out his watch involuntarily. "We have time," said WÃ¼llersdorf. "An hour and a half yet, or almost. I ordered the carriage at a quarter after eight; we have not more than ten minutes to drive."

"Where?"

"Crampas first proposed a corner of the woods, just behind the churchyard. Then he interrupted himself and said: 'No, not there.' Then we agreed upon a place among the dunes, close by the beach. The outer dune has a cut through it and one can look out upon the sea."

Innstetten smiled. "Crampas seems to have selected a beautiful spot. He always had a way of doing that. How did he behave?"

"Marvelously."

"Haughtily? frivolously?"

"Neither the one nor the other. I confess frankly, Innstetten, it staggered me. When I mentioned your name he turned as pale as death, but tried hard to compose himself, and I saw a twitching about the corners of his mouth. But it was only a moment till he had regained his composure and after that he was all sorrowful resignation. I am quite certain he feels that he will not come out of the affair alive, and he doesn't care to. If I judge him correctly he is fond of living and at the same time indifferent about it. He takes life as it comes and knows that it amounts to but little."

139

"Who is his second? Or let me say, rather, whom will he bring along?"

"That was what worried him most after he had recovered himself. He mentioned two or three noblemen of the vicinity, but dropped their names, saying they were too old and too pious, and that he would telegraph to Treptow for his friend Buddenbrook. Buddenbrook came and is a capital man, at once resolute and childlike. He was unable to calm himself, and paced back and forth in the greatest excitement. But when I had told him all he said exactly as you and I: 'You are right, it must be.'"

The coffee came. They lighted their cigars and WÃ¼llersdorf again sought to turn the conversation to more indifferent things. "I am surprised that nobody from Kessin has come to greet you. I know you were very popular. What is the matter with your friend GieshÃ¼bler?"

Innstetten smiled. "You don't know the people here on the coast. They are half Philistines and half wiseacres, not much to my taste. But they have one virt, they are all very mannerly, and none more so than my old GieshÃ¼bler. Everybody knows, of course, what it is about, and for that very reason they take pains not to appear inquisitive."

At this moment there came into view to the left a chaise-like carriage with the top down, which, as it was ahead of time, drove up very slowly.

"Is that ours?" asked Innstetten.

"Presumably."

A moment later the carriage stopped in front of the hotel and Innstetten and WÃ¼llersdorf arose to their feet. WÃ¼llersdorf stepped over to the coachman and said: "To the mole."

The mole lay in the wrong direction of the beach, to the right instead of the left, and the false orders were given merely to avoid any possible interference. Besides, whether they intended to keep to the right or to the left after they were beyond the city limits, they had to pass through the "Plantation" in either case, and so their course led unavoidably past Innstetten's old residence. The house seemed more quiet than formerly. If the rooms on the ground floor looked rather neglected, what must have been the state upstairs! The uncanny feeling that Innstetten had so often combatted in Effi, or had at least laughed at, now came over him, and he was glad when they had driven past.

"That is where I used to live," he said to WÃ¼llersdorf.

140

"It looks strange, rather deserted and abandoned."

"It may be. In the city it was called a haunted house and from the way it stands there today I cannot blame people for thinking so."

"What did they tell about it?"

"Oh, stupid nonsense. An old ship's captain with a granddaughter or a niece, who one fine day disappeared, and then a Chinaman, who was probably her lover. In the hall a small shark and a crocodile, both hung up by strings and always in motion, wonderful to relate, but now is no time for that, when my head is full of all sorts of other phantoms."

"You forget that it may all turn out well yet."

"It must not. A while ago, WÃ¼llersdorf, when you were speaking about Crampas, you yourself spoke differently."

Soon thereafter they had passed through the "Plantation" and the coachman was about to turn to the right toward the mole. "Drive to the left, rather. The mole can wait."

The coachman turned to the left into the broad driveway, which ran behind the men's bathhouse toward the forest. When they were within three hundred paces of the forest WÃ¼llersdorf ordered the coachman to stop. Then the two walked through grinding sand down a rather broad driveway, which here cut at right angles through the three rows of dunes. All along the sides of the road stood thick clumps of lyme grass, and around them immortelles and a few blood-red pinks. Innstetten stooped down and put one of the pinks in his buttonhole. "The immortelles later."

They walked on thus for five minutes. When they had come to the rather deep depression which ran along between the two outer rows of dunes they saw their opponents off to the left, Crampas and Buddenbrook, and with them good Dr. Hannemann, who held his hat in his hand, so that his white hair was waving in the wind.

Innstetten and WÃ¼llersdorf walked up the sand defile; Buddenbrook came to meet them. They exchanged greetings and then the two seconds stepped aside for a brief conference. They agreed that the opponents should advance *a tempo* and shoot when ten paces apart. Then Buddenbrook returned to his place. Everything was attended to quickly, and the shots were fired. Crampas fell.

Innstetten stepped back a few paces and turned his face away from the scene. WÃ¼llersdorf walked over to Buddenbrook and the two awaited the decision of the doctor, who shrugged his shoulders. At the same time Crampas indicated by a motion of

141

his hand that he wished to say something. WÃ¼llersdorf bowed down to him, nodded his assent to the few words, which could scarcely be heard as they came from the lips of the dying man, and then went toward Innstetten.

"Crampas wishes to speak to you, Innstetten. You must comply with his wish. He hasn't three minutes more to live."

Innstetten walked over to Crampas.

"Will you--" were the dying man's last words. Then a painful, yet almost friendly expression in his eyes, and all was over.

CHAPTER XXIX

In the evening of the same day Innstetten was back again in Berlin. He had taken the carriage, which he had left by the crossroad behind the dunes, directly for the railway station, without returning to Kessin, and had left to the seconds the duty of reporting to the authorities. On the train he had a compartment to himself, which enabled him to commune with his own mind and live the event all over again. He had the same thoughts as two days before, except that they ran in the opposite direction, beginning with conviction as to his rights and his duty and ending in doubt. "Guilt, if it is anything at all, is not limited by time and place and cannot pass away in a night. Guilt requires expiation; there is some sense in that. Limitation, on the other hand, only half satisfies; it is weak, or at least it is prosaic." He found comfort in this thought and said to himself over and over that what had happened was inevitable. But the moment he reached this conclusion he rejected it. "There must be a limitation; limitation is the only sensible solution. Whether or not it is prosaic is immaterial. What is sensible is usually prosaic. I am now forty-five. If I had found the letters twenty-five years later I should have been seventy. Then WÃ¼llersdorf would have said: 'Innstetten, don't be a fool.' And if WÃ¼llersdorf didn't say it, Buddenbrook would, and if *he* didn't, either, I myself should. That is clear. When we carry a thing to extremes we carry it too far and make ourselves ridiculous. No doubt about it. But where does it begin? Where is the limit? Within ten years a dl is required and we call it an affair of honor. After eleven years, or perhaps ten and a half, we call it nonsense. The limit, the limit. Where is it? Was it reached? Was it passed? When I recall his last look, resigned and yet smiling in his misery, that look said: 'Innstetten, this is stickling for principle. You might have spared me this, and yourself, too.' Perhaps he was right. I hear some such voice in my soul. Now if I had been full of deadly hatred, if a deep feeling of revenge had found a place in my heart--Revenge is not a thing of beauty, but a human trait and has naturally a human right to exist. But this affair was all for the sake of an idea, a conception, was

142

artificial, half comedy. And now I must contin this comedy, must send Effi away and ruin her, and myself, too--I ought to have burned the letters, and the world should never have been permitted to hear about them. And then when she came, free from suspicion, I ought to have said to her: 'Here is your place,' and ought to have parted from her inwardly, not before the eyes of the world. There are so many marriages that are not marriages. Then happiness would have been gone, but I should not have had the eye staring at me with its searching look and its mild, though mute, accusation."

Shortly before ten o'clock Innstetten alighted in front of his residence. He climbed the stairs and rang the bell. Johanna came and opened the door.

"How is Annie?"

"Very well, your Lordship. She is not yet asleep--If your Lordship--"

"No, no, it would merely excite her. It would be better to wait till morning to see her. Bring me a glass of tea, Johanna. Who has been here?"

"Nobody but the doctor."

Innstetten was again alone. He walked to and fro as he loved to do. "They know all about it. Roswitha is stupid, but Johanna is a clever person. If they don't know accurate details, they have made up a story to suit themselves and so they know anyhow. It is remarkable how many things become indications and the basis for tales, as though the whole world had been present."

Johanna brought the tea, and Innstetten drank it. He was tired to death from the overexertion and went to sleep.

The next morning he was up in good season. He saw Annie, spoke a few words with her, praised her for being a good patient, and then went to the Ministry to make a report to his chief of all that had happened. The minister was very gracious. "Yes, Innstetten, happy is the man who comes out of all that life may bring to us whole. It has gone hard with you." He approved all that had taken place and left the rest to Innstetten.

It was late in the afternoon when Innstetten returned home and found there a few lines from WÃ¼llersdorf. "Returned this morning. A world of experiences--painful, touching--GieshÃ¼bler particularly. The most amiable humpback I ever saw. About you he did not say so very much, but the wife, the wife! He could not calm himself and finally the little man broke out in tears. What strange things happen! It would be better if we had more GieshÃ¼blers. But there are more of the other sort--Then the scene at the home of the major--dreadful. Excuse me from speaking about it. I have learned once more to be on my guard. I shall see you tomorrow. Yours, W."

Innstetten was completely staggered when he read the note. He sat down and wrote a few words in reply. When he had finished he rang the bell. "Johanna, put these letters in the box."

Johanna took the letters and was on the point of going.

"And then, Johanna, one thing more. My wife is not coming back. You will hear from others why. Annie must not know anything about it, at least not now. The poor child. You must break the news to her gradually that she has no mother any more. I can't do it. But be wise about it, and don't let Roswitha spoil it all."

Johanna stood there a moment quite stupefied, and then went up to Innstetten and kissed his hand.

By the time she had reached the kitchen her heart was overflowing with pride and superiority, indeed almost with happiness. His Lordship had not only told her everything, he had even added the final injunction, "and don't let Roswitha spoil it all." That was the most important point. And although she had a kindly feeling and even sympathy for her mistress, nevertheless the thing that above all else occupied her was the triumph of a certain intimate relation to her gracious master.

Under ordinary conditions it would have been easy for her to display and assert this triumph, but today it so happened that her rival, without having been made a confidante, was nevertheless destined to appear the better informed of the two. Just about at the same time as the above conversation was taking place the porter had called Roswitha into his little lodge downstairs and handed her as she entered a newspaper to read. "There, Roswitha, is something that will interest you. You can bring it back to me later. It is only the *Foreigners' Gazette*, but Lena has already gone out to get the *Minor Journal*. There will probably be more in it. They always know everything. Say, Roswitha, who would have thought such a thing!"

Roswitha, who was ordinarily none too curious, had, however, after these words betaken herself as quickly as possible up the back stairs and had just finished reading the account when Johanna came to her.

Johanna laid the letters Innstetten had given her upon the table, glanced over the addresses, or at least pretended to, for she knew very well to whom they were directed, and said with feigned composure: "One goes to Hohen-Cremmen."

"I understand that," said Roswitha.

Johanna was not a little astonished at this remark. "His Lordship does not write to Hohen-Cremmen ordinarily."

144

"Oh, ordinarily? But now--Just think, the porter gave me *this* downstairs only a moment ago."

Johanna took the paper and read in an undertone a passage marked with a heavy ink line: "As we learn from a well informed source, shortly before going to press, there occurred yesterday morning in the watering place Kessin, in Hither Pomerania, a dl between Department Chief von Innstetten of Keith St. and Major von Crampas. Major von Crampas fell. According to rumors, relations are said to have existed between him and the Department Chief's wife, who is beautiful and still very young."

"What don't such papers write?" said Johanna, who was vexed at seeing her news anticipated. "Yes," said Roswitha, "and now the people will read this and say disgraceful things about my poor dear mistress. And the poor major! Now he is dead!"

"Why, Roswitha, what are you thinking of anyhow? Ought he *not* to be dead? Or ought our dear gracious master to be dead?"

"No, Johanna, our gracious master, let him live, let everybody live. I am not for shooting people and can't even bear the report of the pistol. But take into consideration, Johanna, that was half an eternity ago, and the letters, which struck me as so strange the moment I saw them, because they had a red cord, not a ribbon, wrapped around them three or four times and tied--why, they were beginning to look quite yellow, it was so long ago. You see, we have been here now for over six years, and how can a man, just because of such old things--"

"Ah, Roswitha, you speak according to your understanding. If we examine the matter narrowly, you are to blame. It comes from the letters. Why did you come with the chisel and break open the sewing table, which is never permissible? One must never break open a lock in which another has turned a key."

"Why, Johanna, it is really too crl of you to say such a thing to my face, and you know that *you* are to blame, and that you rushed half crazy into the kitchen and told me the sewing table must be opened, the bandage was in it, and then I came with the chisel, and now you say I am to blame. No, I say--"

"Well, I will take it back, Roswitha. But you must not come to me and say: 'the poor major!' What do you mean by the 'poor major?' The poor major was altogether good for nothing. A man who has such a red moustache and twirls it all the time is never good for anything, he does nothing but harm. When one has always been employed in aristocratic homes--but you haven't been, Roswitha, that's where you are lacking--one knows what is fitting and proper and what honor is, and knows that when such a thing comes up there is no way to get around it, and then comes what is called a challenge and one of the men is shot."

145

"Oh, I know that, too; I am not so stupid as you always try to make me appear. But since it happened so long ago--"

"Oh, Roswitha, that everlasting 'so long ago!' It shows plainly enough that you don't know anything about it. You are always telling the same old story about your father with the red-hot tongs and how he came at you with them, and every time I put a red-hot heater in the iron I see him about to kill you on account of the child that died so long ago. Indeed, Roswitha, you talk about it all the time, and all there is left for you to do now is to tell little Annie the story, and as soon as little Annie has been confirmed she will be sure to hear it, perhaps the same day. I am grieved that you should have had all that experience, and yet your father was only a village blacksmith who shod horses and put tires on wheels, and now you come forward and expect our gracious master calmly to put up with all this, merely because it happened so long ago. What do you mean by long ago? Six years is not long ago. And our gracious mistress, who, by the way, is not coming back--his Lordship just told me so--her Ladyship is not yet twenty-six and her birthday is in August, and yet you come to me with the plea of 'long ago.' If she were thirty-six, for at thirty-six, I tell you, one must be particularly cautious, and if his Lordship had done nothing, then aristocratic people would have 'cut' him. But you are not familiar with that word, Roswitha, you know nothing about it."

"No, I know nothing about it and care less, but what I do know is that you are in love with his Lordship."

Johanna struck up a convulsive laugh.

"Well, laugh. I have noticed it for a long time. I don't put it past you, but fortunately his Lordship takes no note of it. The poor wife, the poor wife!"

Johanna was anxious to declare peace. "That will do now, Roswitha. You are mad again, but, I know, all country girls get mad."

"May be."

"I am just going to post these letters now and see whether the porter has got the other paper. I understood you to say, didn't I, that he sent Lena to get one? There must be more in it; this is as good as nothing at all."

CHAPTER XXX

[After Effi and Mrs. Zwicker had been in Ems for nearly three weeks they took breakfast one morning in the open air. The postman was late and Effi was impatient, as she had received no letter from Innstetten for four days. The coming of a pretty waitress to clear away the breakfast dishes started a conversation about pretty housemaids, and Effi spoke enthusiastically of her Johanna's unusual abundance of beautiful flaxen hair. This led to a discussion of painful experiences, in the course of which Effi admitted that she knew what sin meant, but she distinguished between an occasional sin and a habitual sin. Mrs. Zwicker was indulging in a tirade against the pleasure resorts and the ill-sounding names of places in the environs of Berlin, when the postman came. There was nothing from Innstetten, but a large registered letter from Hohen-Cremmen. Effi felt an unaccountable hesitation to open it. Overcoming this she found in the envelope a long letter from her mother and a package of banknotes, upon which her father had written with a red pencil the sum they represented. She leaned back in the rocking chair and began to read. Before she had got very far, the letter fell out of her hands and all the blood left her face. With an effort she picked up the letter and started to go to her room, asking Mrs. Zwicker to send the maid. By holding to the furniture as she dragged herself along she was able to reach her bed, where she fell in a swoon.]

CHAPTER XXXI

Minutes passed. When Effi came to she got up and sat on a chair by the window and gazed out into the quiet street. Oh, if there had only been turmoil and strife outside! But there was only the sunshine on the macadam road and the shadows of the lattice and the trees. The feeling that she was alone in the world came over her with all its might. An hour ago she was a happy woman, the favorite of all who knew her, and now an outcast. She had read only the beginning of the letter, but enough to have the situation clearly before her. Whither? She had no answer to this qstion, and yet she was full of deep longing to escape from her present environment, to get away from this Zwicker woman, to whom the whole affair was merely "an interesting case," and whose sympathy, if she had any such thing in her make-up, would certainly not equal her curiosity.

"Whither?"

On the table before her lay the letter, but she lacked the courage to read any more of it. Finally she said: "What have I further to fear? What else can be said that I have not already said to myself? The man who was the cause of it all is dead, a return to my home is out of the qstion, in a few weeks the divorce will be decreed, and the child will be left with the father. Of course. I am guilty, and a guilty woman cannot bring up her child. Besides, wherewith? I presume I can make my own way. I will see what mama writes about it, how she pictures my life."

With these words she took up the letter again to finish reading it.

"--And now your future, my dear Effi. You will have to rely upon yourself and, so far as outward means are concerned, may count upon our support. You will do best to live in Berlin, for the best place to live such things down is a large city. There you will be one of the many who have robbed themselves of free air and bright sunshine. You will lead a lonely life. If you refuse to, you will probably have to step down out of your sphere. The world in which you have lived will be closed to you. The saddest thing for us and for you--yes, for you, as we know you--is that your parental home will also be closed to you. We can offer you no quiet place in Hohen-Cremmen, no refuge in our house, for it would mean the shutting off of our house from all the world, and we are decidedly not inclined to do that. Not because we are too much attached to the world or that it would seem to us absolutely unbearable to bid farewell to what is called 'society.' No, not for that reason, but simply because we stand by our colors and are going to declare to the whole world our--I cannot spare you the word--our condemnation of your actions, of the actions of our only and so dearly beloved child--"

Effi could read no further. Her eyes filled with tears and after seeking in vain to fight them back she burst into convulsive sobs and wept till her pain was alleviated.

Half an hour later there was a knock at the door and when Effi called: "Come in!" Mrs. Zwicker appeared.

"May I come in?"

"Certainly, my dear," said Effi, who now lay upon the sofa under a light covering and with her hands folded. "I am exhausted and have made myself as comfortable here as I could. Won't you please take a seat?"

Mrs. Zwicker sat down where the table with the bowl of flowers would be between her and Effi. Effi showed no sign of embarrassment and made no change in her position; she did not even unfold her hands. It suddenly became immaterial to her what the woman thought. All she wanted was to get away.

"You have received sad news, dear, gracious Lady?"

"Worse than sad," said Effi. "At any rate sad enough to bring our association here quickly to an end. I must leave today."

"I should not like to appear obtrusive, but has the news anything to do with Annie?"

"No, not with Annie. The news did not come from Berlin at all, it was a letter from my mother. She is worried about me and I am anxious to divert her, or, if I can't do that, at least to be near at hand."

"I appreciate that only too well, much as I lament the necessity of spending these last days in Ems without you. May I offer you my services?"

Before Effi had time to answer, the pretty waitress entered and announced that the gsts were just gathering for lunch, and everybody was greatly excited, for the Emperor was probably coming for three weeks and at the end of his stay there would be grand manoeuvres and the hussars from her home town would be there, too.

Mrs. Zwicker discussed immediately the qstion, whether it would be worth while to stay till then, arrived at a decided answer in the affirmative, and then went to excuse Effi's absence from lunch.

A moment later, as the waitress was about to leave, Effi said: "And then, Afra, when you are free, I hope you can come back to me for a quarter of an hour to help me pack. I am leaving by the seven o'clock train."

"Today? Oh, your Ladyship, what a pity! Why, the beautiful days are just going to begin."

Effi smiled.

CHAPTER XXXII

Three years had passed and for almost that length of time Effi had been living in a small apartment on KÃ¶niggrÃ¤tz Street--a front room and back room, behind which was the kitchen with a servant's bedroom, everything as ordinary and commonplace as possible. And yet it was an unusually pretty apartment, that made an agreeable impression on everybody who saw it, the most agreeable perhaps on old Dr. RummschÃ¼ttel, who called now and then and had long ago forgiven the poor young wife, not only for the rheumatism and neuralgia farce of bygone years, but also for everything else that had happened in the meantime--if there was any need of forgiveness on his part, considering the very different cases he knew about. He was now far along in the seventies, but whenever Effi, who had been ailing considerably for some time, wrote a letter asking him to call, he came the following forenoon and would not listen to any excuses for the number of steps he had to climb. "No excuse, please, dear, most gracious Lady; for in the first place it is my calling, and in the second I am happy and almost proud that I am still able to climb the three flights so well. If I were not afraid of inconveniencing you,-- since, after all, I come as a physician and not as a friend of nature or a landscape enthusiast,--I should probably come oftener, merely to see you and sit down for a few minutes at your back window. I don't believe you fully appreciate the view."

"Oh, yes I do," said Effi; but RummschÃ¼ttel, not allowing himself to be interrupted, contind: "Please, most gracious Lady, step here just for a moment, or allow me to escort you to the window. Simply magnificent again today! Just see the various railroad embankments, three, no, four, and how the trains glide back and forth continually, and now that train yonder disappears again behind a group of trees. Really magnificent! And how the sun shines through the white smoke! If St. Matthew's Churchyard were not immediately behind it it would be ideal."

"I like to look at churchyards."

"Yes, you dare say that. But how about us? We physicians are unavoidably confronted with the qstion, might there, perhaps, not have been some fewer graves here? However, most gracious Lady, I am satisfied with you and my only complaint is that you will not listen to anything about Ems. For your catarrhal affections--"

Effi remained silent.

"Ems would work miracles. But as you don't care to go there--and I understand your reasons--drink the water here. In three minutes you can be in the Prince Albrecht Garden, and even if the music and the costumes and all the diversions of a regular watering-place promenade are lacking, the water itself, you know, is the important thing."

Effi was agreed, and RummschÃ¼ttel took his hat and cane, but stepped once more to the window. "I hear people talking about a plan to terrace the Hill of the Holy Cross. God bless the city government! Once that bare spot yonder is greener--A charming apartment! I could almost envy you--By the way, gracious Lady, I have been wanting for a long time to say to you, you always write me such a lovely letter. Well, who wouldn't enjoy that? But it requires an effort each time. Just send Roswitha for me."

"Just send Roswitha for me," RummschÃ¼ttel had said. Why, was Roswitha at Effi's? Instead of being on Keith Street was she on KÃ¶niggrÃ¤tz Street? Certainly she was, and had been for a long time, just as long as Effi herself had been living on KÃ¶niggrÃ¤tz Street. Three days before they moved Roswitha had gone to see her dear mistress and that was a great day for both of them, so great that we must go back and tell about it.

The day that the letter of renunciation came from Hohen-Cremmen and Effi returned from Ems to Berlin she did not take a separate apartment at once, but tried living in a boarding house, which suited her tolerably well. The two women who kept the boarding house were educated and considerate and had long ago ceased to be inquisitive. Such a variety of people met there that it would have been too much of an undertaking to pry into the secrets of each individual. Such things only interfered with business. Effi, who still remembered the cross-qstionings to which the eyes of Mrs. Zwicker had subjected her, was very agreeably impressed with the reserve of the boarding house keepers. But after two weeks had passed she felt plainly that she could not well endure the prevailing atmosphere of the place, either the physical or the moral. There were usually seven persons at the table. Beside Effi and one of the landladies--the other looked after the kitchen--there were two Englishwomen, who were attending the university, a noblewoman from Saxony, a very pretty Galician Jewess, whose real occupation nobody knew, and a precentor's daughter from Polzin in Pomerania, who wished to become a painter. That was a bad combination, and the attempts of each to show her superiority to the others were unrefreshing. Remarkable to relate, the Englishwomen were not absolutely the worst offenders, but competed for the palm with the girl from Polzin, who was filled with the highest regard for her mission as a painter. Nevertheless Effi, who assumed a passive attitude, could have withstood the pressure of this intellectual atmosphere if it had not been combined with the air of the boarding house, speaking from a purely physical and objective point of view. What this air was actually composed of was perhaps beyond the possibility of determination, but that it took away sensitive Effi's breath was only too certain, and she saw herself compelled for this external reason to go out in search of other rooms, which she found comparatively near by, in the above-described apartment on KÃ¶niggrÃ¤tz St. She was to move in at the beginning of the autumn quarter, had made the necessary purchases, and during the last days of September counted the hours till her liberation from the boarding house. On one of these last days, a quarter of an hour after she had retired from the dining room, planning to enjoy a rest on a sea grass sofa covered with some large-figured woolen material, there was a gentle rap at her door.

"Come in!"

One of the housemaids, a sickly looking person in the middle thirties, who by virt of always being in the hall of the boarding house carried the atmosphere stored there with her everywhere, in her wrinkles, entered the room and said: "I beg your pardon, gracious Lady, but somebody wishes to speak to you."

"Who?"

"A woman."

"Did she tell you her name?"

"Yes. Roswitha."

Before Effi had hardly heard this name she shook off her drowsiness, sprang up, ran out into the corridor, grasped Roswitha by both hands and drew her into her room.

"Roswitha! You! Oh, what joy! What do you bring? Something good, of course. Such a good old face can bring only good things. Oh, how happy I am! I could give a kiss. I should not have thought such joy could ever come to me again. You good old soul, how are you anyhow? Do you still remember how the ghost of the Chinaman used to stalk about? Those were happy times. I thought then they were unhappy, because I did not yet know the hardness of life. Since then I have come to know it. Oh, there are far worse things than ghosts. Come, my good Roswitha, come, sit down by me and tell me--Oh, I have such a longing. How is Annie?"

Roswitha was unable to speak, and so she let her eyes wander around the strange room, whose gray and dusty-looking walls were bordered with narrow gilt molding. Finally she found herself and said that his Lordship was back from Glatz. That the old Emperor had said, "six weeks were quite sufficient (imprisonment) in such a case," and she had only waited for his Lordship's return, on Annie's account, who had to have some supervision. Johanna was no doubt a proper person, but she was still too pretty and too much occupied with herself, and God only knows what all she was thinking about. But now that his Lordship could again keep an eye on Annie and see that everything was right, she herself wanted to try to find out how her Ladyship was getting on.

"That is right, Roswitha."

"And I wanted to see whether your Ladyship lacked anything, and whether you might need me. If so I would stay right here and pitch in and do everything and see to it that your Ladyship was getting on well again."

Effi had been leaning back in the corner of the sofa with her eyes closed, but suddenly she sat up and said: "Yes, Roswitha, what you were saying there is an idea, there is something in it. For I must tell you that I am not going to stay in this boarding house. I have rented an apartment farther down the street and have bought furniture, and in three more days I shall move in. And if, when I arrive there, I could say to you: 'No, Roswitha, not there, the wardrobe must stand here and the mirror there,' why, that would be worth while, and I should like it. Then when we got tired of all the drudgery I should say: 'Now, Roswitha, go over there and get us a decanter of Munich beer, for when one has been working one is thirsty for a drink, and, if you can, bring us also something good from the Habsburg Restaurant. You can return the dishes later.' Yes,

Roswitha, when I think of that it makes my heart feel a great deal lighter. But I must ask you whether you have thought it all over? I will not speak of Annie, to whom you are so attached, for she is almost your own child; nevertheless Annie will be provided for, and Johanna is also attached to her, you know. So leave her out of the consideration. But if you want to come to me remember how everything has changed. I am no longer as I used to be. I have now taken a very small apartment, and the porter will doubtless pay but little attention to you and me. We shall have to be very economical, always have what we used to call our Thursday meal, because that was cleaning day. Do you remember? And do you remember how good Mr. Gieshübler once came in and was urged to sit down with us, and how he said he had never eaten such a delicate dish? You probably remember he was always so frightfully polite, but really he was the only human being in the city who was a connoisseur in matters of eating. The others called everything fine."

Roswitha was enjoying every word and could already see everything running smoothly, when Effi again said: "Have you considered all this? For, while it is my own household, I must not overlook the fact that you have been spoiled these many years, and formerly no qstions were ever asked, for we did not need to be saving; but now I must be saving, for I am poor and have only what is given me, you know, remittances from Hohen-Cremmen. My parents are very good to me, so far as they are able, but they are not rich. And now tell me what you think."

"That I shall come marching along with my trunk next Saturday, not in the evening, but early in the morning, and that I shall be there when the settling process begins. For I can take hold quite differently from your Ladyship."

"Don't say that, Roswitha. I can work too. One can do anything when obliged to."

"And then your Ladyship doesn't need to worry about me, as though I might think: 'that is not good enough for Roswitha.' For Roswitha anything is good that she has to share with your Ladyship, and most to her liking would be something sad. Yes, I look forward to that with real pleasure. Your Ladyship shall see I know what sadness is. Even if I didn't know, I should soon find out. I have not forgotten how I was sitting there in the churchyard, all alone in the world, thinking to myself it would probably be better if I were lying there in a row with the others. Who came along? Who saved my life? Oh, I have had so much to endure. That day when my father came at me with the red-hot tongs--"

"I remember, Roswitha."

"Well, that was bad enough. But when I sat there in the churchyard, so completely poverty stricken and forsaken, that was worse still. Then your Ladyship came. I hope I shall never go to heaven if I forget that."

153

As she said this she arose and went toward the window. "Oh, your Ladyship must see *him* too."

Effi stepped to the window. Over on the other side of the street sat Rollo, looking up at the windows of the boarding house.

A few days later Effi, with the aid of Roswitha, moved into the apartment on KÃ¶niggrÃ¤tz St., and liked it there from the beginning. To be sure, there was no society, but during her boarding house days she had derived so little pleasure from intercourse with people that it was not hard for her to be alone, at least not in the beginning. With Roswitha it was impossible, of course, to carry on an esthetic conversation, or even to discuss what was in the paper, but when it was simply a qstion of things human and Effi began her sentence with, "Oh, Roswitha, I am again afraid," then the faithful soul always had a good answer ready, always comfort and usually advice.

Until Christmas they got on excellently, but Christmas eve was rather sad and when New Year's Day came Effi began to grow quite melancholy. It was not cold, only grizzly and rainy, and if the days were short, the evenings were so much the longer. What was she to do! She read, she embroidered, she played solitaire, she played Chopin, but nocturnes were not calculated to bring much light into her life, and when Roswitha came with the tea tray and placed on the table, beside the tea service, two small plates with an egg and a Vienna cutlet carved in small slices, Effi said, as she closed the piano: "Move up, Roswitha. Keep me company."

Roswitha joined her. "I know, your Ladyship has been playing too much again. Your Ladyship always looks like that and has red spots. The doctor forbade it, didn't he?"

"Ah, Roswitha, it is easy for the doctor to forbid, and also easy for you to repeat everything he says. But what shall I do? I can't sit all day long at the window and look over toward Christ's Church. Sundays, during the evening service, when the windows are lighted up, I always look over that way; but it does me no good, it always makes my heart feel heavier."

"Well, then, your Ladyship ought to go to church. Your Ladyship has been there once."

"Oh, many a time. But I have derived little benefit from it. He preaches quite well and is a very wise man, and I should be happy if I knew the hundredth part of it all. But it seems as though I were merely reading a book. Then when he speaks so loud and saws the air and shakes his long black locks I am drawn, entirely out of my attitude of worship."

"Out of?"

Effi laughed. "You think I hadn't yet got into such an attitude. That is probably tr. But whose fault is it? Certainly not mine. He always talks so much about the Old Testament. Even if that is very good it doesn't edify me. Anyhow, this everlasting listening is not the right thing. You see, I ought to have so much to do that I should not know whither to turn. That would suit me. Now there are societies where young girls learn housekeeping, or sewing, or to be kindergarten teachers. Have you ever heard of these?"

"Yes, I once heard of them. Once upon a time little Annie was to go to a kindergarten."

"Now you see, you know better than I do. I should like to join some such society where I can make myself useful. But it is not to be thought of. The women in charge wouldn't take me, they couldn't. That is the most terrible thing of all, that the world is so closed to one, that it even forbids one to take a part in charitable work. I can't even give poor children a lesson after hours to help them catch up."

"That would not do for your Ladyship. The children always have such greasy shoes on, and in wet weather there is so much steam and smoke, your Ladyship could never stand it."

Effi smiled. "You are probably right, Roswitha, but it is a bad sign that you should be right, and it shows me that I still have too much of the old Effi in me and that I am still too well off."

Roswitha would not agree to that. "Anybody as good as your Ladyship can't be too well off. Now you must not always play such sad music. Sometimes I think all will be well yet, something will surely turn up."

And something did turn up. Effi desired to become a painter, in spite of the precentor's daughter from Polzin, whose conceit as an artist she still remembered as exceedingly disagreeable. Although she laughed about the plan herself, because she was conscious she could never rise above the lowest grade of dilettantism, nevertheless she went at her work with zest, because she at last had an occupation and that, too, one after her own heart, because it was quiet and peaceful. She applied for instruction to a very old professor of painting, who was well-informed concerning the Brandenburgian aristocracy, and was, at the same time, very pious, so that Effi seemed to be his heart's delight from the outset. He probably thought, here was a soul to be saved, and so he received her with extraordinary friendliness, as though she had been his daughter. This made Effi very happy, and the day of her first painting lesson marked for her a turning point toward the good. Her poor life was now no longer so poor, and Roswitha was triumphant when she saw that she had been right and something had turned up after all.

Thus things went on for considerably over a year. Coming again in contact with people made Effi happy, but it also created within her the desire to renew and extend associations. Longing for Hohen-Cremmen came over her at times with the force of a tr passion, and she longed still more passionately to see Annie. After all she was her child, and when she began to turn this thought over in her mind and, at the same time, recalled what Miss Trippelli had once said, to wit: "The world is so small that one could be certain of coming suddenly upon some old acquaintance in Central Africa," she had a reason for being surprised that she had never met Annie. But the time finally arrived when a change was to occur. She was coming from her painting lesson, close by the Zoological Garden, and near the station stepped into a horse car. It was very hot and it did her good to see the lowered curtains blown out and back by the strong current of air passing through the car. She leaned back in the corner toward the front platform and was studying several pictures of bl tufted and tasseled sofas on a stained window pane, when the car began to move more slowly and she saw three school children spring up with school bags on their backs and little pointed hats on their heads. Two of them were blonde and merry, the third brunette and serious. This one was Annie. Effi was badly startled, and the thought of a meeting with the child, for which she had so often longed, filled her now with deadly fright. What was to be done? With quick determination she opened the door to the front platform, on which nobody was standing but the driver, whom she asked to let her get off in front at the next station. "It is forbidden, young lady," said the driver. But she gave him a coin and looked at him so appealingly that the good-natured man changed his mind and mumbled to himself: "I really am not supposed to, but perhaps once will not matter." When the car stopped he took out the lattice and Effi sprang off.

She was still greatly excited when she reached the house.

"Just think, Roswitha, I have seen Annie." Then she told of the meeting in the tram car. Roswitha was displeased that the mother and daughter had not been rejoiced to see each other again, and was very hard to convince that it would not have looked well in the presence of so many people. Then Effi had to tell how Annie looked and when she had done so with motherly pride Roswitha said: "Yes, she is what one might call half and half. Her pretty features and, if I may be permitted to say it, her strange look she gets from her mother, but her seriousness is exactly her father. When I come to think about it, she is more like his Lordship."

"Thank God!" said Effi.

"Now, your Ladyship, there is some qstion about that. No doubt there is many a person who would take the side of the mother."

"Do you think so, Roswitha? I don't."

"Oh, oh, I am not so easily fooled, and I think your Ladyship knows very well, too, how matters really stand and what the men like best."

"Oh, don't speak of that, Roswitha."

The conversation ended here and was never afterward resumed. But even though Effi avoided speaking to Roswitha about Annie, down deep in her heart she was unable to get over that meeting and suffered from the thought of having fled from her own child. It troubled her till she was ashamed, and her desire to meet Annie grew till it became pathological. It was not possible to write to Innstetten and ask his permission. She was fully conscious of her guilt, indeed she nurtured the sense of it with almost zealous care; but, on the other hand, at the same time that she was conscious of guilt, she was also filled with a certain spirit of rebellion against Innstetten. She said to herself, he was right, again and again, and yet in the end he was wrong. All had happened so long before, a new life had begun--he might have let it die; instead poor Crampas died.

No, it would not do to write to Innstetten; but she wanted to see Annie and speak to her and press her to her heart, and after she had thought it over for days she was firmly convinced as to the best way to go about it.

The very next morning she carefully put on a decent black dress and set out for Unter den Linden to call on the minister's wife. She sent in her card with nothing on it but "Effi von Innstetten, nÃ©e von Briest." Everything else was left off, even "Baroness." When the man servant returned and said, "Her Excellency begs you to enter," Effi followed him into an anteroom, where she sat down and, in spite of her excitement, looked at the pictures on the walls. First of all there was Guido Reni's *Aurora*, while opposite it hung English etchings of pictures by Benjamin West, made by the well known aquatint process. One of the pictures was King Lear in the storm on the heath.

Effi had hardly finished looking at the pictures when the door of the adjoining room opened and a tall slender woman of unmistakably prepossessing appearance stepped toward the one who had come to reqst a favor of her and held out her hand. "My dear most gracious Lady," she said, "what a pleasure it is for me to see you again." As she said this she walked toward the sofa and sat down, drawing Effi to a seat beside her.

Effi was touched by the goodness of heart revealed in every word and movement. Not a trace of haughtiness or reproach, only beautiful human sympathy. "In what way can I be of service to you?" asked the minister's wife.

Effi's lips quivered. Finally she said: "The thing that brings me here is a reqst, the fulfillment of which your Excellency may perhaps make possible. I have a ten-year-old daughter whom I have not seen for three years and should like to see again."

The minister's wife took Effi's hand and looked at her in a friendly way.

"When I say, 'not seen for three years,' that is not quite right. Three days ago I saw her again." Then Effi described with great vividness how she had met Annie. "Fleeing from my own child. I know very well that as we sow we shall reap and I do not wish to change anything in my life. It is all right as it is, and I have not wished to have it

157

otherwise. But this separation from my child is really too hard and I have a desire to be permitted to see her now and then, not secretly and clandestinely, but with the knowledge and consent of all concerned."

"With the knowledge and consent of all concerned," repeated the minister's wife. "So that means with the consent of your husband. I see that his bringing up of the child is calculated to estrange her from her mother, a method which I do not feel at liberty to judge. Perhaps he is right. Pardon me for this remark, gracious Lady."

Effi nodded.

"You yourself appreciate the attitude of your husband, and your only desire is that proper respect be shown to a natural impulse, indeed, I may say, the most beautiful of our impulses, at least we women all think so. Am I right?"

"In every particular."

"So you want me to secure permission for occasional meetings, in your home, where you can attempt to win back the heart of your child."

Effi expressed again her acquiescence, and the minister's wife contind: "Then, most gracious Lady, I stall do what I can. But we shall not have an easy task. Your husband-- pardon me for calling him by that name now as before--is a man who is not governed by moods and fancies, but by principles, and it will be hard for him to discard them or even give them up temporarily. Otherwise he would have begun long ago to purs a different method of action and education. What to your heart seems hard he considers right."

"Then your Excellency thinks, perhaps, it would be better to take back my reqst!"

"Oh, no. I wished only to explain the actions of your husband, not to say justify them, and wished at the same time to indicate the difficulties we shall in all probability encounter. But I think we shall overcome them nevertheless. We women are able to accomplish a great many things if we go about them wisely and do not make too great pretensions. Besides, your husband is one of my special admirers and he cannot well refuse to grant what I reqst of him. Tomorrow we have a little circle meeting at which I shall see him and the day after tomorrow morning you will receive a few lines from me telling you whether or not I have approached him wisely, that is to say, successfully. I think we shall come off victorious, and you will see your child again and enjoy her. She is said to be a very pretty girl. No wonder."

CHAPTER XXXIII

Two days later the promised lines arrived and Effi read: "I am glad, dear gracious Lady, to be able to give you good news. Everything turned out as desired. Your husband is too much a man of the world to refuse a Lady a reqst that she makes of him. But I must not keep from you the fact that I saw plainly his consent was not in accord with what he considers wise and right. But let us not pick faults where we ought to be glad. We have arranged that Annie is to come some time on Monday and may good fortune attend your meeting."

It was on the postman's second round that Effi received these lines and it would presumably be less than two hours till Annie appeared. That was a short time and yet too long. Effi walked restlessly about the two rooms and then back to the kitchen, where she talked with Roswitha about everything imaginable: about the ivy over on Christ's Church and the probability that next year the windows would be entirely overgrown; about the porter, who had again turned off the gas so poorly that they were likely to be blown up; and about buying their lamp oil again at the large lamp store on Unter den Linden instead of on Anhalt St. She talked about everything imaginable, except Annie, because she wished to keep down the fear lurking in her soul, in spite of the letter from the minister's wife, or perhaps because of it.

Finally, at noon, the bell was rung timidly and Roswitha went to look through the peephole. Surely enough, it was Annie. Roswitha gave the child a kiss, but said nothing, and then led her very quietly, as though some one were ill in the house, from the corridor into the back room and then to the door opening into the front room.

"Go in there, Annie." With these words she left the child and returned to the kitchen, for she did not wish to be in the way.

Effi was standing at the other end of the room with her back against the post of the mirror when the child entered. "Annie!" But Annie stood still by the half opened door, partly out of embarrassment, but partly on purpose. Effi rushed to her, lifted her up, and kissed her.

"Annie, my sweet child, how glad I am! Come, tell me." She took Annie by the hand and went toward the sofa to sit down. Annie stood and looked shyly at her mother, at the same time reaching her left hand toward the corner of the table cloth, hanging down near her. "Did you know, Annie, that I saw you one day?"

"Yes, I thought you did."

"Now tell me a great deal. How tall you have grown! And that is the scar there. Roswitha told me about it. You were always so wild and hoidenish in your playing. You get that from your mother. She was the same way. And at school? I fancy you are always at the head, you look to me as though you ought to be a model pupil and always bring home the best marks. I have heard also that Miss von Wedelstädt praises you. That is right. I was likewise ambitious, but I had no such good school. Mythology was always my best study. In what are you best?"

"I don't know."

"Oh, you know well enough. Pupils always know that. In what do you have the best marks?"

"In religion."

"Now, you see, you do know after all. Well, that is very fine. I was not so good in it, but it was probably d to the instruction. We had only a young man licensed to preach."

"We had, too."

"Has he gone away?"

Annie nodded.

"Why did he leave?"

"I don't know. Now we have the preacher again."

"And you all love him dearly?"

"Yes, and two of the girls in the highest class are going to change their religion."

"Oh, I understand; that is fine. And how is Johanna?"

"Johanna brought me to the door of the house."

"Why didn't you bring her up with you?"

"She said she would rather stay downstairs and wait over at the church."

"And you are to meet her there?"

"Yes."

"Well, I hope she will not get impatient. There is a little front yard over there and the windows are half overgrown with ivy, as though it were an old church."

"But I should not like to keep her waiting."

"Oh, I see, you are very considerate, and I presume I ought to be glad of it. We need only to make the proper division of the time--Tell me now how Rollo is."

"Rollo is very well, but papa says he is getting so lazy. He lies in the sun all the time."

"That I can readily believe. He was that way when you were quite small. And now, Annie, today we have just seen each other, you know; will you visit me often?"

"Oh, certainly, if I am allowed to."

"We can take a walk in the Prince Albrecht Garden."

"Oh, certainly, if I am allowed to."

"Or we may go to Schilling's and eat ice cream, pineapple or vanilla ice cream. I always liked vanilla best."

"Oh, certainly, if I am allowed to."

At this third "if I am allowed to" the measure was full. Effi sprang up and flashed the child a look of indignation.

"I believe it is high time you were going, Annie. Otherwise Johanna will get impatient." She rang the bell and Roswitha, who was in the next room, entered immediately. "Roswitha, take Annie over to the church. Johanna is waiting there. I hope she has not taken cold. I should be sorry. Remember me to Johanna."

The two went out.

Hardly had Roswitha closed the door behind her when Effi tore open her dress, because she was threatened with suffocation, and fell to laughing convulsively. "So that is the way it goes to meet after a long separation." She rushed forward, opened the window and looked for something to support her. In the distress of her heart she found it. There beside the window was a bookshelf with a few volumes of Schiller and KÃ¶rner on it, and on top of the volumes of poems, which were of equal height, lay a Bible and a songbook. She reached for them, because she had to have something before which she could kneel down and pray. She laid both Bible and songbook on the edge of the table where Annie had been standing, and threw herself violently down before them and spoke in a half audible tone: "O God in Heaven, forgive me what I have done. I was a child--No, no, I was not a child, I was old enough to know what I was doing. I *did* know, too, and I will not minimize my guilt. But this is too much. This action of the child is not the work of my God who would punish me, it is the work of *him*, and *him* alone. I thought he had a noble heart and have always felt small beside him, but now I know that it is he who is small. And because he is small he is crl. Everything that is small is crl. *He* taught the child to say that. He always was a school-master, Crampas called him one, scoffingly at the time, but he was right. 'Oh, certainly if I am allowed to!' You don't *have* to be allowed to. I don't want you any more, I hate you both, even my own child. Too much is too much. He was ambitious, but nothing more. Honor, honor, honor. And then he shot the poor fellow whom I never even loved and whom I had forgotten, because I didn't love him. It was all stupidity in the first place, but then came blood and murder, with me to blame. And now he sends me the child, because he cannot refuse a minister's wife anything, and before he sends the child he trains it like a parrot and teaches it the phrase, 'if I am allowed to.' I am disgusted at what I did; but the thing that disgusts me most is your virt. Away with you! I must live, but I doubt if it will be long."

When Roswitha came back Effi lay on the floor seemingly lifeless, with her face turned away.

CHAPTER XXXIV

RummschÃ¼ttel was called and pronounced Effi's condition serious. He saw that the hectic flush he had noticed for over a year was more pronounced than ever, and, what was worse, she showed the first symptoms of nervous fever. But his quiet, friendly manner, to which he added a dash of humor, did Effi good, and she was calm so long as RummschÃ¼ttel was with her. When he left, Roswitha accompanied him as far as the outer hall and said: "My, how I am scared, Sir Councillor; if it ever comes back, and it may--oh, I shall never have another quiet hour. But it was too, too much, the way the child acted. Her poor Ladyship! And still so young; at her age many are only beginning life."

"Don't worry, Roswitha. It may all come right again. But she must get away. We will see to that. Different air, different people."

Two days later there arrived in Hohen-Cremmen a letter which ran: "Most gracious Lady: My long-standing friendly relations to the houses of Briest and Belling, and above all the hearty love I cherish for your daughter, will justify these lines. Things cannot go on any longer as they are. Unless something is done to resc your daughter from the loneliness and sorrow of the life she has been leading for years she will soon pine away. She always had a tendency to consumption, for which reason I sent her to Ems years ago. This old trouble is now aggravated by a new one; her nerves are giving out. Nothing but a change of air can check this. But whither shall I send her? It would not be hard to make a proper choice among the watering places of Silesia. Salzbrunn is good, and Reinerz still better, on account of the nervous complication. But no place except Hohen-Cremmen will do. For, most gracious Lady, air alone cannot restore your daughter's health. She is pining away because she has nobody but Roswitha. The fidelity of a servant is beautiful, but parental love is better. Pardon an old man for meddling in affairs that lie outside of his calling as a physician. No, not outside, either, for after all it is the physician who is here speaking and making demands--pardon the word--in accordance with his duty. I have seen so much of life--But enough on this topic. With kindest regards to your husband, your humble servant, Dr. Rummschüttel."

Mrs. von Briest had read the letter to her husband. They were sitting on the shady tile walk, with their backs to the drawing room and facing the circular bed and the sundial. The wild grapevine twining around the windows was rustling gently in the breeze and over the water a few dragon-flies were hovering in the bright sunshine.

Briest sat speechless, drumming on the tea-tray.

"Please don't drum, I had rather you would talk."

"Ah, Luise, what shall I say? My drumming says quite enough. You have known for over a year what I think about it. At the time when Innstetten's letter came, a flash from a clear sky, I was of your opinion. But that was half an eternity ago. Am I to play the grand inquisitor till the end of my days? I tell you, I have had my fill of it for a long time."

"Don't reproach me, Briest. I love her as much as you, perhaps more; each in his own way. But it is not our only purpose in life to be weak and affectionate and to tolerate things that are contrary to the law and the commandments, things that men condemn, and in the present instance rightly."

"Hold on! One thing comes first."

"Of course, one thing comes first; but what is the one thing?"

"The love of parents for their children, especially when they have only one child."

"Then good-by catechism, morality, and the claims of 'society.'"

"Ah, Luise, talk to me about the catechism as much as you like, but don't speak to me about 'society.'"

"It is very hard to get along without 'society.'"

"Also without a child. Believe me, Luise, 'society' can shut one eye when it sees fit. Here is where I stand in the matter: If the people of Rathenow come, all right, if they don't come, all right too. I am simply going to telegraph: 'Effi, come.' Are you agreed?"

She got up and kissed him on the forehead. "Of course I am. Only you must not find fault with me. An easy step it is not, and from now on our life will be different."

"I can stand it. There is a good rape crop and in the autumn I can hunt an occasional hare. I still have a taste for red wine, and it will taste even better when we have the child back in the house. Now I am going to send the telegram."

* * * * *

Effi had been in Hohen-Cremmen for over six months. She occupied the two rooms on the second floor which she had formerly had when there for a visit. The larger one was furnished for her personally, and Roswitha slept in the other. What Rummschüttel had expected from this sojourn and the good that went with it, was realized, so far as it could be realized. The coughing diminished, the bitter expression that had robbed Effi's unusually kind face of a good part of its charm disappeared, and there came days when she could laugh again. About Kessin and everything back there little was said, with the single exception of Mrs. von Padden--and Gieshübler, of course, for whom old Mr. von Briest had a very tender spot in his heart. "This Alonzo, this fastidious Spaniard, who harbors a Mirambo and brings up a Trippelli--well, he must be a genius, and you can't make me believe he isn't." Then Effi had to yield and act for him the part of Gieshübler, with hat in hand and endless bows of politeness. By virt of her peculiar talent for mimicry, she could do the bows very well, although it went against the grain, because she always felt that it was an injustice to the dear good man.--They never talked about Innstetten and Annie, but it was settled that Annie was to inherit Hohen-Cremmen.

Effi took a new lease on life, and her mother, who in tr womanly fashion was not altogether averse to regarding the affair, painful though it was, as merely an interesting case, vied with her father in expressions of love and devotion.

"Such a good winter we have not had for a long time," said Briest. Then Effi arose from her seat and stroked back the sparse hairs from his forehead. But beautiful as everything seemed from the point of view of Effi's health, it was all illusion, for in reality the disease was gaining ground and quietly consuming her vitality. Effi again wore, as on the day of her betrothal to Innstetten, a bl and white striped smock with a loose belt, and when she walked up to her parents with a quick elastic step, to bid them good morning, they looked at each other with joyful surprise--with joyful surprise and yet at the same time with sadness, for they could not fail to see that it was not the freshness of youth, but a transformation, that gave her slender form and beaming eyes this peculiar appearance. All who observed her closely saw this, but Effi herself did not. Her whole attention was engaged by the happy feeling at being back in this place, to her so charmingly peaceful, and living reconciled with those whom she had always loved and who had always loved her, even during the years of her misery and exile.

She busied herself with all sorts of things about the home and attended to the decorations and little improvements in the household. Her appreciation of the beautiful enabled her always to make the right choice. Reading and, above all, study of the arts she had given up entirely. "I have had so much of it that I am happy to be able to lay my hands in my lap." Besides, it doubtless reminded her too much of her days of sadness. She cultivated instead the art of contemplating nature with calmness and delight, and when the leaves fell from the plane trees, or the sunbeams glistened on the ice of the little pond, or the first crocuses blossomed in the circular plot, still half in the grip of winter--it did her good, and she could gaze on all these things for hours, forgetting what life had denied her, or, to be more accurate, what she had robbed herself of.

Callers were not altogether a minus quantity, not everybody shunned her; but her chief associates were the families at the schoolhouse and the parsonage.

It made little difference that the Jahnke daughters had left home; there could have been no very cordial friendship with them anyhow. But she found a better friend than ever in old Mr. Jahnke himself, who considered not only all of Swedish Pomerania, but also the Kessin region as Scandinavian outposts, and was always asking qstions about them. "Why, Jahnke, we had a steamer, and, as I wrote to you, I believe, or may perhaps have told you, I came very near going over to Wisby. Just think, I almost went to Wisby. It is comical, but I can say 'almost' with reference to many things in my life."

"A pity, a pity," said Jahnke.

"Yes, indeed, a pity. But I actually did make a tour of Rügen. You would have enjoyed that, Jahnke. Just think, Arcona with its great camping place of the Wends, that is said still to be visible. I myself did not go there, but not very far away is the Hertha

165

Lake with white and yellow water lilies. The place made one think a great deal of your Hertha."

"Yes, yes, Hertha. But you were about to speak of the Hertha Lake."

"Yes, I was. And just think, Jahnke, close by the lake stood two large shining sacrificial stones, with the grooves still showing, in which the blood used to run off. Ever since then I have had an aversion for the Wends."

"Oh, pardon me, gracious Lady, but they were not Wends. The legends of the sacrificial stones and the Hertha Lake go back much, much farther, clear back before the birth of Christ. They were the pure Germans, from whom we are all descended."

"Of course," laughed Effi, "from whom we are all descended, the Jahnkes certainly, and perhaps the Briests, too."

Then she dropped the subject of Rügen and the Hertha Lake and asked about his grandchildren and which of them he liked best, Bertha's or Hertha's.

Indeed Effi was on a very friendly footing with Jahnke. But in spite of his intimate relation to Hertha Lake, Scandinavia, and Wisby, he was only a simple man and so the lonely young woman could not fail to val her chats with Niemeyer much higher. In the autumn, so long as promenades in the park were possible, she had an abundance of such chats, but with the beginning of winter came an interruption for several months, because she did not like to go to the parsonage. Mrs. Niemeyer had always been a very disagreeable woman, but she pitched her voice higher than ever now, in spite of the fact that in the opinion of the parish she herself was not altogether above reproach.

The situation remained the same throughout the winter, much to Effi's sorrow. But at the beginning of April when the bushes showed a fringe of green and the park paths dried off, the walks were resumed.

Once when they were sauntering along they heard a cuckoo in the distance, and Effi began to count to see how many times it called. She was leaning on Niemeyer's arm. Suddenly she said: "The cuckoo is calling yonder, but I don't want to consult him about the length of my life. Tell me, friend, what do you think of life?"

"Ah, dear Effi, you must not lay such doctors' qstions before me. You must apply to a philosopher or offer a prize to a faculty. What do I think of life? Much and little. Sometimes it is very much and sometimes very little."

"That is right, friend, I like that; I don't need to know anymore." As she said this they came to the swing. She sprang into it as nimbly as in her earliest girlhood days, and

166

before the old man, who watched her, could recover from his fright, she crouched down between the two ropes and set the swing board in motion by a skillful lifting and dropping of the weight of her body. In a few seconds she was flying through the air. Then, holding on with only one hand, she tore a little silk handkerchief from around her neck and waved it happily and haughtily. Soon she let the swing stop, sprang out, and took Niemeyer's arm again.

"Effi, you are just as you always were."

"No, I wish I were. But I am too old for this; I just wanted to try it once more. Oh, how fine it was and how much good the air did me! It seemed as though I were flying up to heaven. I wonder if I shall go to heaven? Tell me, friend, you ought to know. Please, please."

Niemeyer took her hand into his two wrinkled ones and gave her a kiss on the forehead, saying: "Yes, Effi, you will."

CHAPTER XXXV

Effi spent the whole day out in the park, because she needed to take the air. Old Dr. Wiesike of Friesack approved of it, but in his instructions gave her too much liberty to do what she liked, and during the cold days in May she took a severe cold. She became feverish, coughed a great deal, and the doctor, who had been calling every third day, now came daily. He was put to it to know what to do, for the sleeping powders and cough medicines Effi asked for could not be given, because of the fever.

"Doctor," said old von Briest, "what is going to come of this? You have known her since she was a little thing, in fact you were here at her birth. I don't like all these symptoms: her noticeable falling away, the red spots, and the gleam of her eyes when she suddenly turns to me with a pleading look. What do you think it will amount to? Must she die?"

Wiesike shook his head gravely. "I will not say that, von Briest, but I don't like the way her fever keeps up. However, we shall bring it down soon, for she must go to Switzerland or Mentone for pure air and agreeable surroundings that will make her forget the past."

"Lethe, Lethe."

"Yes, Lethe," smiled Wiesike. "It's a pity that while the ancient Swedes, the Greeks, were leaving us the name they did not leave us also the spring itself."

"Or at least the formula for it. Waters are imitated now, you know. My, Wiesike, what a business we could build up here if we could only start such a sanatorium! Friesack the spring of forgetfulness! Well, let us try the Riviera for the present. Mentone is the Riviera, is it not? To be sure, the price of grain is low just now, but what must be must be. I shall talk with my wife about it."

That he did, and his wife consented immediately, inflnced in part by her own ardent desire to see the south, particularly since she had felt like one retired from the world. But Effi would not listen to it. "How good you are to me! And I am selfish enough to accept the sacrifice, if I thought it would do any good. But I am certain it would only harm me."

"You try to make yourself think that, Effi."

"No. I have become so irritable that everything annoys me. Not here at home, for you humor me and clear everything out of my way. But when traveling that is impossible, the disagreeable element cannot be eliminated so easily. It begins with the conductor and ends with the waiter. Even when I merely think of their self-satisfied countenances my temperature runs right up. No, no, keep me here. I don't care to leave Hohen-Cremmen any more; my place is here. The heliotrope around the sundial is dearer to me than Mentone."

After this conversation the plan was dropped and in spite of the great benefit Wiesike had expected from the Riviera he said: "We must respect these wishes, for they are not mere whims. Such patients have a very fine sense and know with remarkable certainty what is good for them and what not. What Mrs. Effi has said about the conductor and the waiter is really quite correct, and there is no air with healing power enough to counterbalance hotel annoyances, if one is at all affected by them. So let us keep her here. If that is not the best thing, it is certainly not the worst."

This proved to be tr. Effi got better, gained a little in weight (old von Briest belonged to the weight fanatics), and lost much of her irritability. But her need of fresh air kept growing steadily, and even when the west wind blew and the sky was overcast with gray clouds, she spent many hours out of doors. On such days she would usually go out into the fields or the marsh, often as far as two miles, and when she grew tired would sit down on the hurdle fence, where, lost in dreams, she would watch the ranunculi and red sorrel waving in the wind.

"You go out so much alone," said Mrs. von Briest. "Among our people you are safe, but there are so many strange vagabonds prowling around."

That made an impression on Effi, who had never thought of danger, and when she was alone with Roswitha, she said: "I can't well take you with me, Roswitha; you are too fat and no longer sure-footed."

"Oh, your Ladyship, it is hardly yet as bad as that. Why, I could still be married."

"Of course," laughed Effi. "One is never too old for that. But let me tell you, Roswitha, if I had a dog to accompany me--Papa's hunting dog has no attachment for me--hunting dogs are so stupid--and he never stirs till the hunter or the gardener takes the gun from the rack. I often have to think of Rollo."

"Tr," said Roswitha, "they have nothing like Rollo here. But I don't mean anything against 'here.' Hohen-Cremmen is very good."

Three or four days after this conversation between Effi and Roswitha, Innstetten entered his office an hour earlier than usual. The morning sun, which shone very brightly, had wakened him and as he had doubtless felt he could not go to sleep again he had got out of bed to take up a piece of work that had long been waiting to be attended to.

At a quarter past eight he rang. Johanna brought the breakfast tray, on which, beside the morning papers, there were two letters. He glanced at the addresses and recognized by the handwriting that one was from the minister. But the other? The postmark could not be read plainly and the address, "Baron von Innstetten, Esq.," showed a happy lack of familiarity with the customary use of titles. In keeping with this was the very primitive character of the writing. But the address was remarkably accurate: "W., Keith St. 1c, third story."

Innstetten was enough of an official to open first the letter from "His Excellency." "My dear Innstetten: I am happy to be able to announce to you that His Majesty has deigned to sign your appointment and I congratulate you sincerely." Innstetten was pleased at the friendly lines from the minister, almost more than at the appointment itself, for, since the morning in Kessin, when Crampas had bidden him farewell with that look which still haunted him, he had grown somewhat sceptical of such things as climbing higher on the ladder. Since then he had measured with a different measure and viewed things in a different light. Distinction--what did that amount to in the end? As the days passed by with less and less joy for him, he more than once recalled a half-forgotten minister's anecdote from the time of the elder Ladenberg, who, upon receiving the Order of the Red Eagle, for which he had long been waiting, threw it down in a rage and exclaimed: "Lie there till you turn black." It probably did turn into a black one subseqntly, but many days too late and certainly without real satisfaction for the receiver. Everything that is to give us pleasure must come at the right time and in the right circumstances, for what delights us today may be valless tomorrow. Innstetten felt this deeply, and as certainly as he had formerly laid store by honors and distinctions coming from his highest superiors, just so certainly was he now firmly convinced that the glittering appearance of things amounted to but little, and that what is called happiness, if it existed at all, is something other than this appearance. "Happiness, if I am right, lies in two things: being exactly where one belongs--but what official can say that of himself?--and, especially, performing comfortably the most commonplace functions, that is, getting enough sleep and not having new boots that pinch. When the 720 minutes of a twelve-hour day pass without any special annoyance that can be called a happy day."

Innstetten was today in the mood for such gloomy reflections. When he took up the second letter and read it he ran his hand over his forehead, with the painful feeling that there is such a thing as happiness, that he had once possessed it, but had lost it and could never again recover it. Johanna entered and announced Privy Councillor WÃ¼llersdorf, who was already standing on the threshold and said: "Congratulations, Innstetten."

"I believe you mean what you say; the others will be vexed. However--"

"However. You are surely not going to be pessimistic at a moment like this."

"No. The graciousness of His Majesty makes me feel ashamed, and the friendly feeling of the minister, to whom I owe all this, almost more."

"But--"

"But I have forgotten how to rejoice. If I said that to anybody but you my words would be considered empty phrases. But you understand me. Just look around you. How empty and deserted everything is! When Johanna comes in, a so-called jewel, she startles me and frightens me. Her stage entry," contind Innstetten, imitating Johanna's pose, "the half comical shapeliness of her bust, which comes forward claiming special attention, whether of mankind or me, I don't know--all this strikes me as so sad and pitiable, and if it were not so ridiculous, it might drive me to suicide."

"Dear Innstetten, are you going to assume the duties of a permanent secretary in this frame of mind?"

"Oh, bah! How can I help it? Read these lines I have just received."

WÃ¼llersdorf took the second letter with the illegible postmark, was amused at the "Esq.," and stepped to the window that he might read more easily.

"Gracious Sir: I suppose you will be surprised that I am writing to you, but it is about Rollo. Little Annie told us last year Rollo was so lazy now, but that doesn't matter here. He can be as lazy as he likes here, the lazier the better. And her Ladyship would like it so much. She always says, when she walks upon the marsh or over the fields: 'I am

170

really afraid, Roswitha, because I am so alone; but who is there to accompany me? Rollo, oh yes, he would do. He bears no grudge against me either. That is the advantage, that animals do not trouble themselves so much about such things.' These are her Ladyship's words and I will say nothing further, and merely ask your Lordship to remember me to my little Annie. Also to Johanna. From your faithful, most obedient servant, Roswitha Gellenbagen."

"Well," said WÃ¼llersdorf, as he folded the letter again, "she is ahead of us."

"I think so, too."

"This is also the reason why everything else seems so doubtful to you."

"You are right. It has been going through my head for a long time, and these simple words with their intended, or perhaps unintended complaint, have put me completely beside myself again. It has been troubling me for over a year and I should like to get clear out of here. Nothing pleases me any more. The more distinctions I receive the more I feel that it is all vanity. My life is bungled, and so I have thought to myself I ought to have nothing more to do with strivings and vanities, and ought to be able to employ my pedagogical inclinations, which after all are my most characteristic quality, as a superintendent of public morals. It would not be anything new. If the plan were feasible I should surely become a very famous character, such as Dr. Wichern of the Rough House in Hamburg, for example, that man of miracles, who tamed all criminals with his glance and his piety."

"Hm, there is nothing to be said against that; it would be possible."

"No, it is not possible either. Not even *that*. Absolutely every aven is closed to me. How could I touch the soul of a murderer? To do that one must be intact himself. And if one no longer is, but has a like spot on his own hands, then he must at least be able to play the crazy penitent before his confreres, who are to be converted, and entertain them with a scene of gigantic contrition."

WÃ¼llersdorf nodded.

"Now you see, you agree. But I can't do any of these things any more. I can no longer play the man in the hair shirt, let alone the dervish or the fakir, who dances himself to death in the midst of his self-accusations. And inasmuch as all such things are impossible I have puzzled out, as the best thing for me, to go away from here and off to the coal black fellows who know nothing of culture and honor. Those fortunate creatures! For culture and honor and such rubbish are to blame for all my trouble. We don't do such things out of passion, which might be an acceptable excuse. We do them for the sake of mere notions--notions! And then the one fellow collapses and later the other collapses, too, only in a worse way."

171

"Oh pshaw! Innstetten, those are whims, mere fancies. Go to Africa! What does that mean! It will do for a lieutenant who is in debt. But a man like you! Are you thinking of presiding over a palaver, in a red fez, or of entering into blood relationship with a son-in-law of King Mtesa? Or will you feel your way along the Congo in a tropical helmet, with six holes in the top of it, until you come out again at Kamerun or thereabouts? Impossible!"

"Impossible? Why? If *that* is impossible, what then?"

"Simply stay here and practice resignation. Who, pray, is unoppressed! Who could not say every day: 'Really a very qstionable affair.' You know, I have also a small burden to bear, not the same as yours, but not much lighter. That talk about creeping around in the primeval forest or spending the night in an ant hill is folly. Whoever cares to, may, but it is not the thing for us. The best thing is to stand in the gap and hold out till one falls, but, until then, to get as much out of life as possible in the small and even the smallest things, keeping one eye open for the violets when they bloom, or the Luise monument when it is decorated with flowers, or the little girls with high lace shoes when they skip the rope. Or drive out to Potsdam and go into the Church of Peace, where Emperor Frederick lies, and where they are just beginning to build him a tomb. As you stand there consider the life of that man, and if you are not pacified then, there is no help for you, I should say."

"Good, good! But the year is long and every single day--and then the evening."

"That is always the easiest part of the day to know what to do with. Then we have *Sardanapal*, or *Coppelia*, with Del Era, and when that is out we have Siechen's, which is not to be despised. Three steins will calm you every time. There are always many, a great many others, who are in exactly the same general situation as we are, and one of them who had had a great deal of misfortune once said to me: 'Believe me, WÃ¼llersdorf, we cannot get along without "false work."' The man who said it was an architect and must have known about it. His statement is correct. Never a day passes but I am reminded of the 'false work.'"

After WÃ¼llersdorf had thus expressed himself he took his hat and cane. During these words Innstetten may have recalled his own earlier remarks about little happiness, for he nodded his head half agreeing, and smiled to himself.

"Where are you going now, WÃ¼llersdorf? It is too early yet for the Ministry."

"I am not going there at all today. First I shall take an hour's walk along the canal to the Charlottenburg lock and then back again. And then make a short call at Huth's on Potsdam St., going cautiously up the little wooden stairway. Below there is a flower store."

"And that affords you pleasure? That satisfies you?"

"I should not say that exactly, but it will help a bit. I shall find various regular gsts there drinking their morning glass, but their names I wisely keep secret. One will tell about the Duke of Ratibor, another about the Prince-Bishop Kopp, and a third perhaps about Bismarck. There is always a little something to be learned. Three-fourths of what is said is inaccurate, but if it is only witty I do not waste much time criticising it and always listen gratefully."

With that he went out.

CHAPTER XXXVI

May was beautiful, June more beautiful, and after Effi had happily overcome the first painful feeling aroused in her by Rollo's arrival, she was full of joy at having the faithful dog about her again. Roswitha was praised and old von Briest launched forth into words of recognition for Innstetten, who, he said, was a cavalier, never petty, but always stout-hearted. "What a pity that the stupid affair had to come between them! As a matter of fact, they were a model couple." The only one who remained calm during the welcoming scene was Rollo himself, who either had no appreciation of time or considered the separation as an irregularity which was now simply removed. The fact that he had grown old also had something to do with it, no doubt. He remained sparing with his demonstrations of affection as he had been with his evidences of joy, during the welcoming scene. But he had grown in fidelity, if such a thing were possible. He never left the side of his mistress. The hunting dog he treated benevolently, but as a being of a lower order. At night he lay on the rush mat before Effi's door; in the morning, when breakfast was served out of doors by the sundial, he was always quiet, always sleepy, and only when Effi arose from the breakfast table and walked toward the hall to take her straw hat and umbrella from the rack, did his youth return. Then, without troubling himself about whether his strength was to be put to a hard or easy test, he ran up the village road and back again and did not calm down till they were out in the fields. Effi, who cared more for fresh air than for landscape beauty, avoided the little patches of forest and usually kept to the main road, which 'at first was bordered with very old elms and then, where the turnpike began, with poplars. This road led to the railway station about an hour's walk away. She enjoyed everything, breathing in with delight the fragrance wafted to her from the rape and clover fields, or watching the soaring of the larks, and counting the draw-wells and troughs, to which the cattle went to drink. She could hear a soft ringing of bells that made her feel as though she must close her eyes and pass away in sweet forgetfulness. Near the station, close by the turnpike, lay a road roller. This was her daily resting place, from which she could observe what took place on the railroad. Trains came and went and sometimes she could see two columns of

173

smoke which for a moment seemed to blend into one and then separated, one going to the right, the other to the left, till they disappeared behind the village and the grove. Rollo sat beside her, sharing her lunch, and when he had caught the last bite, he would run like mad along some plowed furrow, doubtless to show his gratitude, and stop only when a pair of pheasants scared from their nest flew up from a neighboring furrow close by him.

"How beautiful this summer is! A year ago, dear mama, I should not have thought I could ever again be so happy," said Effi every day as she walked with her mother around the pond or picked an early apple from a tree and bit into it vigorously, for she had beautiful teeth. Mrs. von Briest would stroke her hand and say: "Just wait till you are well again, Effi, quite well, and then we shall find happiness, not that of the past, but a new kind. Thank God, there are several kinds of happiness. And you shall see, we shall find something for you."

"You are so good. Really I have changed your lives and made you prematurely old."

"Oh, my dear Effi, don't speak of it. I thought the same about it, when the change came. Now I know that our quiet is better than the noise and loud turmoil of earlier years. If you keep on as you are we can go away yet. When Wiesike proposed Mentone you were ill and irritable, and because you were ill, you were right in saying what you did about conductors and waiters. When you have steadier nerves again you can stand that. You will no longer be offended, but will laugh at the grand manners and the curled hair. Then the bl sea and white sails and the rocks all overgrown with red cactus--I have never seen them, to be sure, but that is how I imagine them. I should like to become acquainted with them."

Thus the summer went by and the meteoric showers were also past. During these evenings Effi had sat at her window till after midnight and yet never grew tired of watching. "I always was a weak Christian, but I wonder whether we ever came from up there and whether, when all is over here, we shall return to our heavenly home, to the stars above or further beyond. I don't know and don't care to know. I just have the longing."

Poor Effi! She had looked up at the wonders of the sky and thought about them too long, with the result that the night air, and the fog rising from the pond, made her so ill she had to stay in bed again. When Wiesike was summoned and had examined her he took Briest aside and said: "No more hope; be prepared for an early end."

What he said was only too tr, and a few days later, comparatively early in the evening, it was not yet ten o'clock, Roswitha came down stairs and said to Mrs. von Briest: "Most gracious Lady, her Ladyship upstairs is very ill. She talks continually to herself in a soft voice and sometimes it seems as though she were praying, but she says she is not, and I don't know, it seems to me as though the end might come any hour."

174

"Does she wish to speak to me?"

"She hasn't said so, but I believe she does. You know how she is; she doesn't want to disturb you and make you anxious. But I think it would be well."

"All right, Roswitha, I will come."

Before the clock began to strike Mrs. von Briest mounted the stairway and entered Effi's room. Effi lay on a reclining chair near the open window. Mrs. von Briest drew up a small black chair with three gilt spindles in its ebony back, took Effi's hand and said: "How are you, Effi! Roswitha says you are so feverish."

"Oh, Roswitha worries so much about everything. I could see by her looks she thought I was dying. Well, I don't know. She thinks everybody ought to be as much worried as she is."

"Are you so calm about dying, dear Effi?"

"Entirely calm, mama."

"Aren't you deceiving yourself? Everybody clings to life, especially the young, and you are still so young, dear Effi."

Effi remained silent for a while. Then she said: "You know, I haven't read much. Innstetten was often surprised at it, and he didn't like it."

This was the first time she had mentioned Innstetten's name, and it made a deep impression on her mother and showed clearly that the end was come.

"But I thought," said Mrs. von Briest, "you were going to tell me something."

"Yes, I was, because you spoke of my still being so young. Certainly I am still young; but that makes no difference. During our happy days Innstetten used to read aloud to me in the evening. He had very good books, and in one of them there was a story about a man who had been called away from a merry table. The following morning he asked how it had been after he left. Somebody answered: 'Oh, there were all sorts of things, but you really didn't miss anything.' You see, mama, these words have impressed themselves upon my memory--It doesn't signify very much if one is called away from the table a little early."

Mrs. von Briest remained silent. Effi lifted herself up a little higher and said: "Now that I have talked to you about old times and also about Innstetten, I must tell you something else, dear mama."

"You are getting excited, Effi."

"No, no, to tell about the burden of my heart will not excite me, it will quiet me. And so I wanted to tell you that I am dying reconciled to God and men, reconciled also to *him*."

"Did you cherish in your heart such great bitterness against him? Really--pardon me, my dear Effi, for mentioning it now--really it was you who brought down sorrow upon yourself and your husband."

Effi assented. "Yes, mama, and how sad that it should be so. But when all the terrible things happened, and finally the scene with Annie--you know what I mean--I turned the tables on him, mentally, if I may use the ridiculous comparison, and came to believe seriously that he was to blame, because he was prosaic and calculating, and toward the end crl. Then curses upon him crossed my lips."

"Does that trouble you now?"

"Yes. And I am anxious that he shall know how, during my days of illness here, which have been almost my happiest, how it has become clear to my mind that he was right in his every act. In the affair with poor Crampas--well, after all, what else could he have done? Then the act by which he wounded me most deeply, the teaching of my own child to shun me, even in that he was right, hard and painful as it is for me to admit it. Let him know that I died in this conviction. It will comfort and console him, and may reconcile him. He has much that is good in his nature and was as noble as anybody can be who is not truly in love."

Mrs. von Briest saw that Effi was exhausted and seemed to be either sleeping or about to go to sleep. She rose quietly from her chair and went out. Hardly had she gone when Effi also got up, and sat at the open window to breathe in the cool night air once more. The stars glittered and not a leaf stirred in the park. But the longer she listened the more plainly she again heard something like soft rain falling on the plane trees. A feeling of liberation came over her. "Rest, rest."

* * * * *

It was a month later and September was drawing to an end. The weather was beautiful, but the foliage in the park began to show a great deal of read and yellow and since the equinox, which had brought three stormy days, the leaves lay scattered in every direction. In the circular plot a slight change had been made. The sundial was gone and in the place where it had stood there lay since yesterday a white marble slab with

176

nothing on it but "Effi Briest" and a cross beneath. This had been Em's last reqst. "I should like to have back my old name on my stone; I brought no honor to the other." This had been promised her.

The marble slab had arrived and been placed in position yesterday, and Briest and his wife were sitting in view of it, looking at it and the heliotrope, which had been spared, and which now bordered the stone. Rollo lay beside them with his head on his paws.

Wilke, whose spats were growing wider and wider, brought the breakfast and the mail, and old Mr. von Briest said: "Wilke, order the little carriage. I am going to drive across the country with my wife."

Mrs. von Briest had meanwhile poured the coffee and was looking at the circle and its flower bed. "See, Briest, Rollo is lying by the stone again. He is really taking it harder than we. He wont eat any more, either."

"Well, Luise, it is the brute creature. That is just what I have always said. We don't amount to as much as we think. But here we always talk about instinct. In the end I think it is the best."

"Don't speak that way. When you begin to philosophize--don't take offense--Briest, you show your incompetence. You have a good understanding, but you can't tackle such qstions."

"That's tr."

"And if it is absolutely necessary to discuss qstions there are entirely different ones, Briest, and I can tell you that not a day passes, since the poor child has been lying here, but such qstions press themselves on me."

"What qstions?"

"Whether after all we are perhaps not to blame?"

"Nonsense, Luise. What do you mean?"

"Whether we ought not to have disciplined her differently. You and I particularly, for Niemeyer is only a cipher; he leaves everything in doubt. And then, Briest, sorry as I am--your continual use of ambiguous expressions--and finally, and here I accuse myself too, for I do not desire to come off innocent in this matter, I wonder if she was not too young, perhaps?"

177

Rollo, who awoke at these words, shook his head gravely and Briest said calmly: "Oh, Luise, don't--that is *too* wide a field."

2000,

CPSIA information can be obtained at www.ICGtesting.com
Printed in the USA
LVOW102317160112

264112LV00017B/130/P